XENA™
WARRIOR PRINCESS
tooth & claw

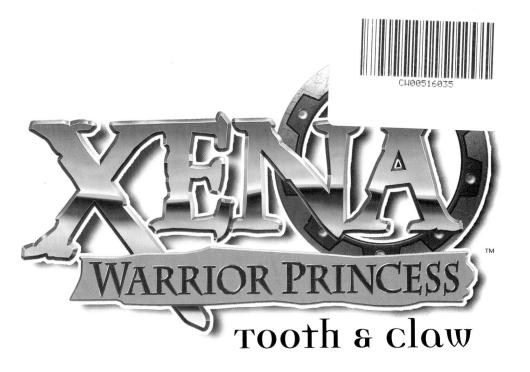

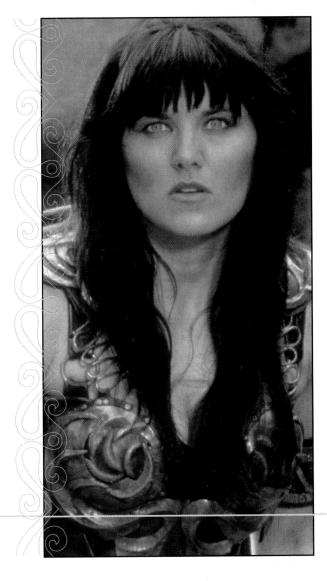

XENA: WARRIOR PRINCESS ™ **created by ROB TAPERT &
JOHN SCHULIAN**

Roy Thomas, Tom and Mary Bierbaum: Writers

Robert Teranishi, June Brigman and Aaron Lopresti: Pencillers

Steve Montano and Claude St Aubin: Inkers

Kenny Lopez and John Workman: Letterers

Digital Chameleon: Colour designs/separations

Renée Witterstaetter and Dwight Jon Zimmerman: Editors

XENA: WARRIOR PRINCESS – TOOTH & CLAW
ISBN 1 84023 073 8

Published by Titan Books Ltd
42 - 44 Dolben St
London SE1 0UP

© 1999 Studios USA Television Distribution LLC

Originally published in single magazine form in the USA by Topps
Comics as *Xena: Warrior Princess: The Dragon's Teeth* #1-3 and *The
Marriage of Hercules and Xena.*

British Library Cataloguing-In-Publication data. A catalogue record for
this book is available from the British Library.

First edition: March 1999
10 9 8 7 6 5 4 3 2 1

Printed in Italy.

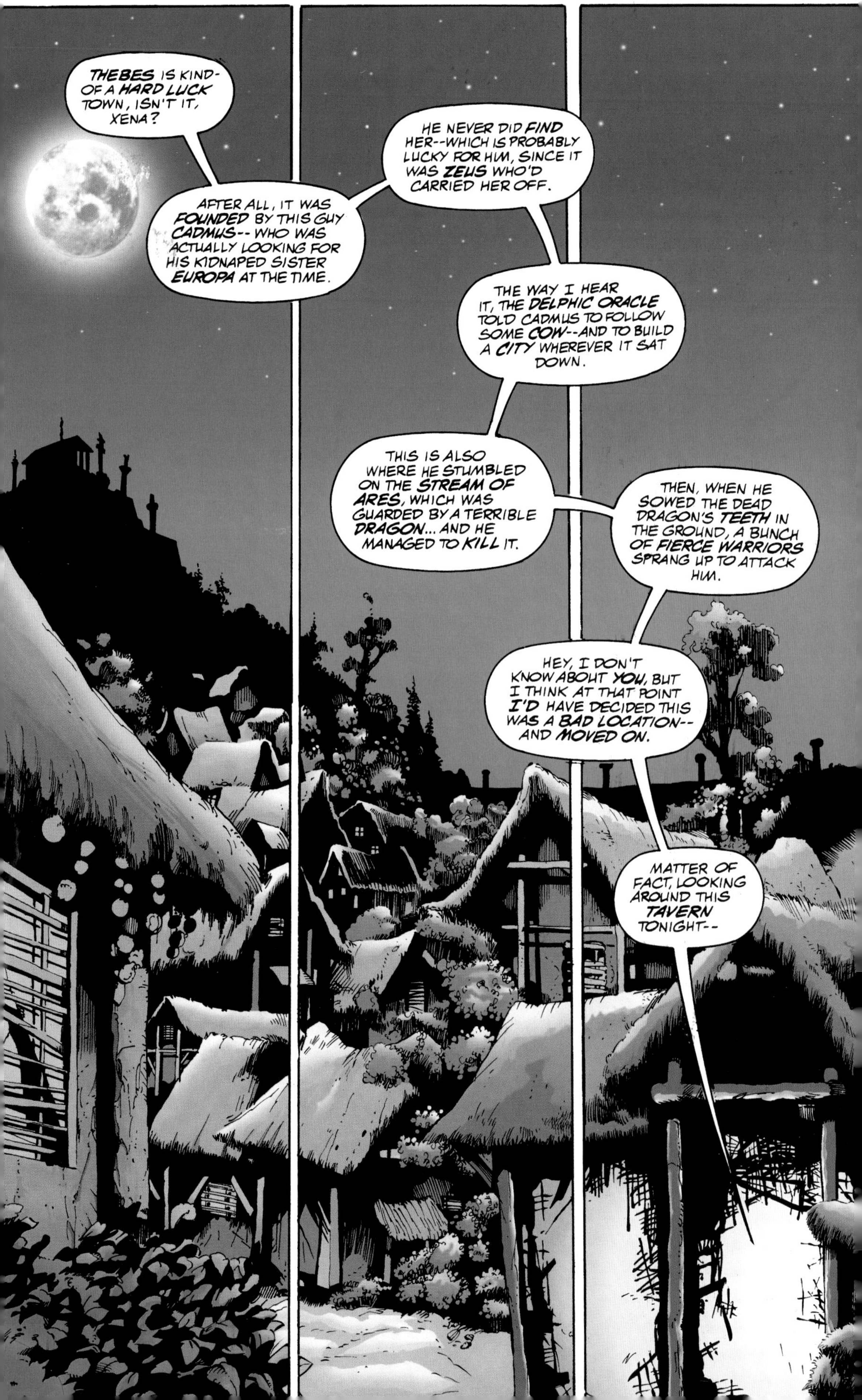
THEBES IS KIND-OF A HARD LUCK TOWN, ISN'T IT, XENA?
AFTER ALL, IT WAS FOUNDED BY THIS GUY CADMUS-- WHO WAS ACTUALLY LOOKING FOR HIS KIDNAPED SISTER EUROPA AT THE TIME.
HE NEVER DID FIND HER--WHICH IS PROBABLY LUCKY FOR HIM, SINCE IT WAS ZEUS WHO'D CARRIED HER OFF.
THE WAY I HEAR IT, THE DELPHIC ORACLE TOLD CADMUS TO FOLLOW SOME COW--AND TO BUILD A CITY WHEREVER IT SAT DOWN.
THIS IS ALSO WHERE HE STUMBLED ON THE STREAM OF ARES, WHICH WAS GUARDED BY A TERRIBLE DRAGON... AND HE MANAGED TO KILL IT.
THEN, WHEN HE SOWED THE DEAD DRAGON'S TEETH IN THE GROUND, A BUNCH OF FIERCE WARRIORS SPRANG UP TO ATTACK HIM.
HEY, I DON'T KNOW ABOUT YOU, BUT I THINK AT THAT POINT I'D HAVE DECIDED THIS WAS A BAD LOCATION-- AND MOVED ON.
MATTER OF FACT, LOOKING AROUND THIS TAVERN TONIGHT--

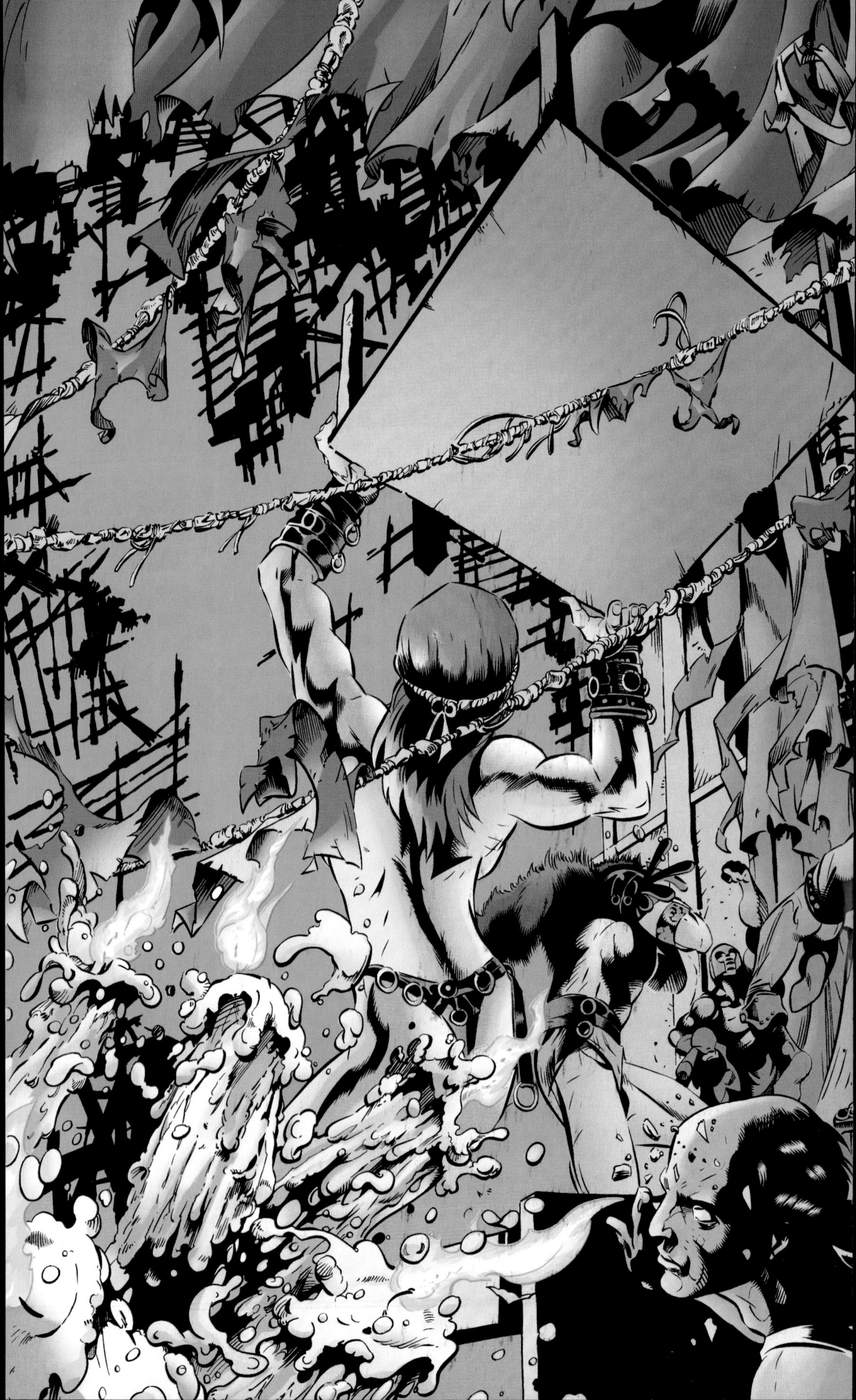

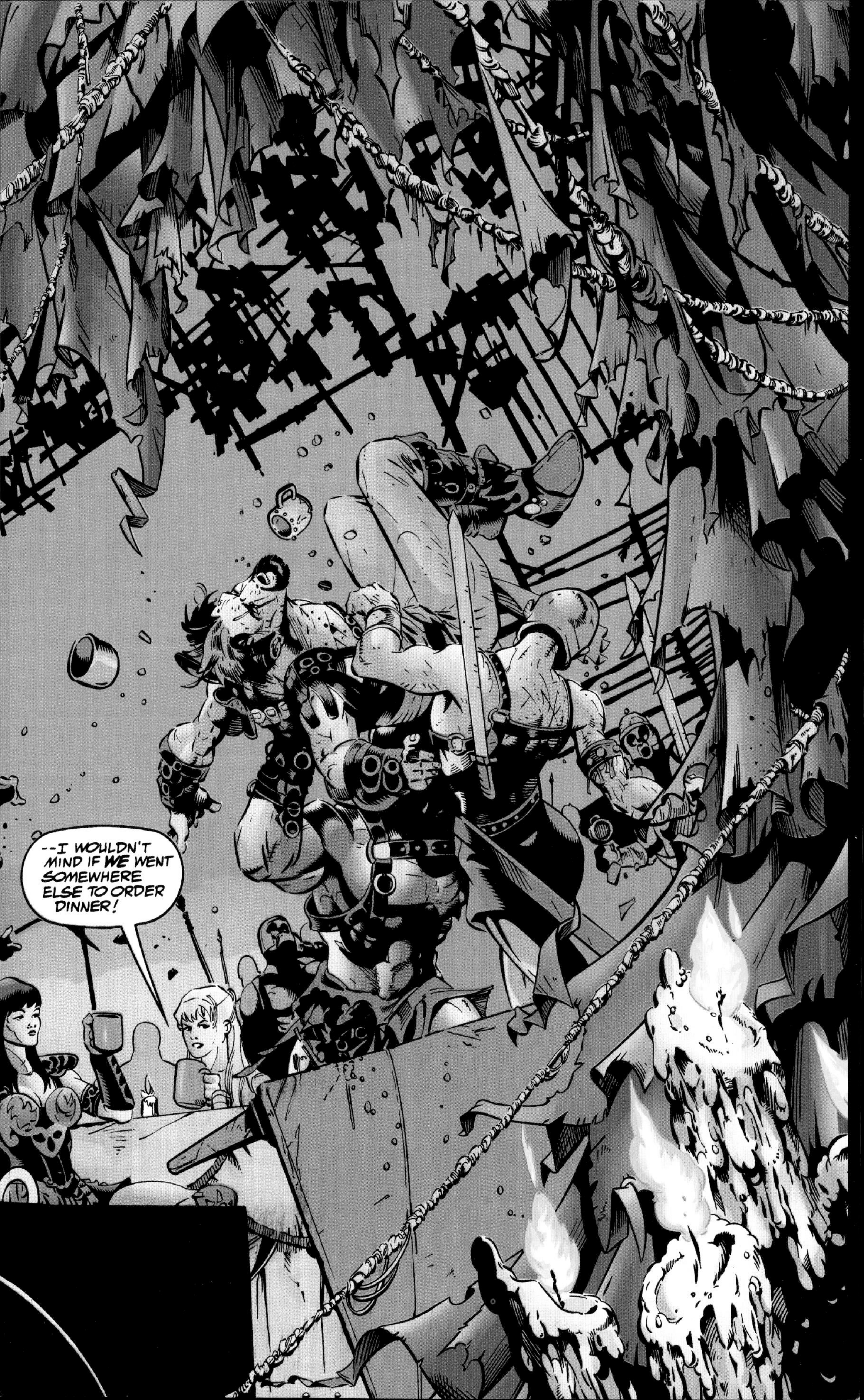
--I WOULDN'T MIND IF WE WENT SOMEWHERE ELSE TO ORDER DINNER!

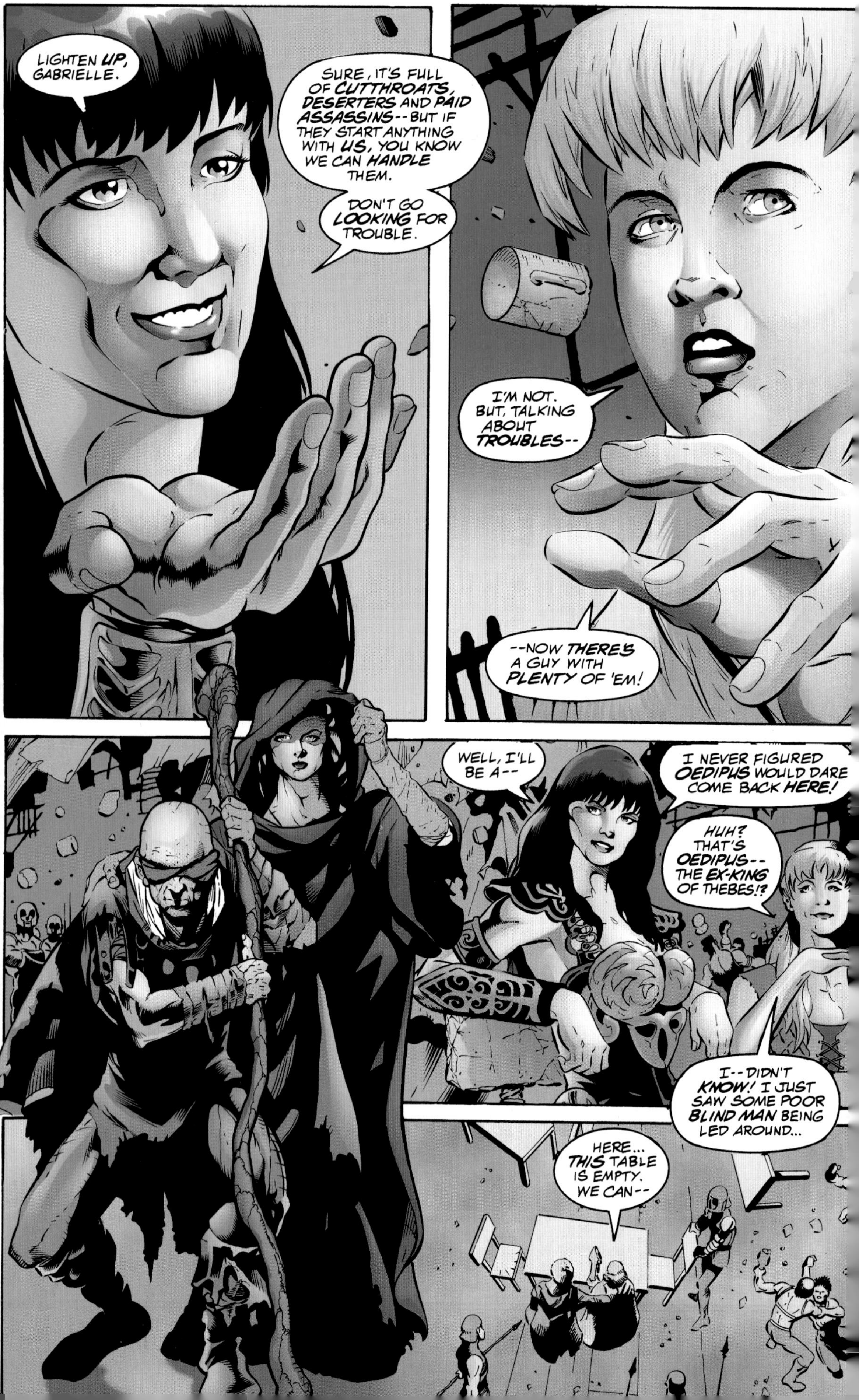
LIGHTEN UP, GABRIELLE.
SURE, IT'S FULL OF CUTTHROATS, DESERTERS AND PAID ASSASSINS--BUT IF THEY START ANYTHING WITH US, YOU KNOW WE CAN HANDLE THEM.
DON'T GO LOOKING FOR TROUBLE.
I'M NOT. BUT, TALKING ABOUT TROUBLES--
--NOW THERE'S A GUY WITH PLENTY OF 'EM!
WELL, I'LL BE A--
I NEVER FIGURED OEDIPUS WOULD DARE COME BACK HERE!
HUH? THAT'S OEDIPUS--THE EX-KING OF THEBES!?
I--DIDN'T KNOW! I JUST SAW SOME POOR BLIND MAN BEING LED AROUND...
HERE... THIS TABLE IS EMPTY. WE CAN--

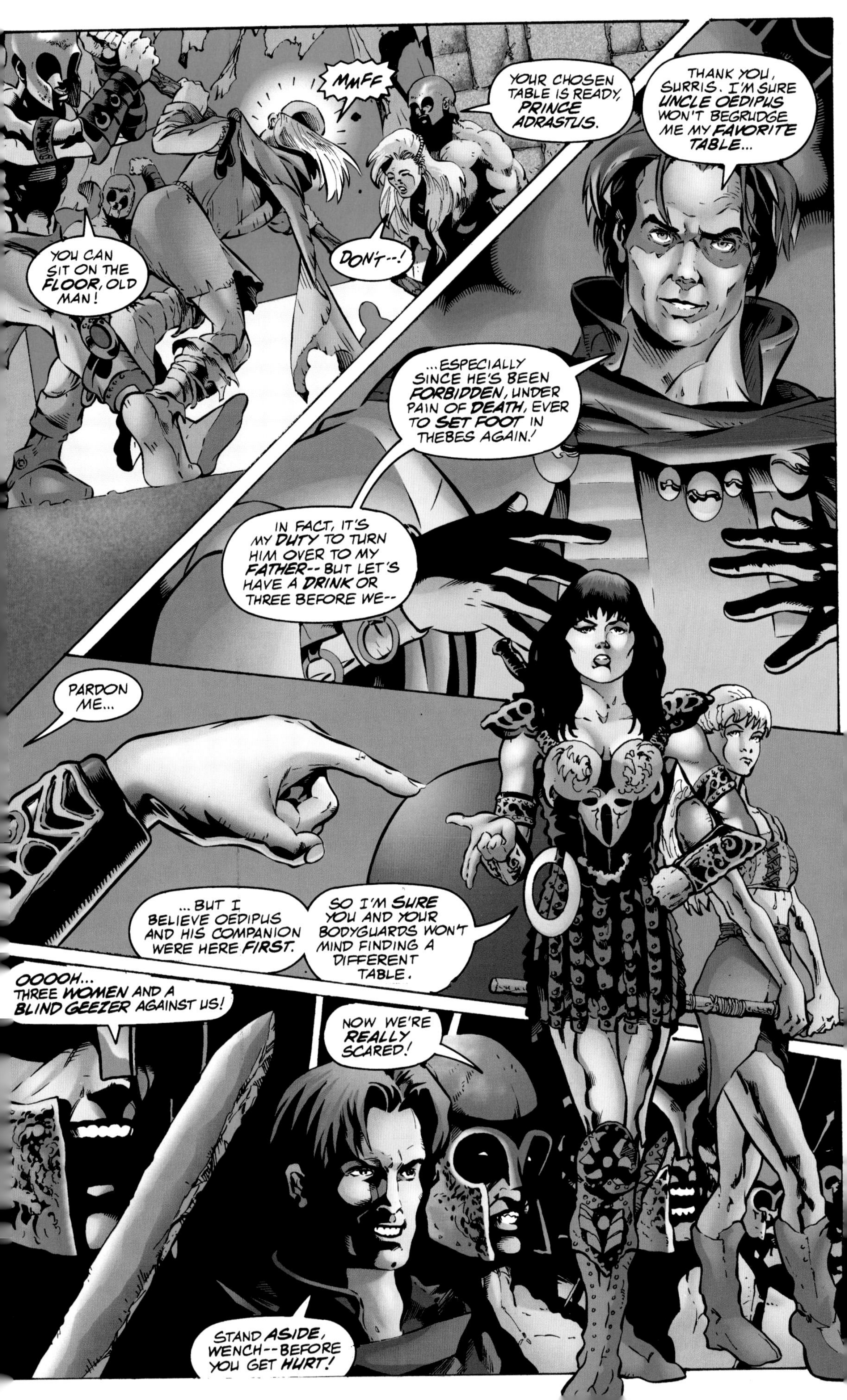
MMFF
YOUR CHOSEN TABLE IS READY, PRINCE ADRASTUS.
YOU CAN SIT ON THE FLOOR, OLD MAN!
DON'T--!
THANK YOU, SURRIS. I'M SURE UNCLE OEDIPUS WON'T BEGRUDGE ME MY FAVORITE TABLE...
...ESPECIALLY SINCE HE'S BEEN FORBIDDEN, UNDER PAIN OF DEATH, EVER TO SET FOOT IN THEBES AGAIN.
IN FACT, IT'S MY DUTY TO TURN HIM OVER TO MY FATHER-- BUT LET'S HAVE A DRINK OR THREE BEFORE WE--
PARDON ME...
...BUT I BELIEVE OEDIPUS AND HIS COMPANION WERE HERE FIRST.
SO I'M SURE YOU AND YOUR BODYGUARDS WON'T MIND FINDING A DIFFERENT TABLE.
OOOOH... THREE WOMEN AND A BLIND GEEZER AGAINST US!
NOW WE'RE REALLY SCARED!
STAND ASIDE, WENCH--BEFORE YOU GET HURT!

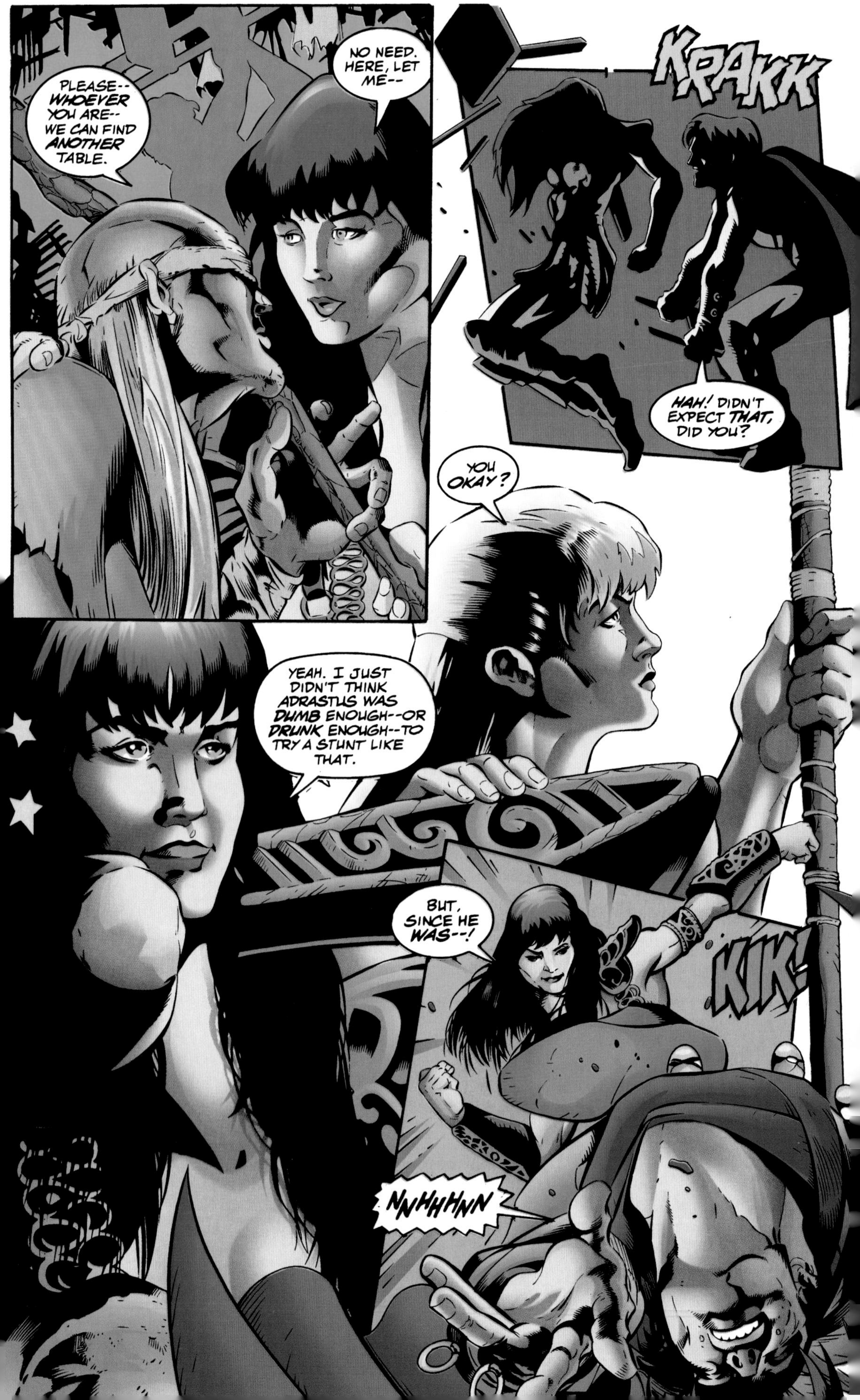
PLEASE-- WHOEVER YOU ARE-- WE CAN FIND ANOTHER TABLE.
NO NEED. HERE, LET ME--
KRAKK
HAH! DIDN'T EXPECT THAT, DID YOU?
YOU OKAY?
YEAH. I JUST DIDN'T THINK ADRASTUS WAS DUMB ENOUGH--OR DRUNK ENOUGH--TO TRY A STUNT LIKE THAT.
BUT, SINCE HE WAS--!
KIK!
NNHHHNN

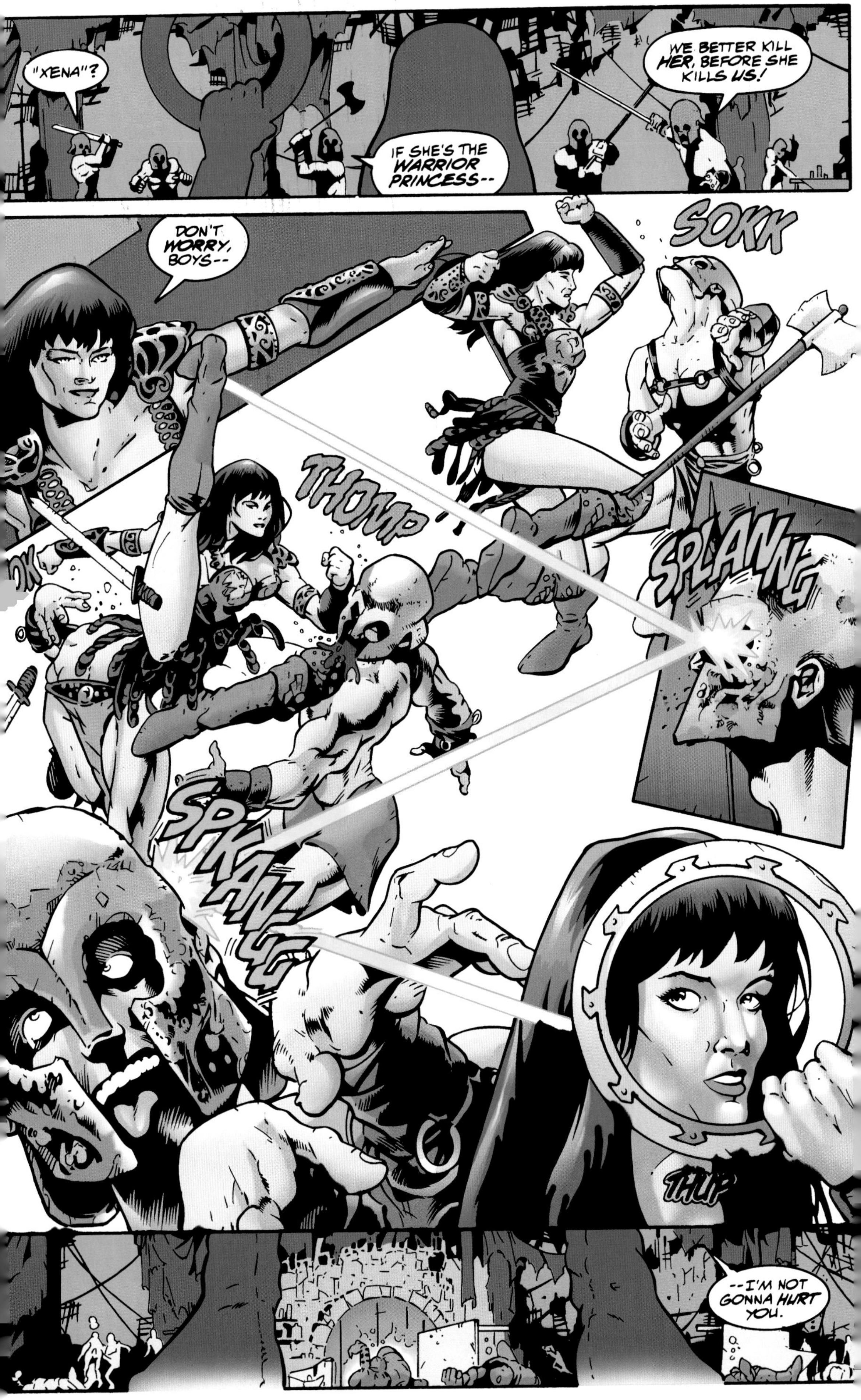
"XENA"?
IF SHE'S THE WARRIOR PRINCESS--
WE BETTER KILL HER, BEFORE SHE KILLS US!
DON'T WORRY, BOYS--
SOKK
THOMP
SPLANNG
SPKANG
THUP
--I'M NOT GONNA HURT YOU.

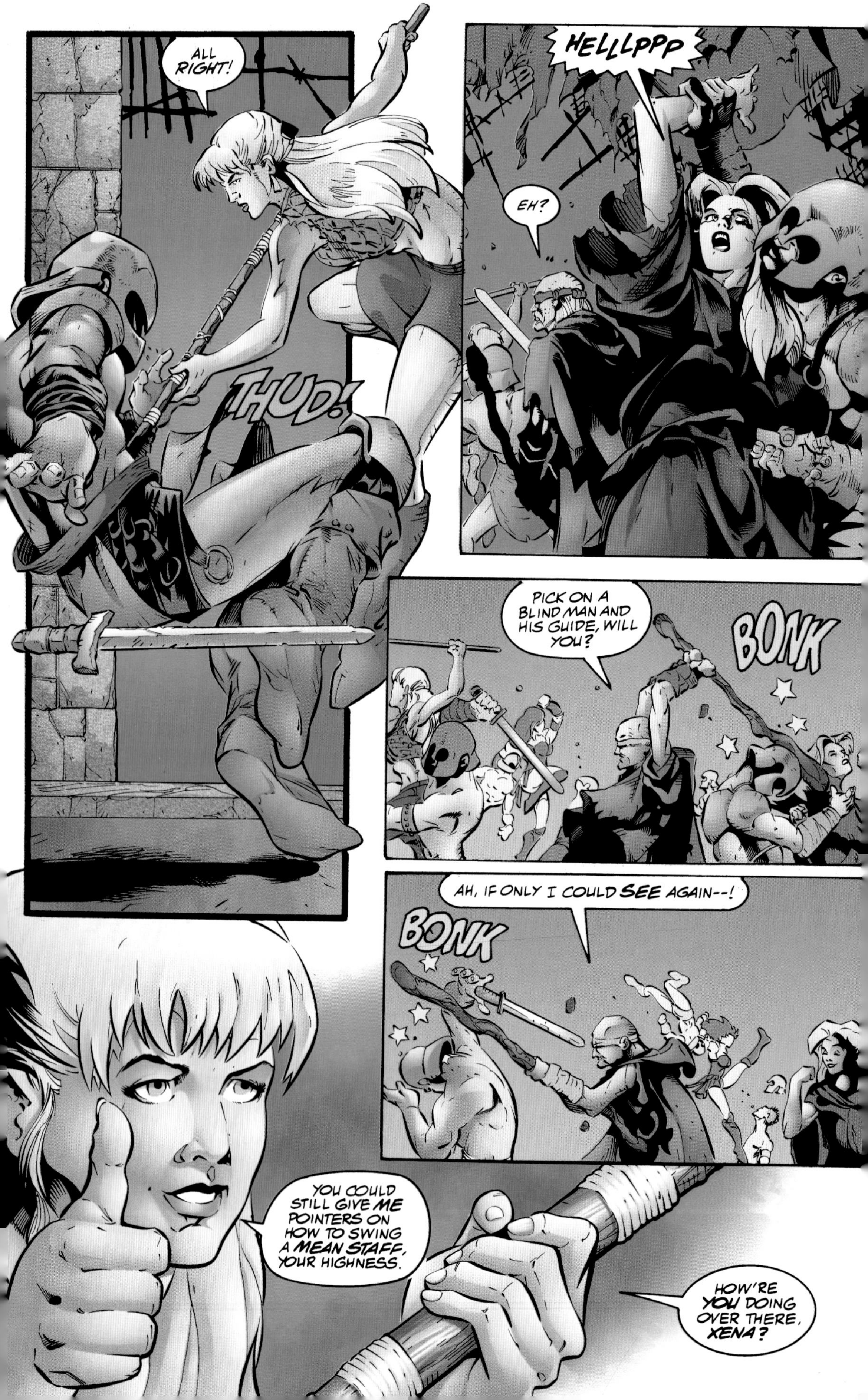
ALL RIGHT!
THUD!
HELLLPPP
EH?
PICK ON A BLIND MAN AND HIS GUIDE, WILL YOU?
BONK
AH, IF ONLY I COULD SEE AGAIN--!
BONK
YOU COULD STILL GIVE ME POINTERS ON HOW TO SWING A MEAN STAFF, YOUR HIGHNESS.
HOW'RE YOU DOING OVER THERE, XENA?

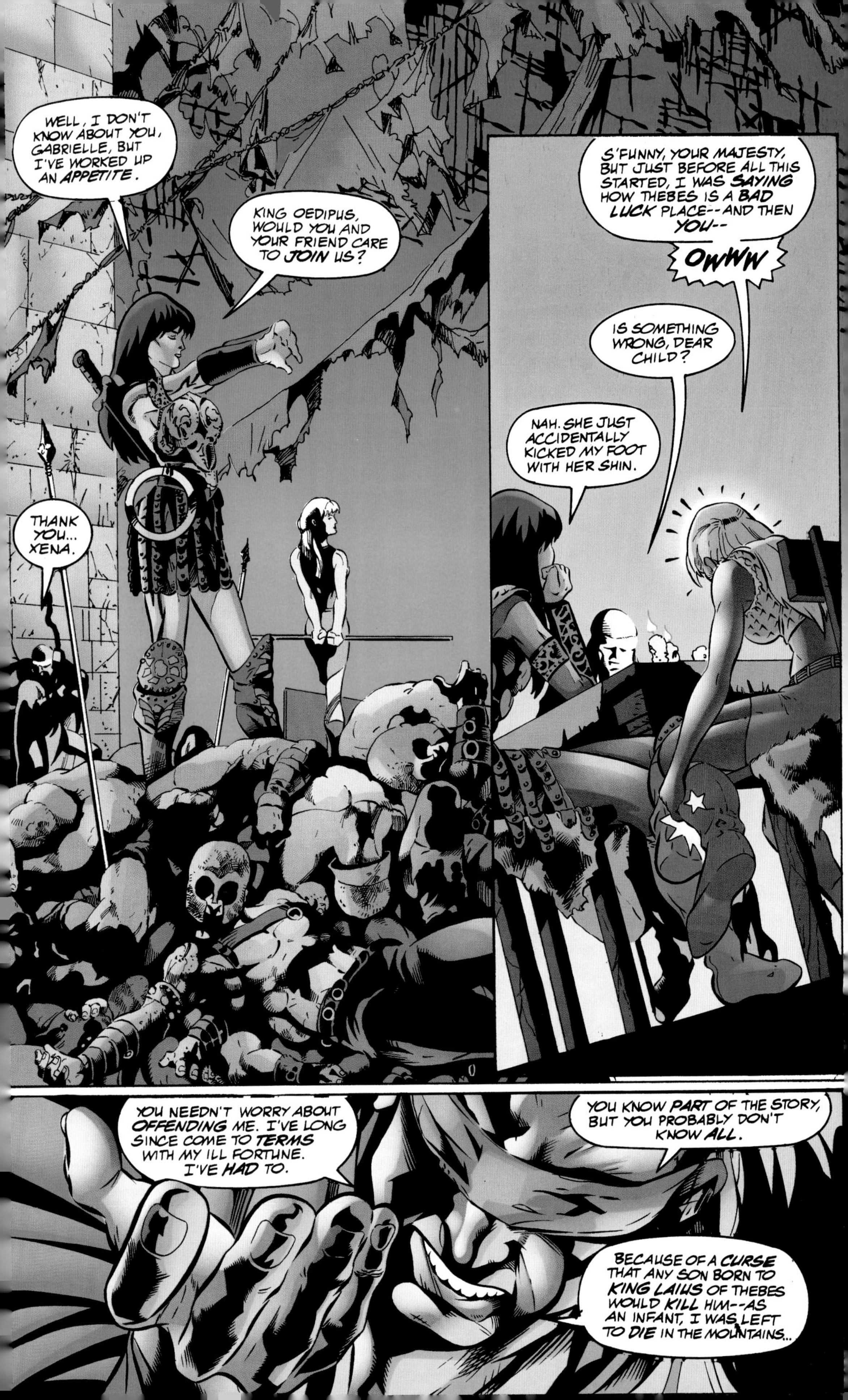
WELL, I DON'T KNOW ABOUT YOU, GABRIELLE, BUT I'VE WORKED UP AN APPETITE.
KING OEDIPUS, WOULD YOU AND YOUR FRIEND CARE TO JOIN US?
THANK YOU... XENA.
S'FUNNY, YOUR MAJESTY, BUT JUST BEFORE ALL THIS STARTED, I WAS SAYING HOW THEBES IS A BAD LUCK PLACE--AND THEN YOU--
OWWW
IS SOMETHING WRONG, DEAR CHILD?
NAH. SHE JUST ACCIDENTALLY KICKED MY FOOT WITH HER SHIN.
YOU NEEDN'T WORRY ABOUT OFFENDING ME. I'VE LONG SINCE COME TO TERMS WITH MY ILL FORTUNE. I'VE HAD TO.
YOU KNOW PART OF THE STORY, BUT YOU PROBABLY DON'T KNOW ALL.
BECAUSE OF A CURSE THAT ANY SON BORN TO KING LAIUS OF THEBES WOULD KILL HIM--AS AN INFANT, I WAS LEFT TO DIE IN THE MOUNTAINS...

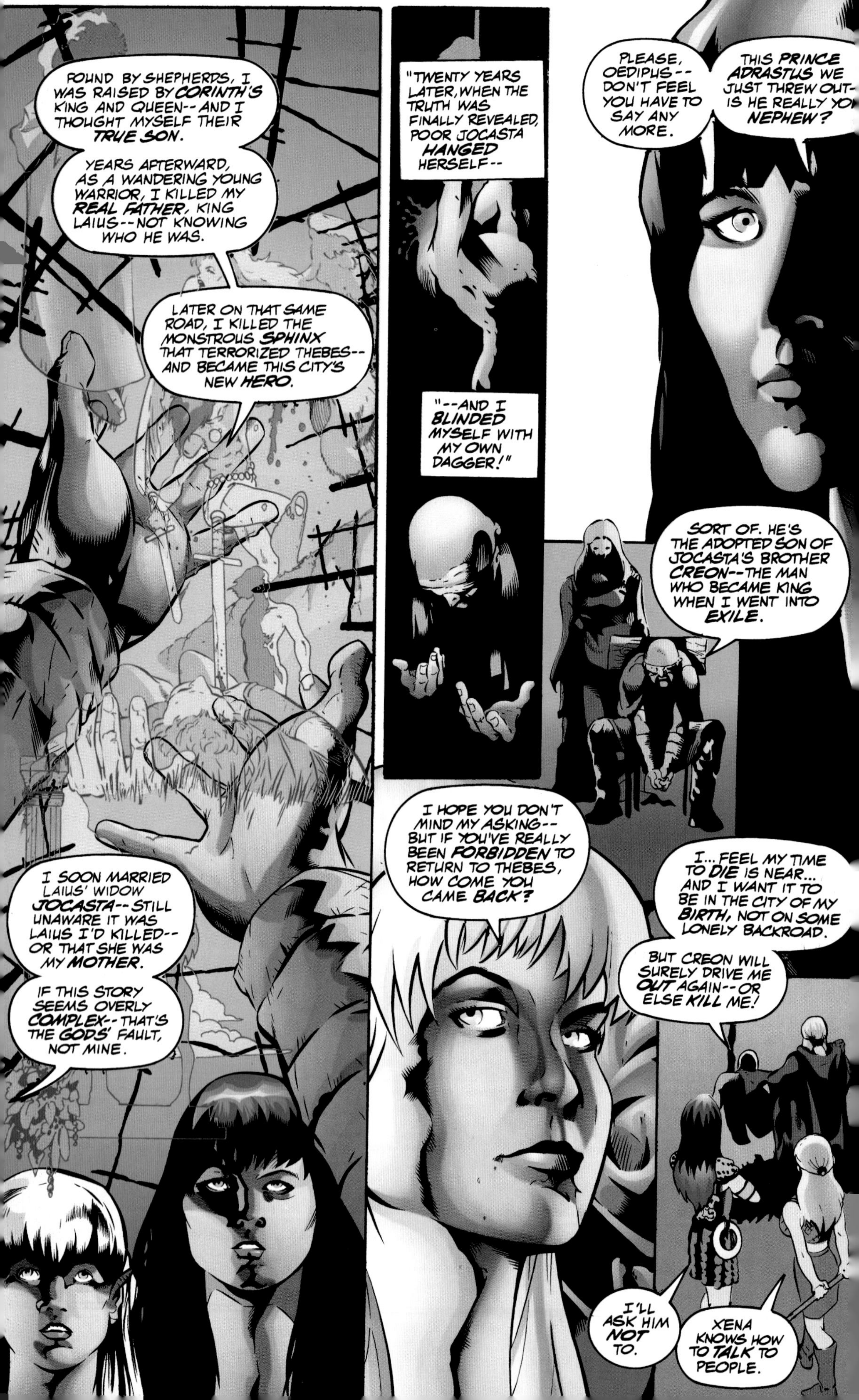

FOUND BY SHEPHERDS, I WAS RAISED BY CORINTH'S KING AND QUEEN-- AND I THOUGHT MYSELF THEIR TRUE SON.
YEARS AFTERWARD, AS A WANDERING YOUNG WARRIOR, I KILLED MY REAL FATHER, KING LAIUS--NOT KNOWING WHO HE WAS.
LATER ON THAT SAME ROAD, I KILLED THE MONSTROUS SPHINX THAT TERRORIZED THEBES-- AND BECAME THIS CITY'S NEW HERO.
I SOON MARRIED LAIUS' WIDOW JOCASTA-- STILL UNAWARE IT WAS LAIUS I'D KILLED-- OR THAT SHE WAS MY MOTHER.
IF THIS STORY SEEMS OVERLY COMPLEX-- THAT'S THE GODS' FAULT, NOT MINE.
"TWENTY YEARS LATER, WHEN THE TRUTH WAS FINALLY REVEALED, POOR JOCASTA HANGED HERSELF--
"--AND I BLINDED MYSELF WITH MY OWN DAGGER!"
PLEASE, OEDIPUS-- DON'T FEEL YOU HAVE TO SAY ANY MORE.
THIS PRINCE ADRASTUS WE JUST THREW OUT-- IS HE REALLY YO NEPHEW?
SORT OF. HE'S THE ADOPTED SON OF JOCASTA'S BROTHER CREON--THE MAN WHO BECAME KING WHEN I WENT INTO EXILE.
I HOPE YOU DON'T MIND MY ASKING-- BUT IF YOU'VE REALLY BEEN FORBIDDEN TO RETURN TO THEBES, HOW COME YOU CAME BACK?
I... FEEL MY TIME TO DIE IS NEAR... AND I WANT IT TO BE IN THE CITY OF MY BIRTH, NOT ON SOME LONELY BACKROAD.
BUT CREON WILL SURELY DRIVE ME OUT AGAIN-- OR ELSE KILL ME!
I'LL ASK HIM NOT TO.
XENA KNOWS HOW TO TALK TO PEOPLE.

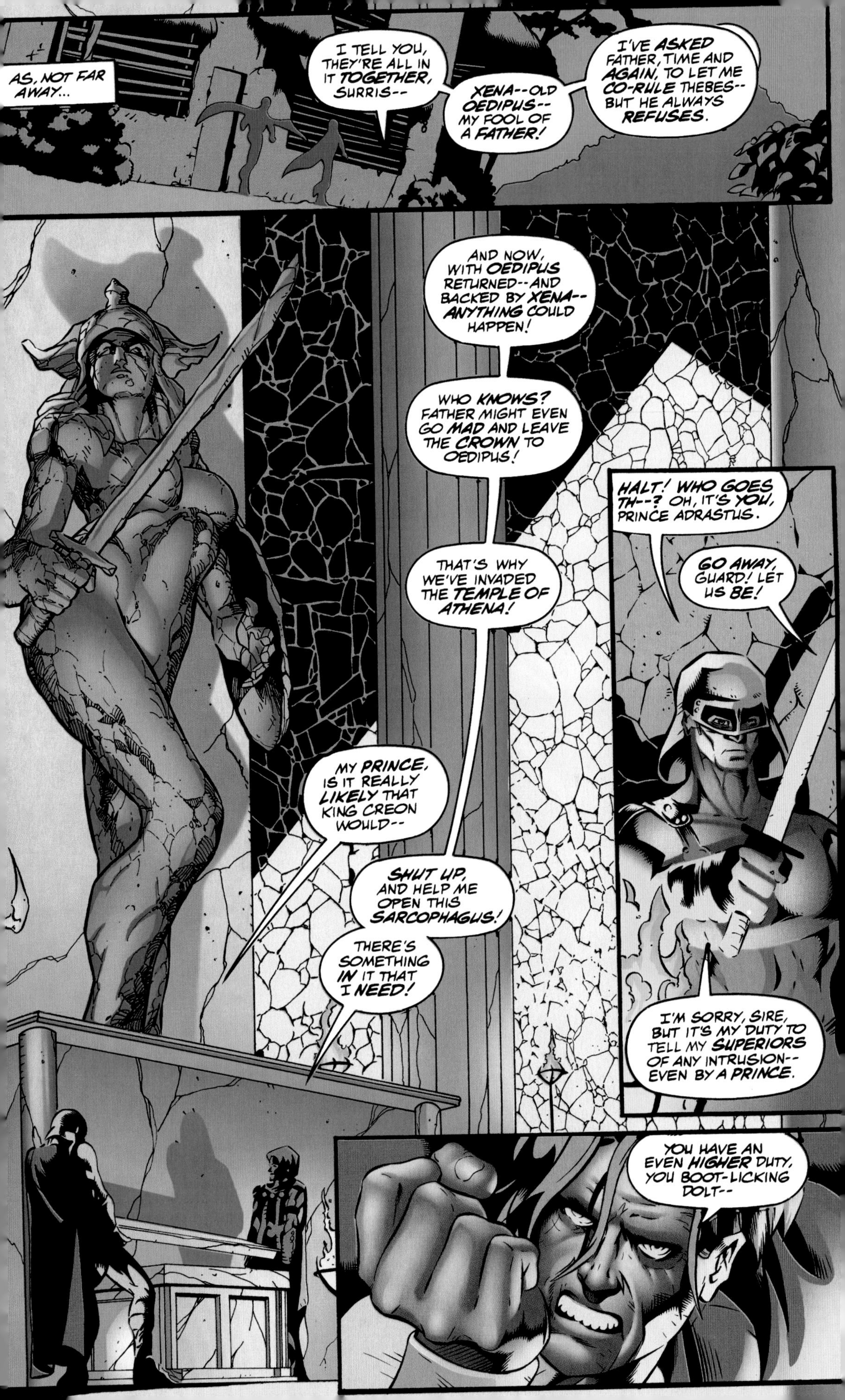
AS, NOT FAR AWAY...
I TELL YOU, THEY'RE ALL IN IT TOGETHER, SURRIS--
XENA--OLD OEDIPUS--MY FOOL OF A FATHER!
I'VE ASKED FATHER, TIME AND AGAIN, TO LET ME CO-RULE THEBES--BUT HE ALWAYS REFUSES.
AND NOW, WITH OEDIPUS RETURNED--AND BACKED BY XENA--ANYTHING COULD HAPPEN!
WHO KNOWS? FATHER MIGHT EVEN GO MAD AND LEAVE THE CROWN TO OEDIPUS!
THAT'S WHY WE'VE INVADED THE TEMPLE OF ATHENA!
MY PRINCE, IS IT REALLY LIKELY THAT KING CREON WOULD--
SHUT UP, AND HELP ME OPEN THIS SARCOPHAGUS!
THERE'S SOMETHING IN IT THAT I NEED!
HALT! WHO GOES TH--? OH, IT'S YOU, PRINCE ADRASTUS.
GO AWAY, GUARD! LET US BE!
I'M SORRY, SIRE, BUT IT'S MY DUTY TO TELL MY SUPERIORS OF ANY INTRUSION--EVEN BY A PRINCE.
YOU HAVE AN EVEN HIGHER DUTY, YOU BOOT-LICKING DOLT--

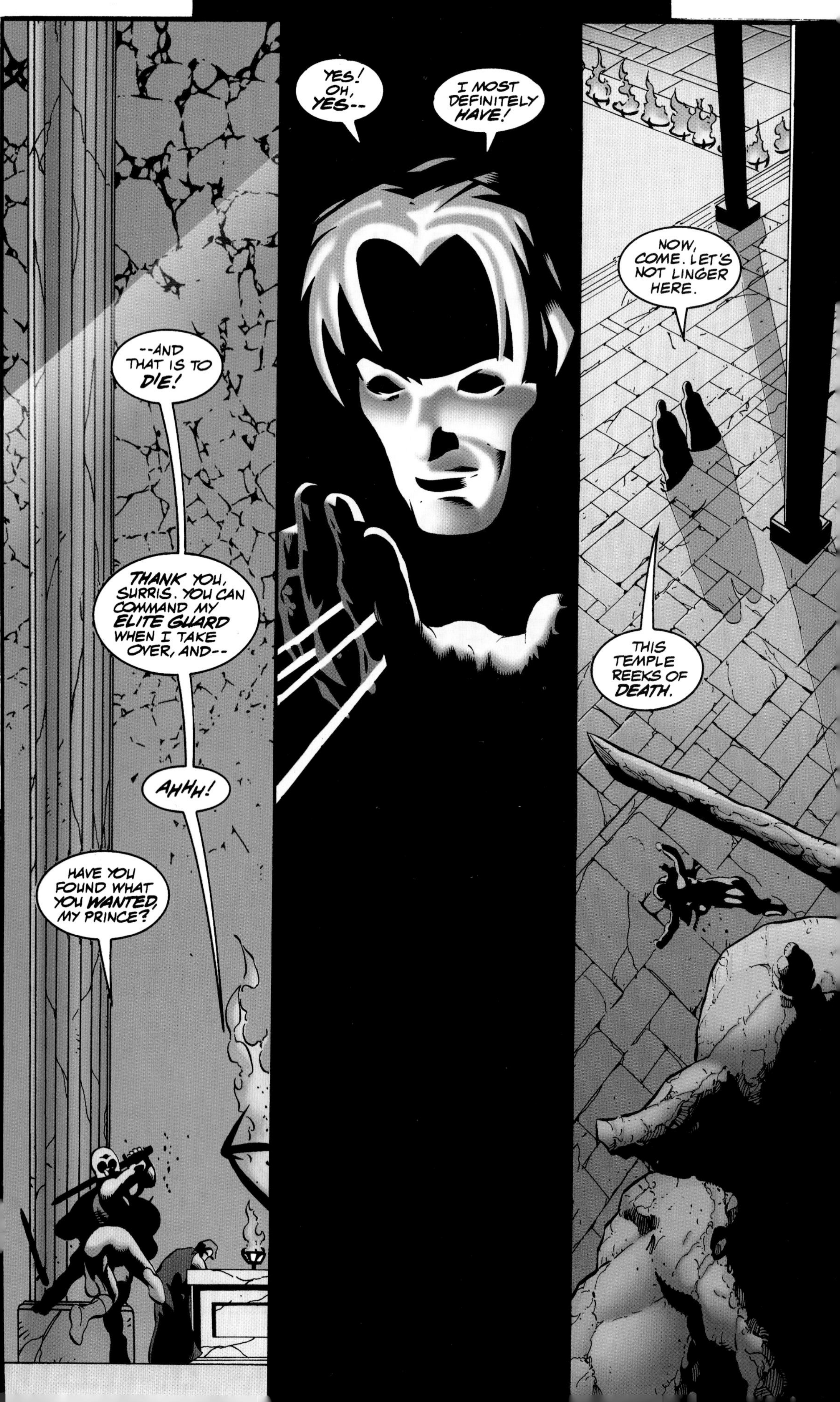
--AND THAT IS TO DIE!
THANK YOU, SURRIS. YOU CAN COMMAND MY ELITE GUARD WHEN I TAKE OVER, AND--
AHHH!
HAVE YOU FOUND WHAT YOU WANTED, MY PRINCE?
YES! OH, YES--
I MOST DEFINITELY HAVE!
NOW, COME. LET'S NOT LINGER HERE.
THIS TEMPLE REEKS OF DEATH.

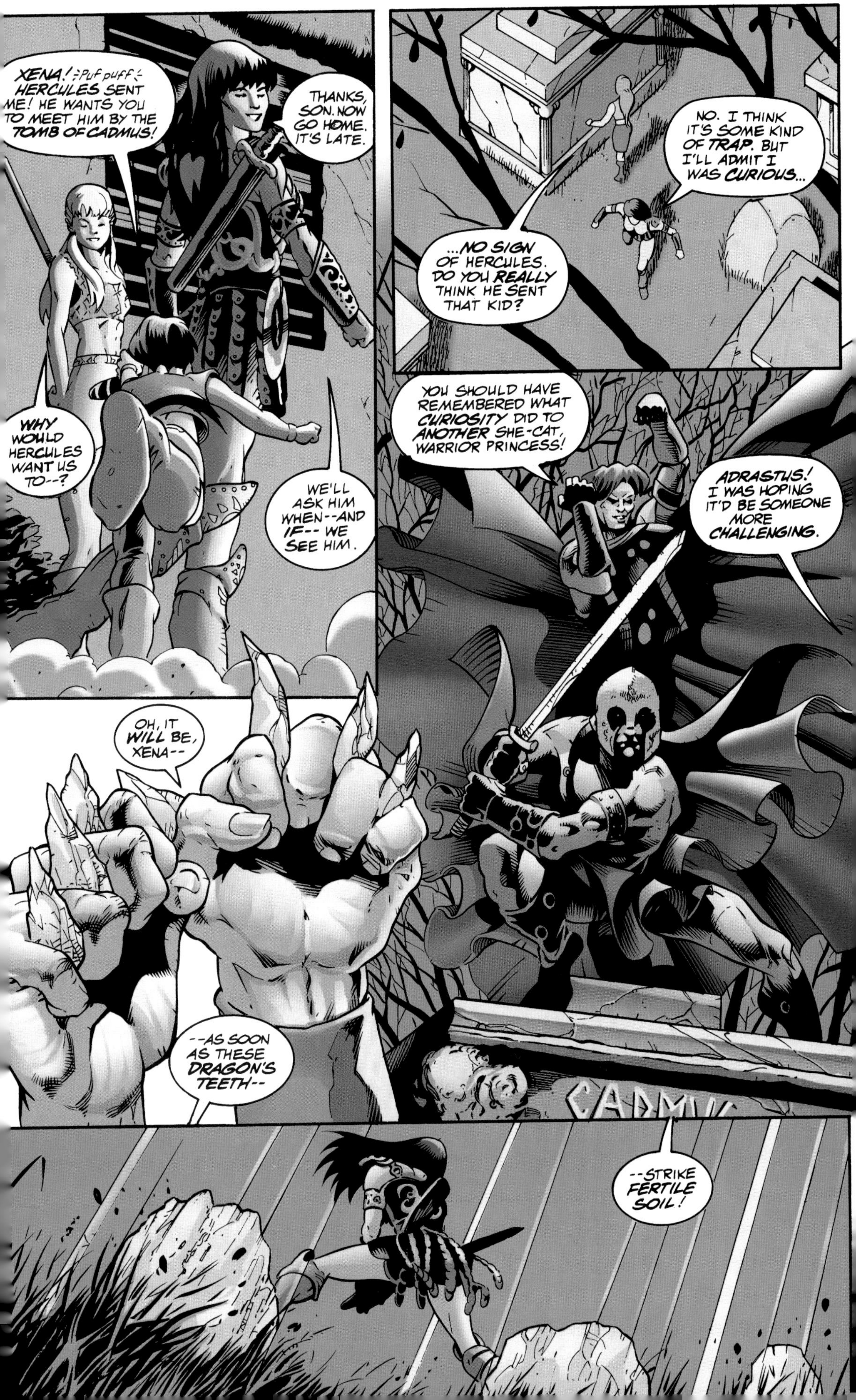
XENA! ≈Puf puff≈ HERCULES SENT ME! HE WANTS YOU TO MEET HIM BY THE TOMB OF CADMUS!
THANKS, SON. NOW GO HOME. IT'S LATE.
WHY WOULD HERCULES WANT US TO--?
WE'LL ASK HIM WHEN--AND IF-- WE SEE HIM.
...NO SIGN OF HERCULES. DO YOU REALLY THINK HE SENT THAT KID?
NO. I THINK IT'S SOME KIND OF TRAP. BUT I'LL ADMIT I WAS CURIOUS...
YOU SHOULD HAVE REMEMBERED WHAT CURIOSITY DID TO ANOTHER SHE-CAT, WARRIOR PRINCESS!
ADRASTUS! I WAS HOPING IT'D BE SOMEONE MORE CHALLENGING.
OH, IT WILL BE, XENA--
--AS SOON AS THESE DRAGON'S TEETH--
--STRIKE FERTILE SOIL!

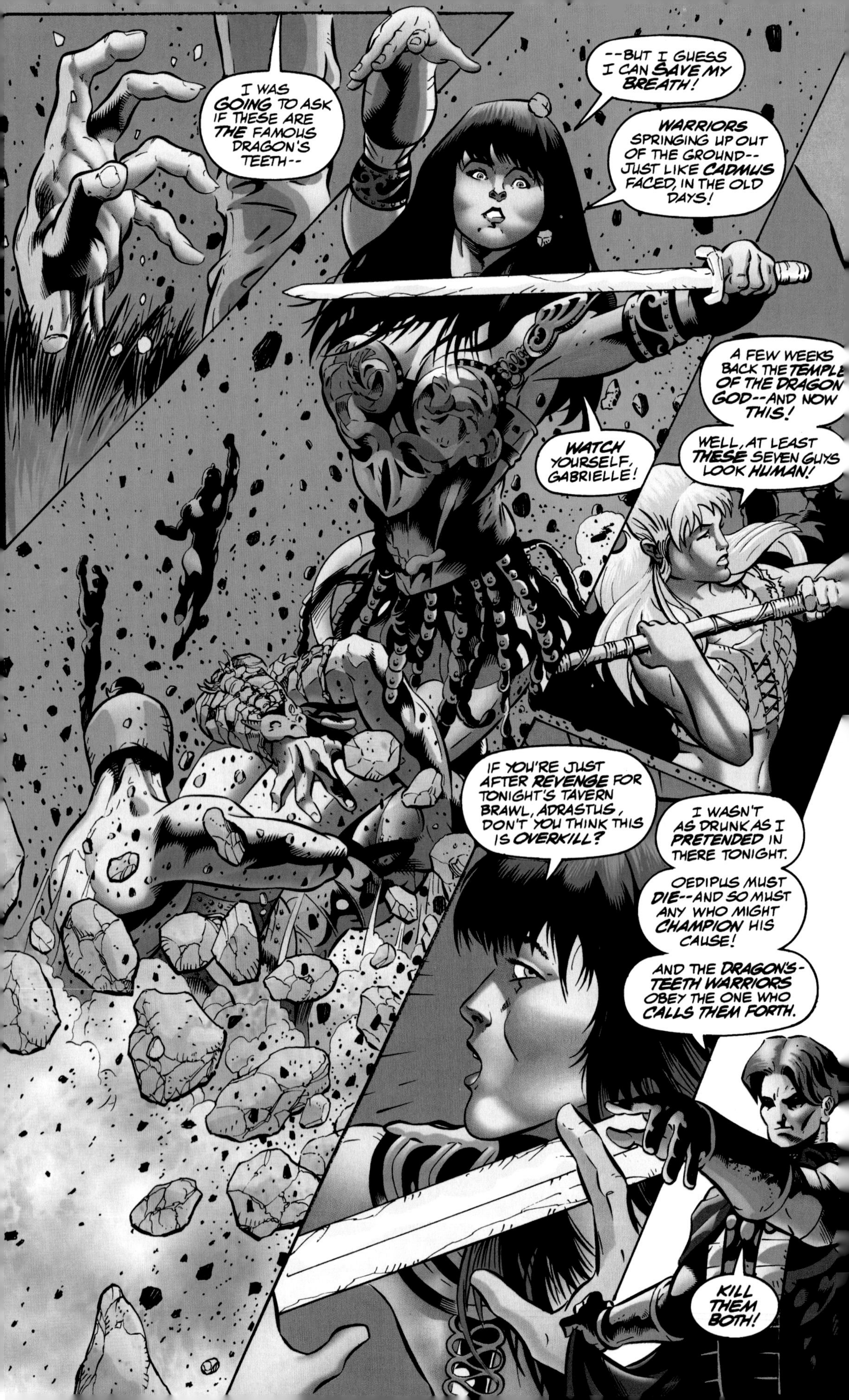
I WAS GOING TO ASK IF THESE ARE THE FAMOUS DRAGON'S TEETH--
--BUT I GUESS I CAN SAVE MY BREATH!
WARRIORS SPRINGING UP OUT OF THE GROUND-- JUST LIKE CADMUS FACED, IN THE OLD DAYS!
WATCH YOURSELF, GABRIELLE!
A FEW WEEKS BACK THE TEMPLE OF THE DRAGON GOD--AND NOW THIS!
WELL, AT LEAST THESE SEVEN GUYS LOOK HUMAN!
IF YOU'RE JUST AFTER REVENGE FOR TONIGHT'S TAVERN BRAWL, ADRASTUS, DON'T YOU THINK THIS IS OVERKILL?
I WASN'T AS DRUNK AS I PRETENDED IN THERE TONIGHT.
OEDIPUS MUST DIE--AND SO MUST ANY WHO MIGHT CHAMPION HIS CAUSE!
AND THE DRAGON'S-TEETH WARRIORS OBEY THE ONE WHO CALLS THEM FORTH.
KILL THEM BOTH!

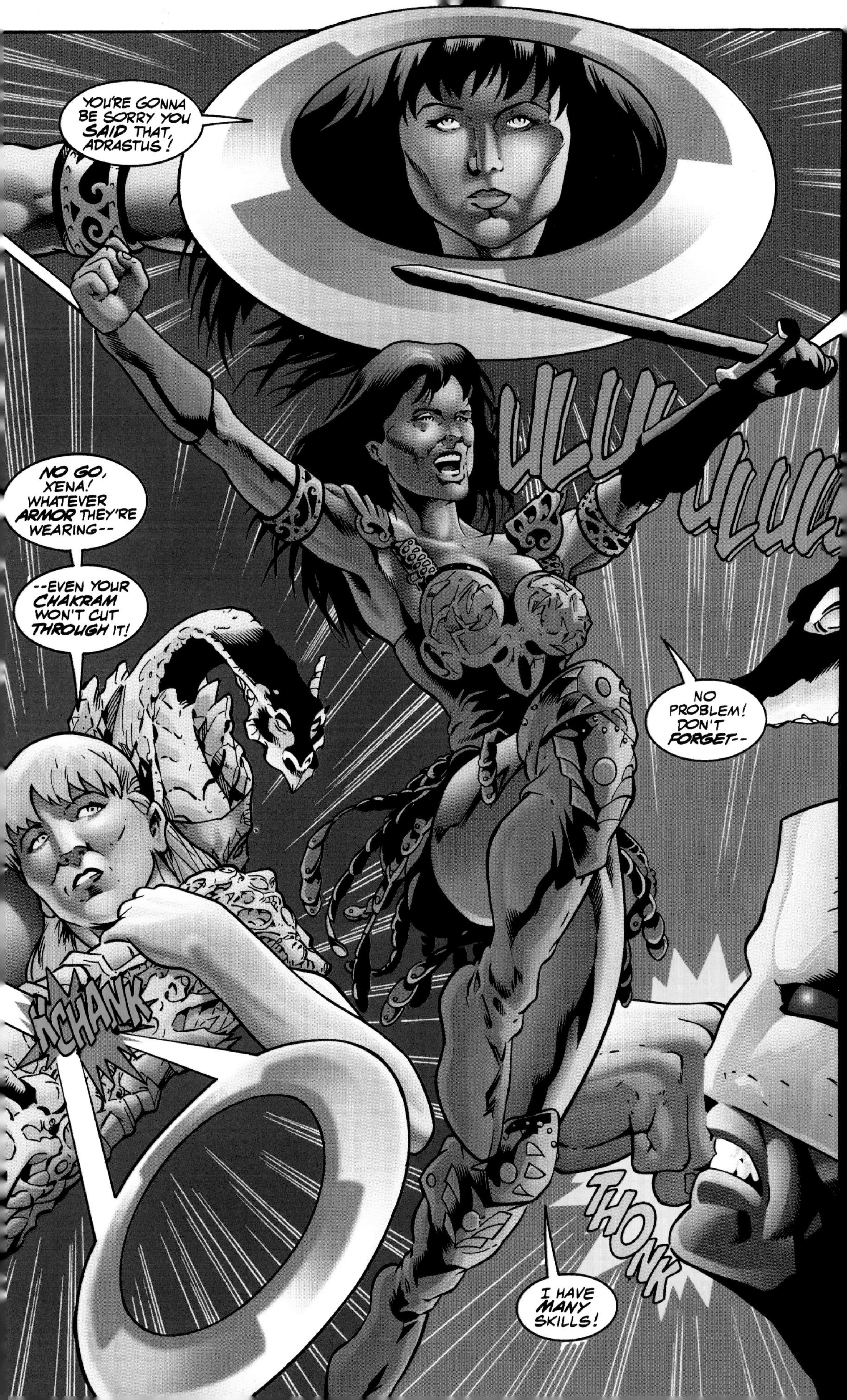

YOU'RE GONNA BE SORRY YOU SAID THAT, ADRASTUS!
ULULU
ULULU
NO GO, XENA! WHATEVER ARMOR THEY'RE WEARING--
--EVEN YOUR CHAKRAM WON'T CUT THROUGH IT!
NO PROBLEM! DON'T FORGET--
KCHANK
THONK
I HAVE MANY SKILLS!

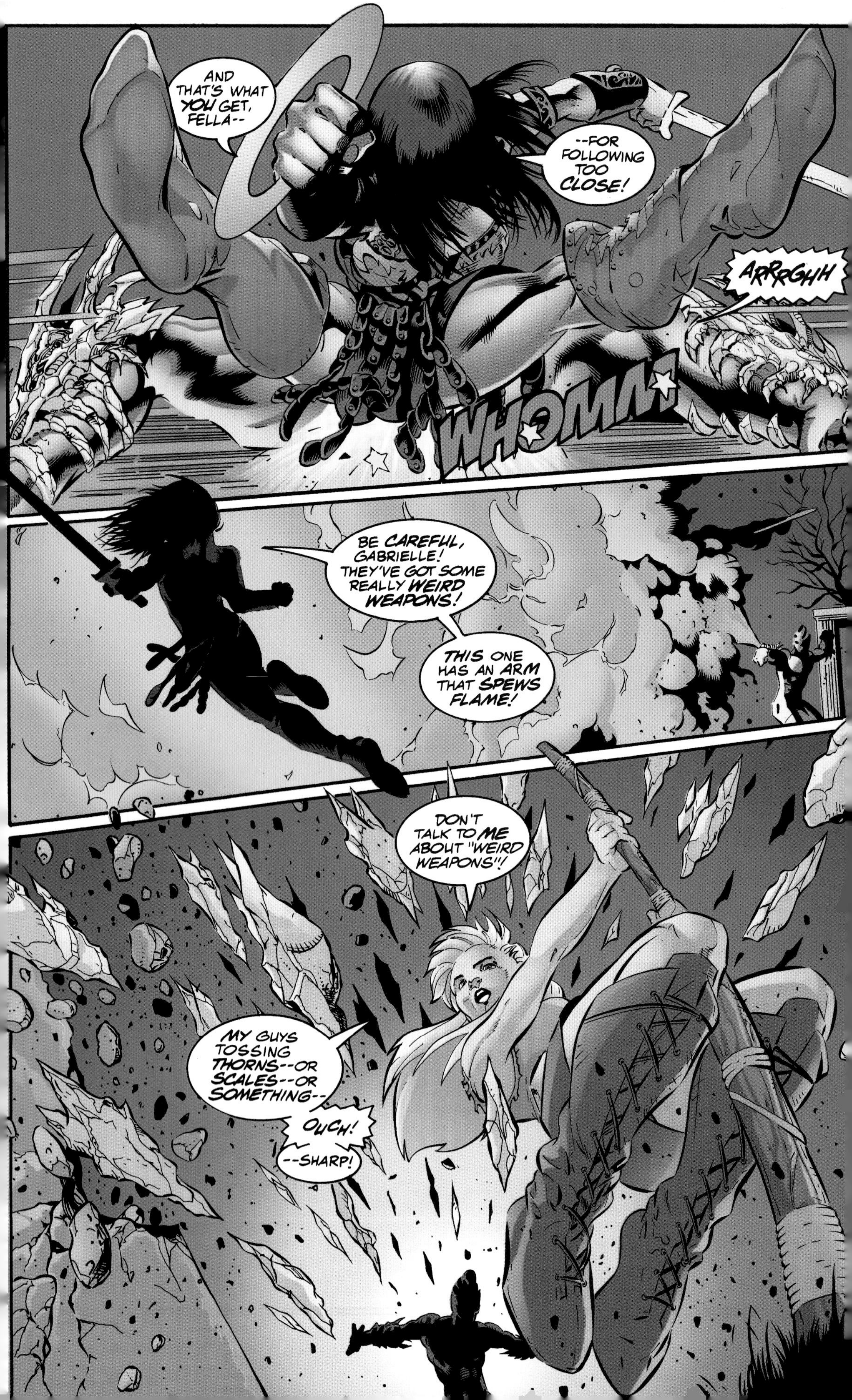
AND THAT'S WHAT YOU GET, FELLA--
--FOR FOLLOWING TOO CLOSE!
ARRRGHH
WHOMM!
BE CAREFUL, GABRIELLE! THEY'VE GOT SOME REALLY WEIRD WEAPONS!
THIS ONE HAS AN ARM THAT SPEWS FLAME!
DON'T TALK TO ME ABOUT "WEIRD WEAPONS"!
MY GUYS TOSSING THORNS--OR SCALES--OR SOMETHING--
OUCH!
--SHARP!

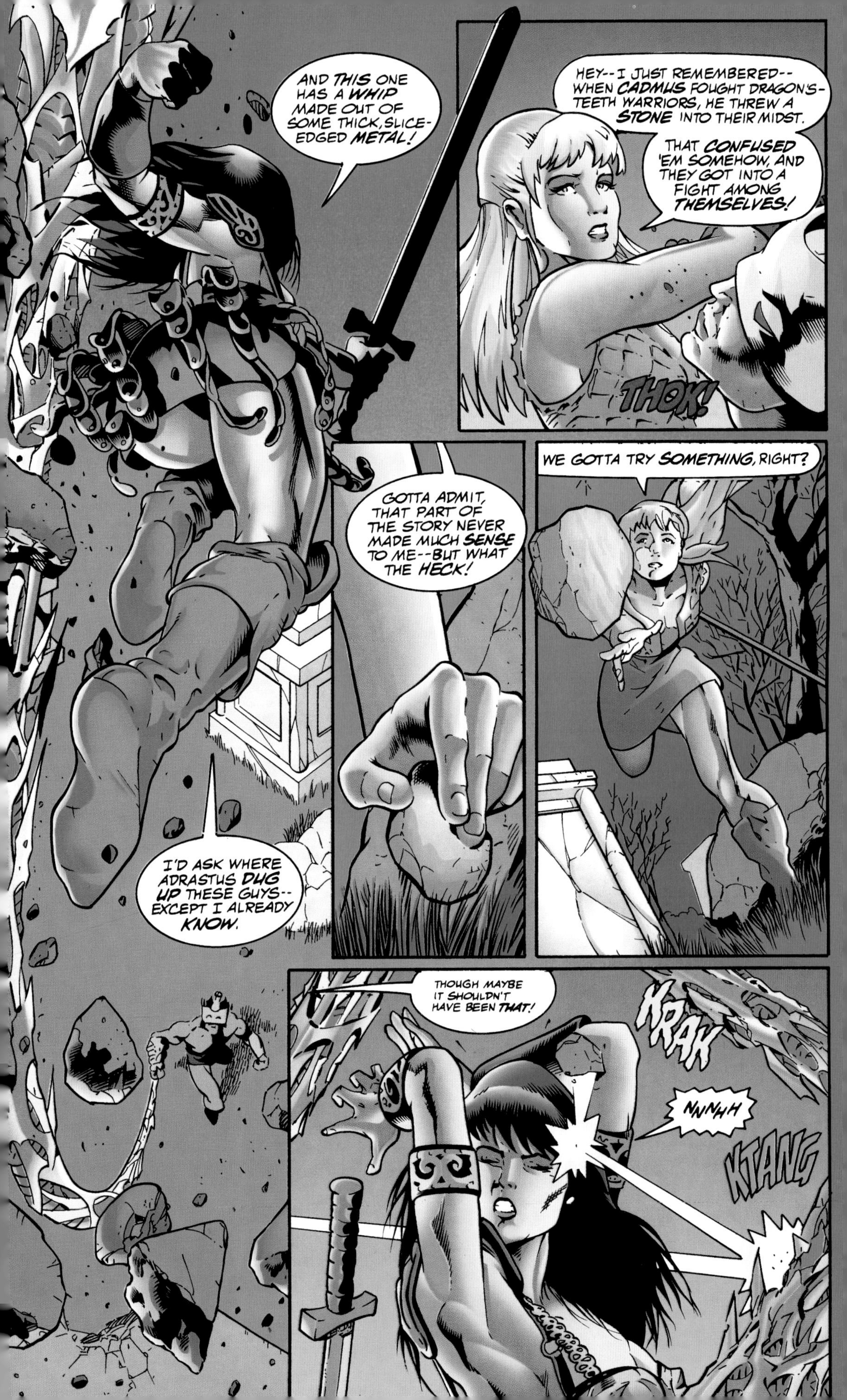
AND THIS ONE HAS A WHIP MADE OUT OF SOME THICK, SLICE-EDGED METAL!
I'D ASK WHERE ADRASTUS DUG UP THESE GUYS--EXCEPT I ALREADY KNOW.
HEY--I JUST REMEMBERED--WHEN CADMUS FOUGHT DRAGON'S-TEETH WARRIORS, HE THREW A STONE INTO THEIR MIDST.
THAT CONFUSED 'EM SOMEHOW, AND THEY GOT INTO A FIGHT AMONG THEMSELVES!
THOK!
GOTTA ADMIT, THAT PART OF THE STORY NEVER MADE MUCH SENSE TO ME--BUT WHAT THE HECK!
WE GOTTA TRY SOMETHING, RIGHT?
THOUGH MAYBE IT SHOULDN'T HAVE BEEN THAT!
KRAK
NNNHH
KTANG

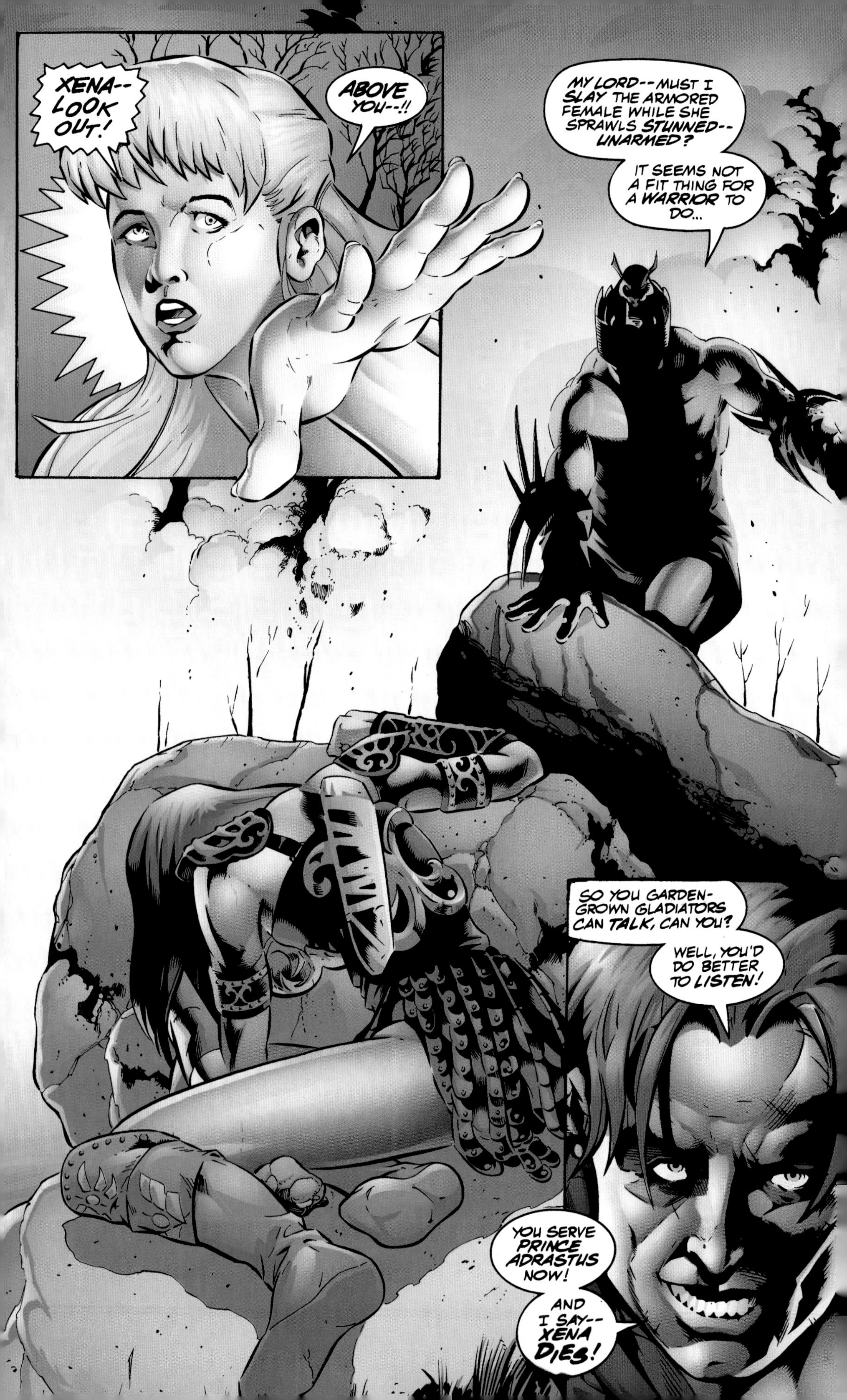
XENA-- LOOK OUT!
ABOVE YOU--!!
MY LORD--MUST I SLAY THE ARMORED FEMALE WHILE SHE SPRAWLS STUNNED--UNARMED?
IT SEEMS NOT A FIT THING FOR A WARRIOR TO DO...
SO YOU GARDEN-GROWN GLADIATORS CAN TALK, CAN YOU?
WELL, YOU'D DO BETTER TO LISTEN!
YOU SERVE PRINCE ADRASTUS NOW!
AND I SAY-- XENA DIES!

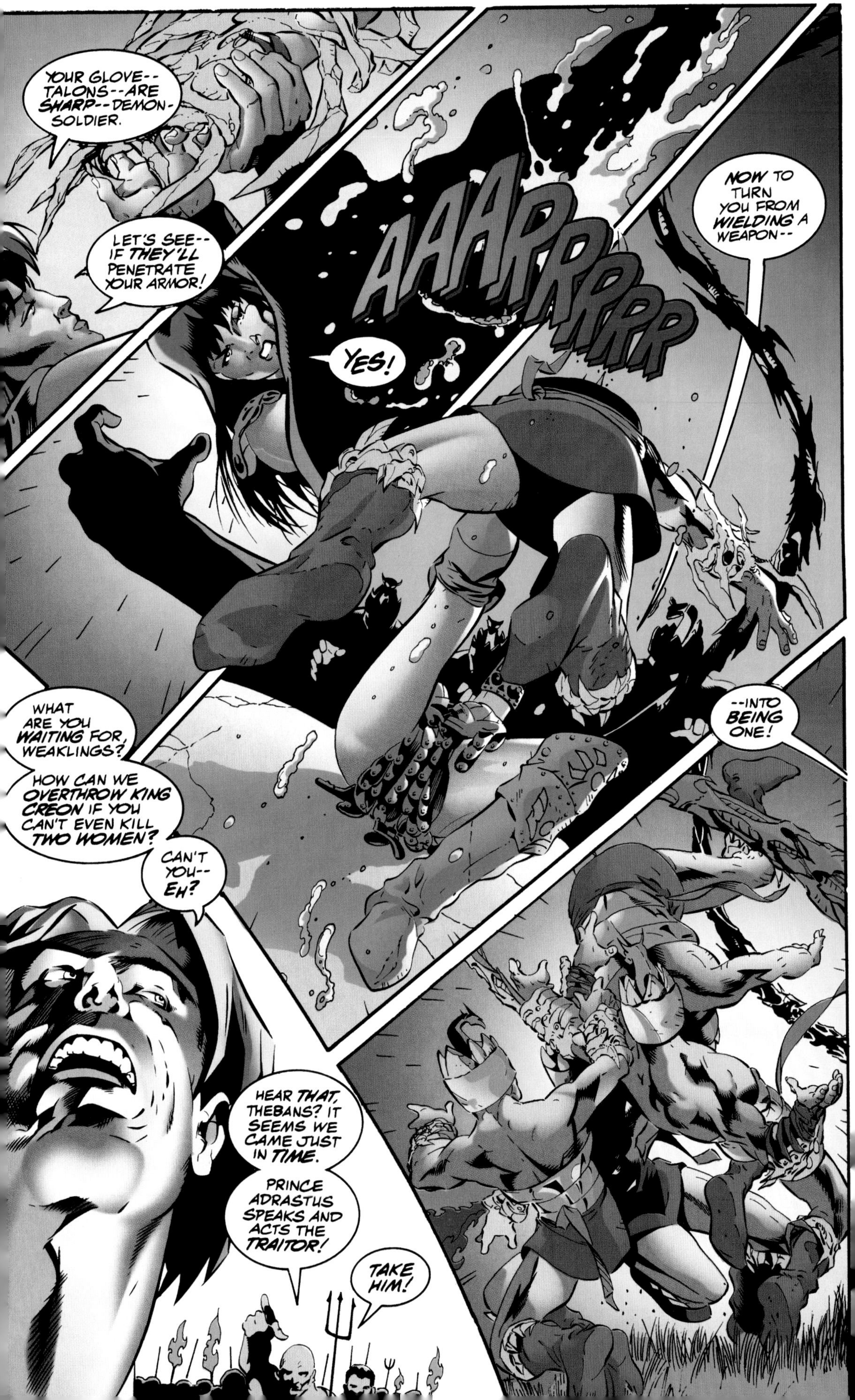
YOUR GLOVE--TALONS--ARE SHARP--DEMON-SOLDIER.
LET'S SEE--IF THEY'LL PENETRATE YOUR ARMOR!
AAARRRRRR
YES!
NOW TO TURN YOU FROM WIELDING A WEAPON--
--INTO BEING ONE!
WHAT ARE YOU WAITING FOR, WEAKLINGS?
HOW CAN WE OVERTHROW KING CREON IF YOU CAN'T EVEN KILL TWO WOMEN?
CAN'T YOU--EH?
HEAR THAT, THEBANS? IT SEEMS WE CAME JUST IN TIME.
PRINCE ADRASTUS SPEAKS AND ACTS THE TRAITOR!
TAKE HIM!

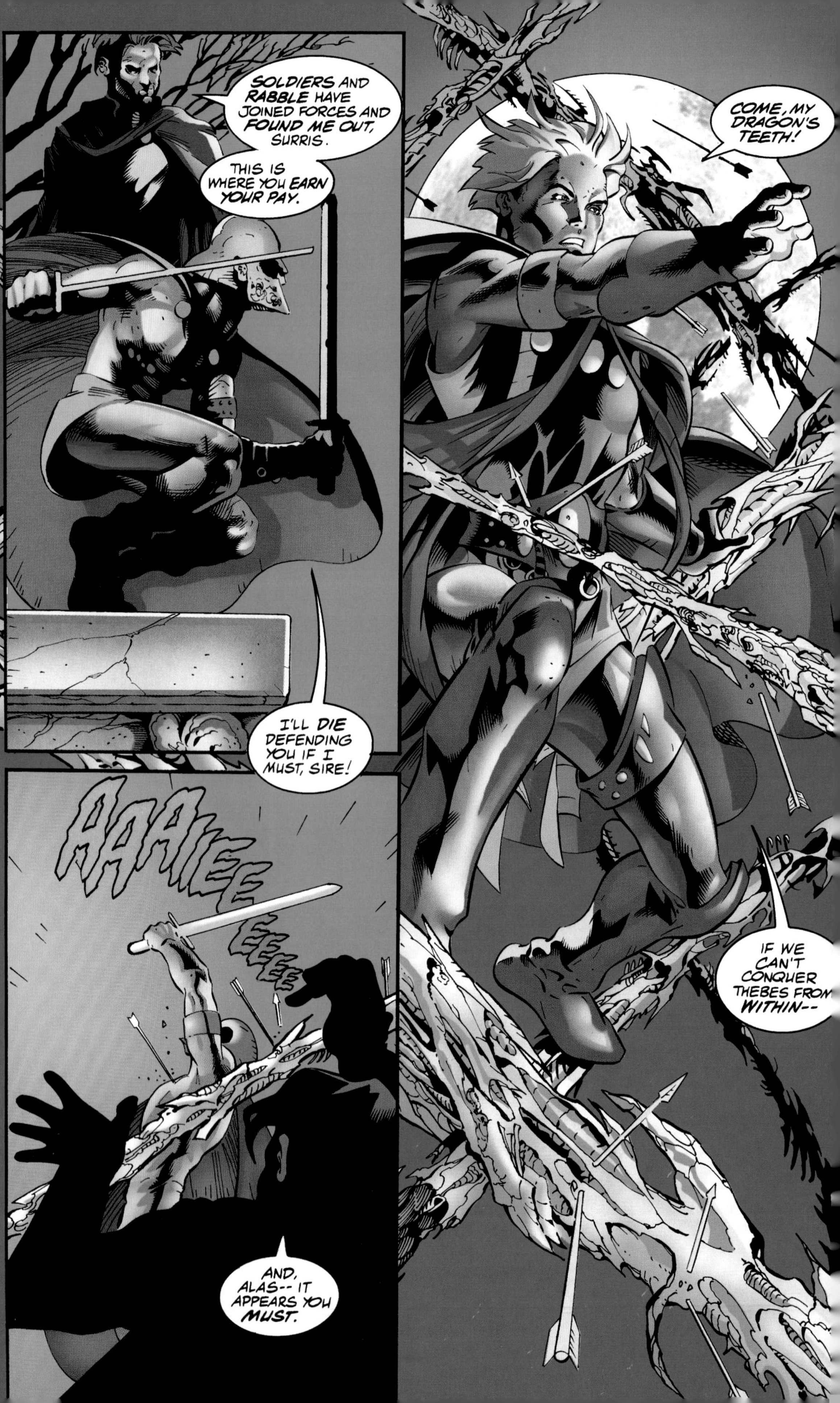

SOLDIERS AND RABBLE HAVE JOINED FORCES AND FOUND ME OUT, SURRIS.
THIS IS WHERE YOU EARN YOUR PAY.
I'LL DIE DEFENDING YOU IF I MUST, SIRE!
AAAIEEEEEEE
AND, ALAS-- IT APPEARS YOU MUST.
COME, MY DRAGON'S TEETH!
IF WE CAN'T CONQUER THEBES FROM WITHIN--

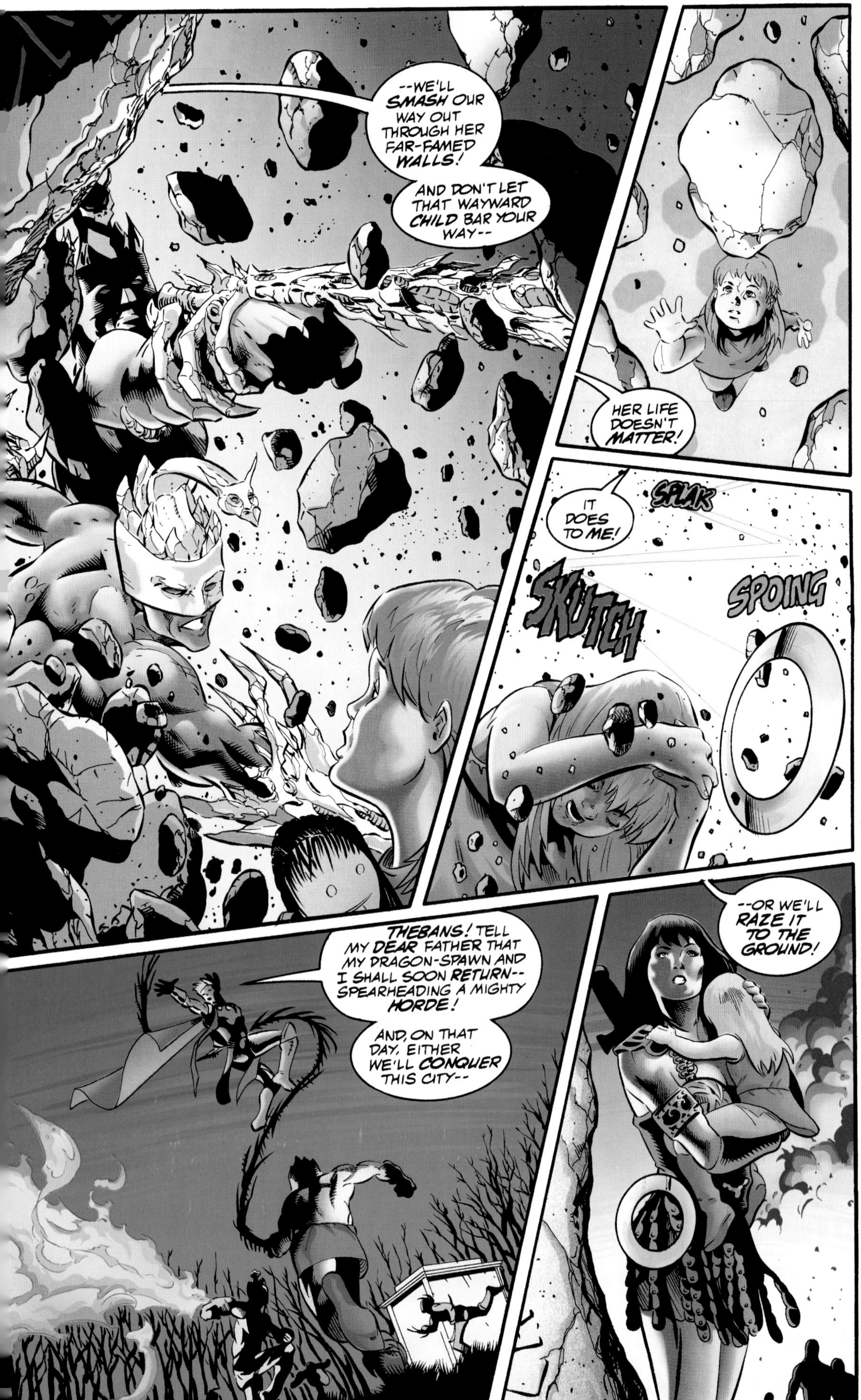
--WE'LL SMASH OUR WAY OUT THROUGH HER FAR-FAMED WALLS!
AND DON'T LET THAT WAYWARD CHILD BAR YOUR WAY--
HER LIFE DOESN'T MATTER!
IT DOES TO ME!
SPLAK
SKUTCH
SPOING
THEBANS! TELL MY DEAR FATHER THAT MY DRAGON-SPAWN AND I SHALL SOON RETURN-- SPEARHEADING A MIGHTY HORDE!
AND, ON THAT DAY, EITHER WE'LL CONQUER THIS CITY--
--OR WE'LL RAZE IT TO THE GROUND!

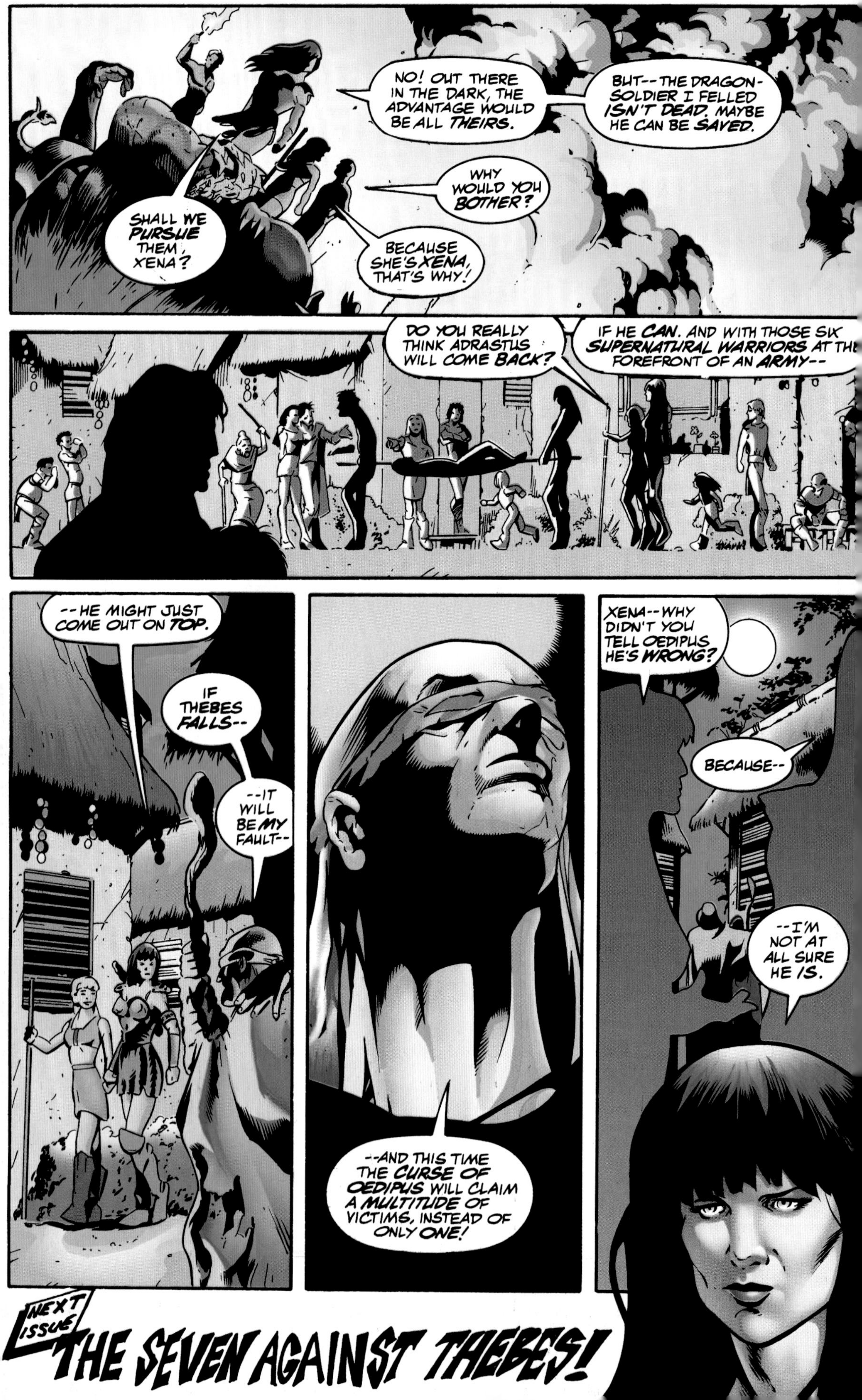
NO! OUT THERE IN THE DARK, THE ADVANTAGE WOULD BE ALL THEIRS.
BUT--THE DRAGON-SOLDIER I FELLED ISN'T DEAD. MAYBE HE CAN BE SAVED.
SHALL WE PURSUE THEM, XENA?
WHY WOULD YOU BOTHER?
BECAUSE SHE'S XENA, THAT'S WHY!
DO YOU REALLY THINK ADRASTUS WILL COME BACK?
IF HE CAN. AND WITH THOSE SIX SUPERNATURAL WARRIORS AT THE FOREFRONT OF AN ARMY--
--HE MIGHT JUST COME OUT ON TOP.
IF THEBES FALLS--
--IT WILL BE MY FAULT--
--AND THIS TIME THE CURSE OF OEDIPUS WILL CLAIM A MULTITUDE OF VICTIMS, INSTEAD OF ONLY ONE!
XENA--WHY DIDN'T YOU TELL OEDIPUS HE'S WRONG?
BECAUSE--
--I'M NOT AT ALL SURE HE IS.
NEXT ISSUE
THE SEVEN AGAINST THEBES!

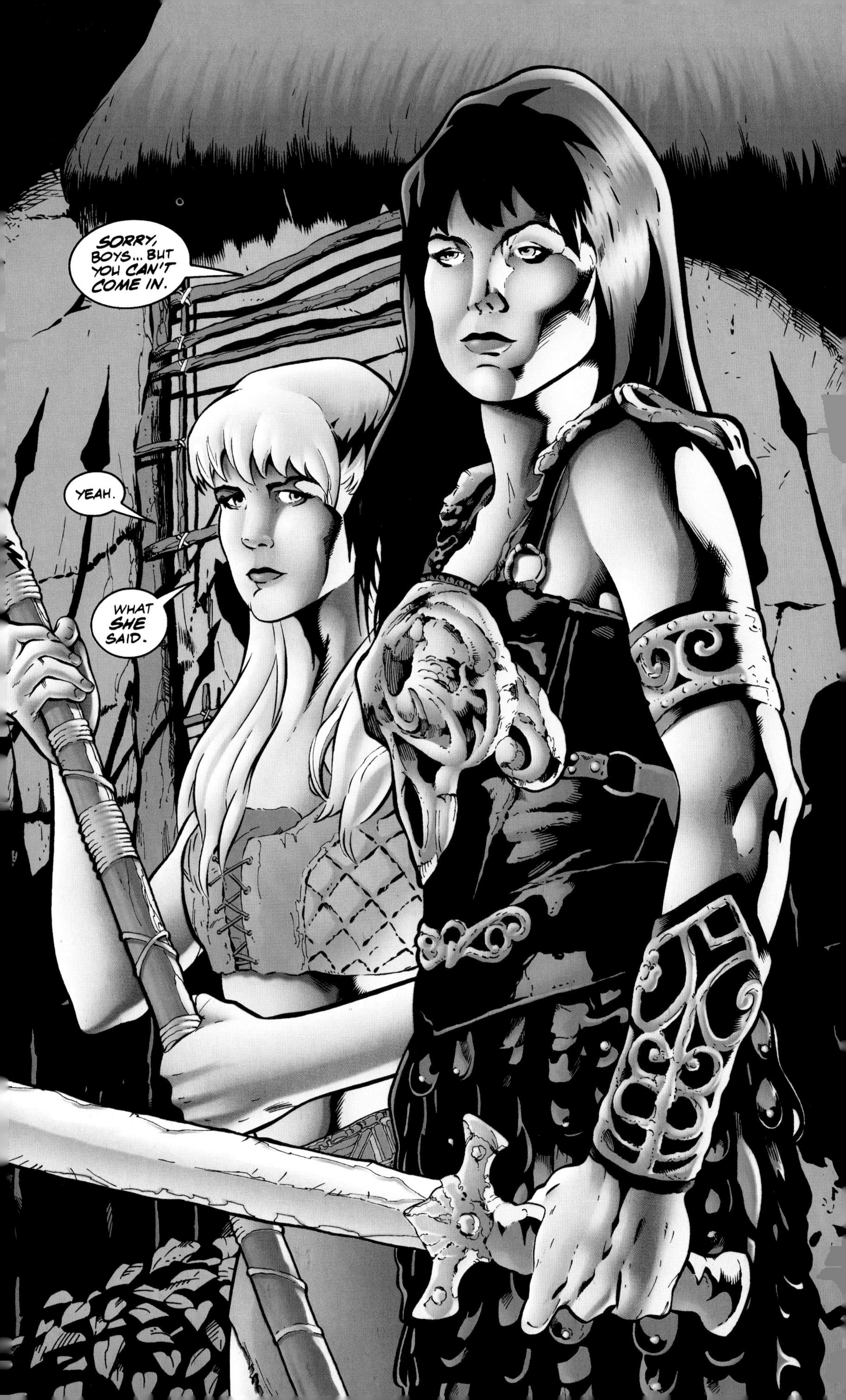
SORRY, BOYS... BUT YOU CAN'T COME IN.
YEAH.
WHAT SHE SAID.

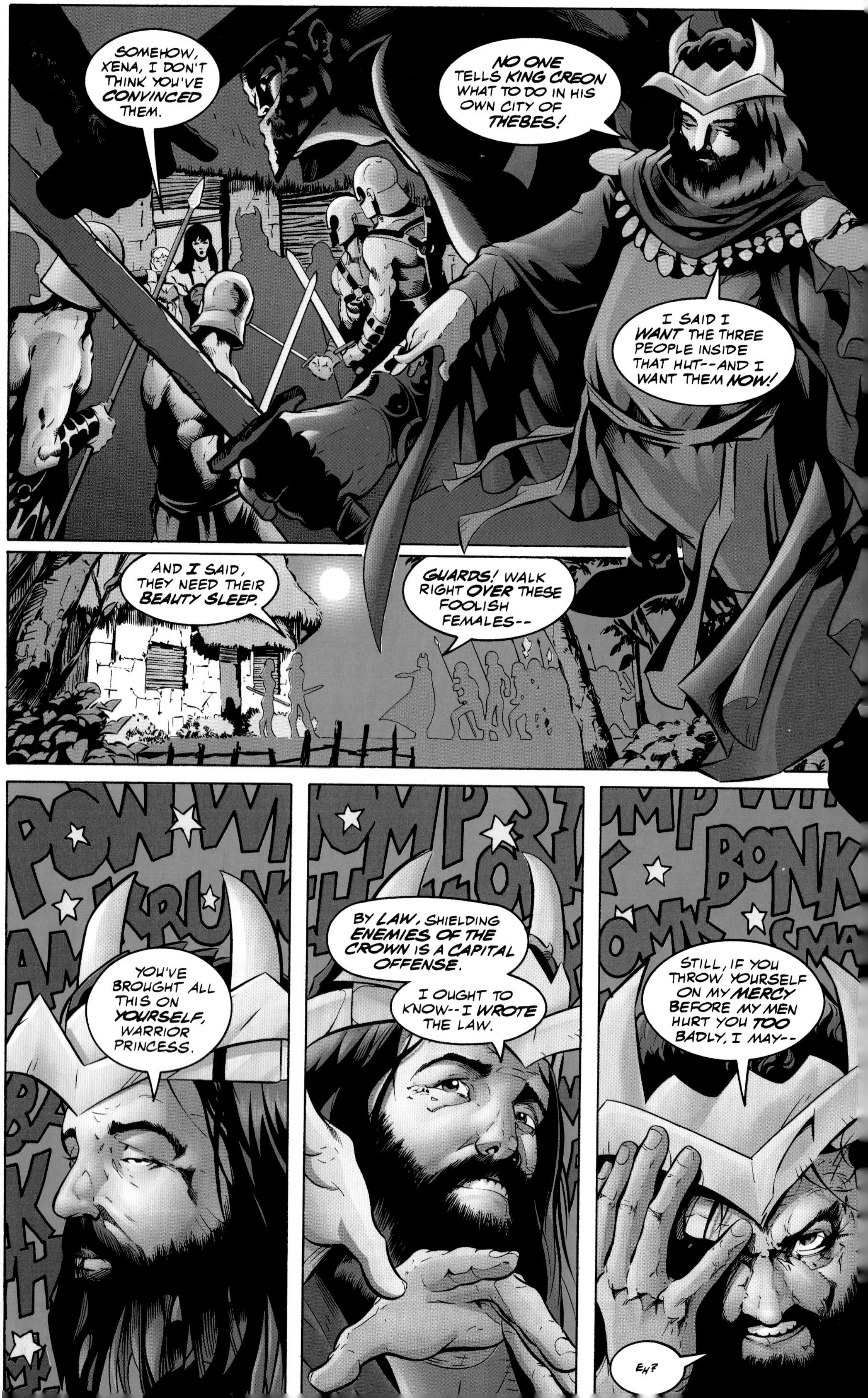
SOMEHOW, XENA, I DON'T THINK YOU'VE CONVINCED THEM.
NO ONE TELLS KING CREON WHAT TO DO IN HIS OWN CITY OF THEBES!
I SAID I WANT THE THREE PEOPLE INSIDE THAT HUT--AND I WANT THEM NOW!
AND I SAID, THEY NEED THEIR BEAUTY SLEEP.
GUARDS! WALK RIGHT OVER THESE FOOLISH FEMALES--
POW
YOU'VE BROUGHT ALL THIS ON YOURSELF, WARRIOR PRINCESS.
BY LAW, SHIELDING ENEMIES OF THE CROWN IS A CAPITAL OFFENSE.
I OUGHT TO KNOW--I WROTE THE LAW.
BONK
STILL, IF YOU THROW YOURSELF ON MY MERCY BEFORE MY MEN HURT YOU TOO BADLY, I MAY--
EH?

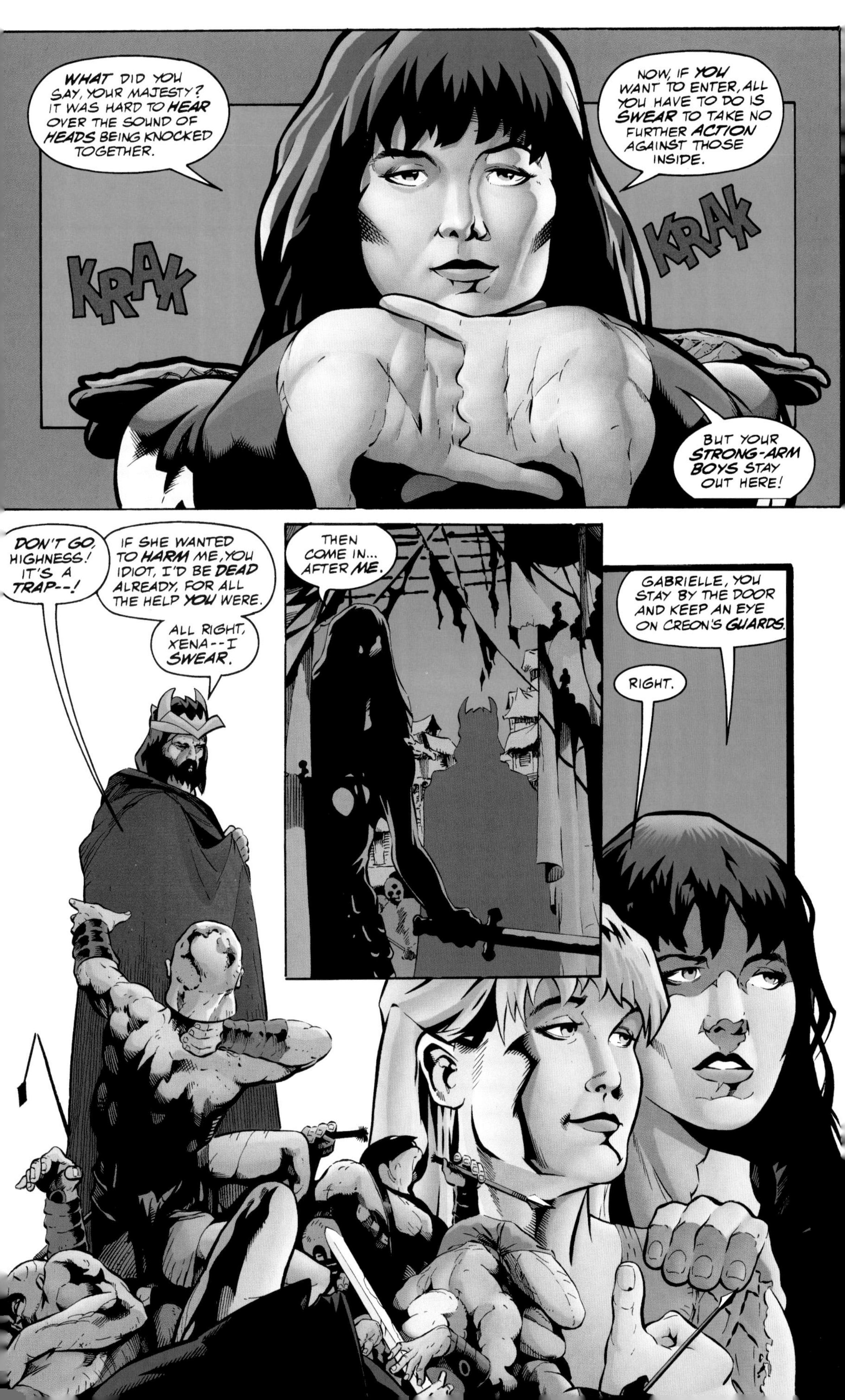
WHAT DID YOU SAY, YOUR MAJESTY? IT WAS HARD TO HEAR OVER THE SOUND OF HEADS BEING KNOCKED TOGETHER.
NOW, IF YOU WANT TO ENTER, ALL YOU HAVE TO DO IS SWEAR TO TAKE NO FURTHER ACTION AGAINST THOSE INSIDE.
KRAK
KRAK
BUT YOUR STRONG-ARM BOYS STAY OUT HERE!
DON'T GO, HIGHNESS! IT'S A TRAP--!
IF SHE WANTED TO HARM ME, YOU IDIOT, I'D BE DEAD ALREADY, FOR ALL THE HELP YOU WERE.
ALL RIGHT, XENA--I SWEAR.
THEN COME IN... AFTER ME.
GABRIELLE, YOU STAY BY THE DOOR AND KEEP AN EYE ON CREON'S GUARDS.
RIGHT.

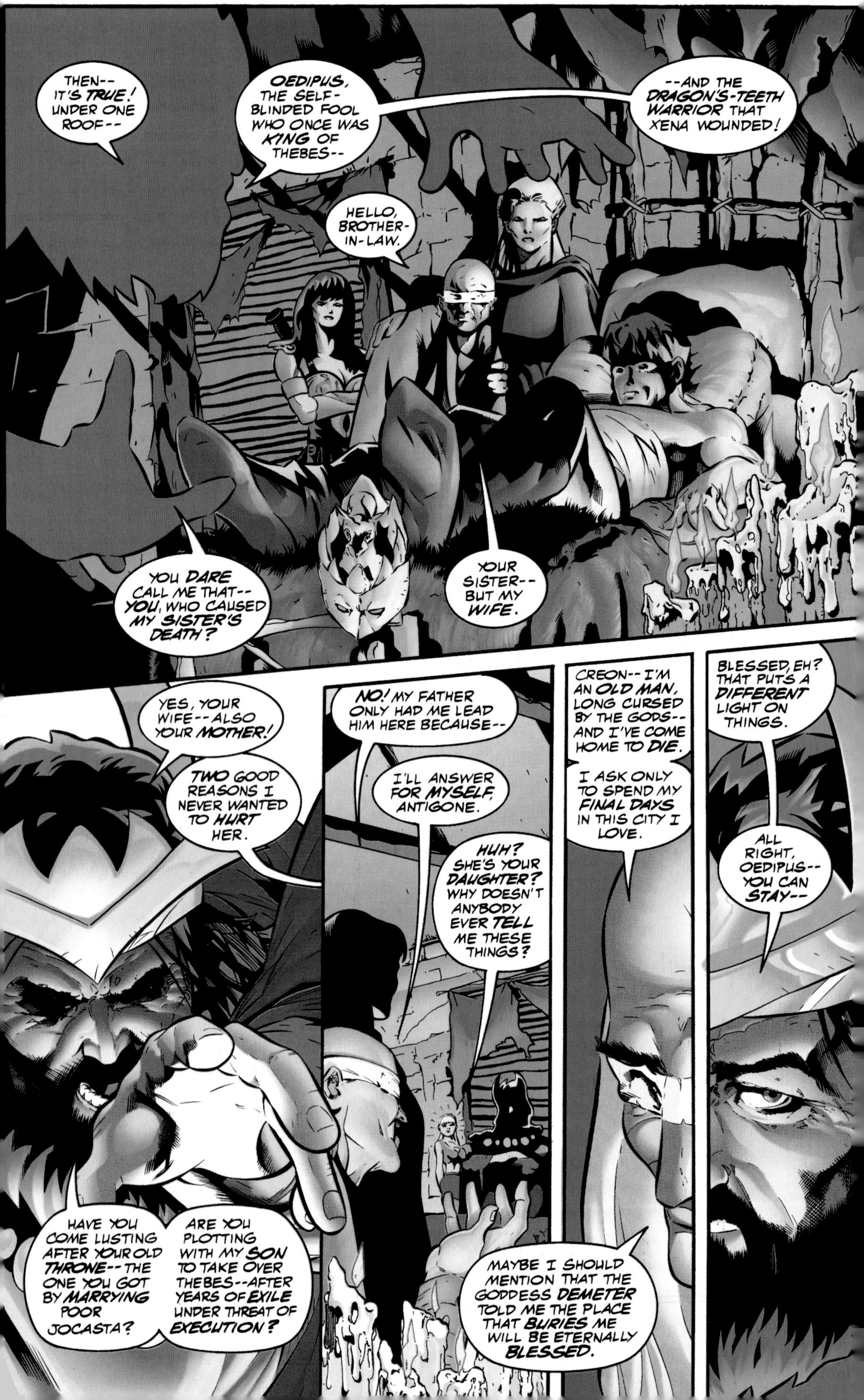
THEN-- IT'S TRUE! UNDER ONE ROOF--
OEDIPUS, THE SELF-BLINDED FOOL WHO ONCE WAS KING OF THEBES--
--AND THE DRAGON'S-TEETH WARRIOR THAT XENA WOUNDED!
HELLO, BROTHER-IN-LAW.
YOU DARE CALL ME THAT-- YOU, WHO CAUSED MY SISTER'S DEATH?
YOUR SISTER-- BUT MY WIFE.
YES, YOUR WIFE--ALSO YOUR MOTHER!
TWO GOOD REASONS I NEVER WANTED TO HURT HER.
HAVE YOU COME LUSTING AFTER YOUR OLD THRONE-- THE ONE YOU GOT BY MARRYING POOR JOCASTA?
ARE YOU PLOTTING WITH MY SON TO TAKE OVER THEBES--AFTER YEARS OF EXILE UNDER THREAT OF EXECUTION?
NO! MY FATHER ONLY HAD ME LEAD HIM HERE BECAUSE--
I'LL ANSWER FOR MYSELF, ANTIGONE.
HUH? SHE'S YOUR DAUGHTER? WHY DOESN'T ANYBODY EVER TELL ME THESE THINGS?
CREON-- I'M AN OLD MAN, LONG CURSED BY THE GODS-- AND I'VE COME HOME TO DIE.
I ASK ONLY TO SPEND MY FINAL DAYS IN THIS CITY I LOVE.
MAYBE I SHOULD MENTION THAT THE GODDESS DEMETER TOLD ME THE PLACE THAT BURIES ME WILL BE ETERNALLY BLESSED.
BLESSED, EH? THAT PUTS A DIFFERENT LIGHT ON THINGS.
ALL RIGHT, OEDIPUS-- YOU CAN STAY--

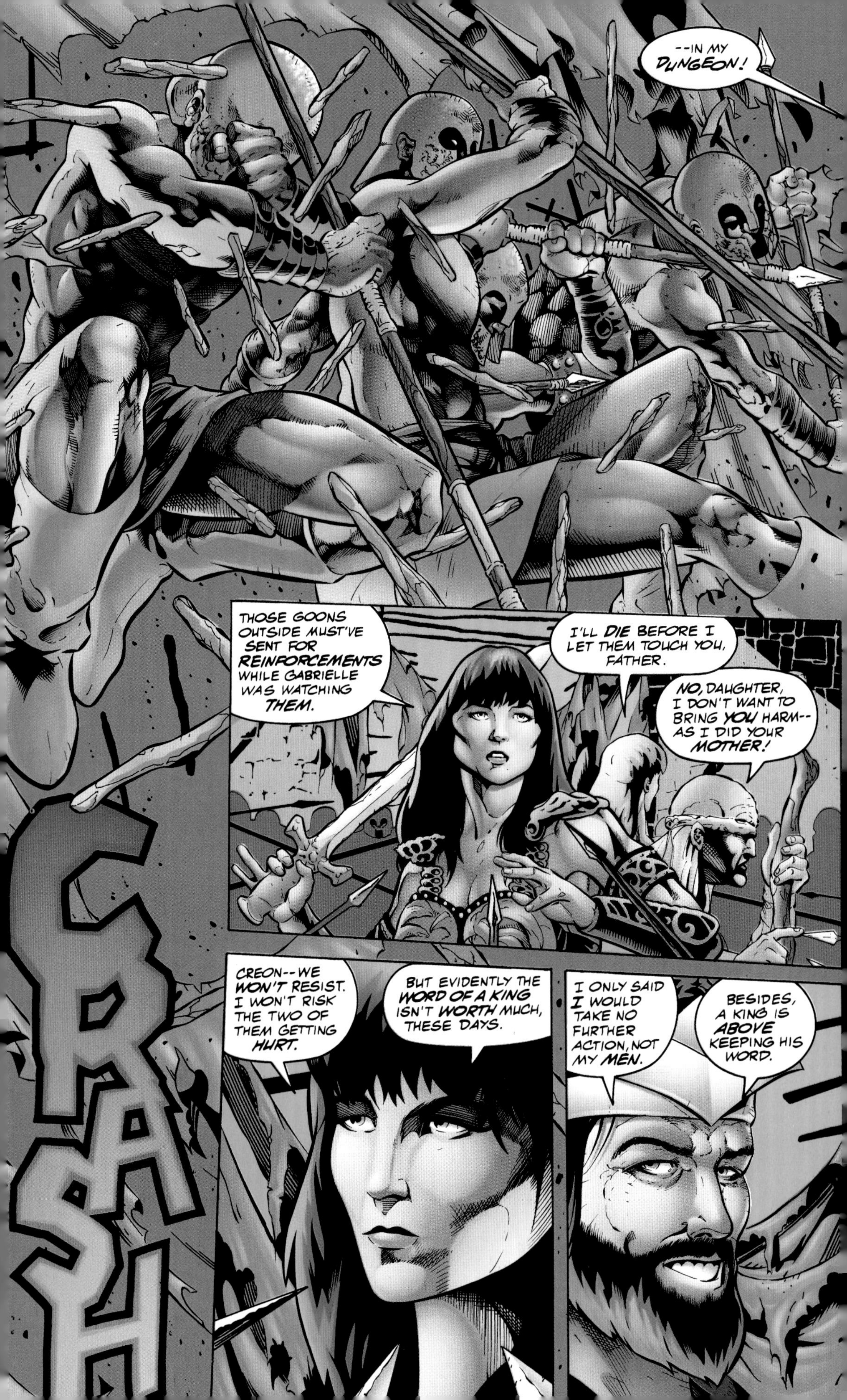
--IN MY DUNGEON!
CRASH
THOSE GOONS OUTSIDE MUST'VE SENT FOR REINFORCEMENTS WHILE GABRIELLE WAS WATCHING THEM.
I'LL DIE BEFORE I LET THEM TOUCH YOU, FATHER.
NO, DAUGHTER, I DON'T WANT TO BRING YOU HARM--AS I DID YOUR MOTHER!
CREON--WE WON'T RESIST. I WON'T RISK THE TWO OF THEM GETTING HURT.
BUT EVIDENTLY THE WORD OF A KING ISN'T WORTH MUCH, THESE DAYS.
I ONLY SAID I WOULD TAKE NO FURTHER ACTION, NOT MY MEN.
BESIDES, A KING IS ABOVE KEEPING HIS WORD.

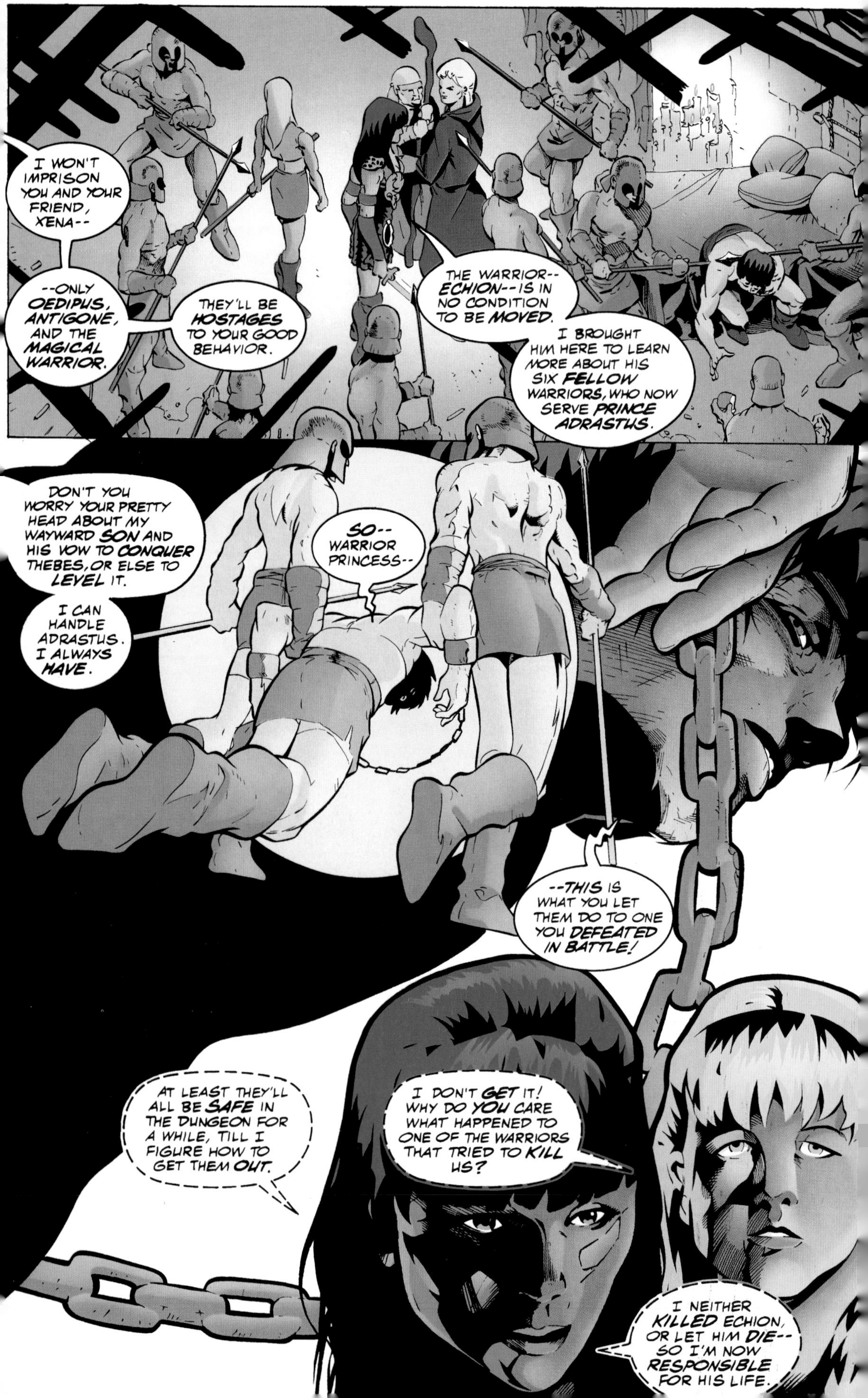
I WON'T IMPRISON YOU AND YOUR FRIEND, XENA--
--ONLY OEDIPUS, ANTIGONE, AND THE MAGICAL WARRIOR.
THEY'LL BE HOSTAGES TO YOUR GOOD BEHAVIOR.
THE WARRIOR--ECHION--IS IN NO CONDITION TO BE MOVED.
I BROUGHT HIM HERE TO LEARN MORE ABOUT HIS SIX FELLOW WARRIORS, WHO NOW SERVE PRINCE ADRASTUS.
DON'T YOU WORRY YOUR PRETTY HEAD ABOUT MY WAYWARD SON AND HIS VOW TO CONQUER THEBES, OR ELSE TO LEVEL IT.
I CAN HANDLE ADRASTUS. I ALWAYS HAVE.
SO--WARRIOR PRINCESS--
--THIS IS WHAT YOU LET THEM DO TO ONE YOU DEFEATED IN BATTLE!
AT LEAST THEY'LL ALL BE SAFE IN THE DUNGEON FOR A WHILE, TILL I FIGURE HOW TO GET THEM OUT.
I DON'T GET IT! WHY DO YOU CARE WHAT HAPPENED TO ONE OF THE WARRIORS THAT TRIED TO KILL US?
I NEITHER KILLED ECHION, OR LET HIM DIE--SO I'M NOW RESPONSIBLE FOR HIS LIFE.

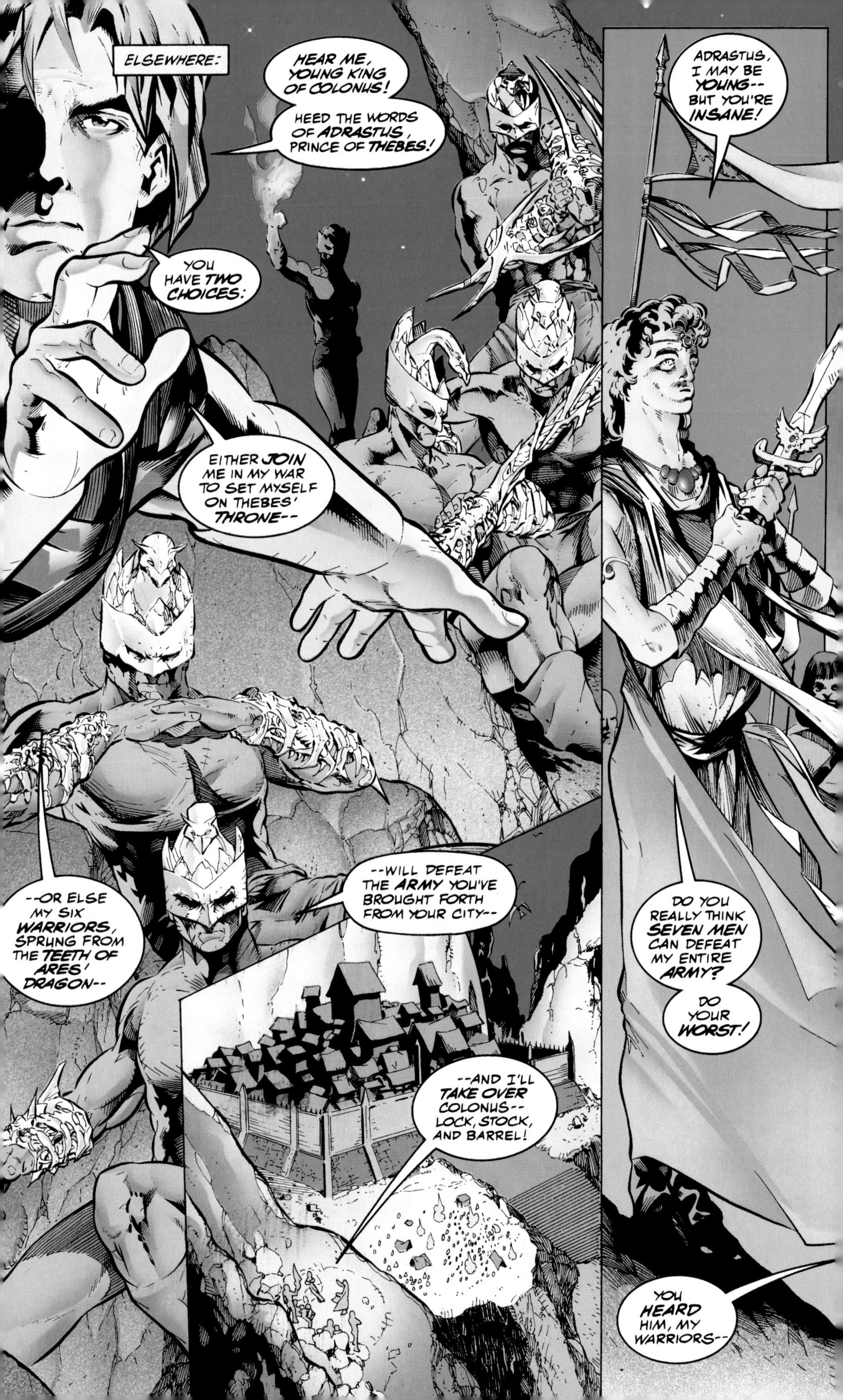
ELSEWHERE:
HEAR ME, YOUNG KING OF COLONUS!
HEED THE WORDS OF ADRASTUS, PRINCE OF THEBES!
YOU HAVE TWO CHOICES:
EITHER JOIN ME IN MY WAR TO SET MYSELF ON THEBES' THRONE--
--OR ELSE MY SIX WARRIORS, SPRUNG FROM THE TEETH OF ARES' DRAGON--
--WILL DEFEAT THE ARMY YOU'VE BROUGHT FORTH FROM YOUR CITY--
--AND I'LL TAKE OVER COLONUS-- LOCK, STOCK, AND BARREL!
ADRASTUS, I MAY BE YOUNG-- BUT YOU'RE INSANE!
DO YOU REALLY THINK SEVEN MEN CAN DEFEAT MY ENTIRE ARMY?
DO YOUR WORST!
YOU HEARD HIM, MY WARRIORS--

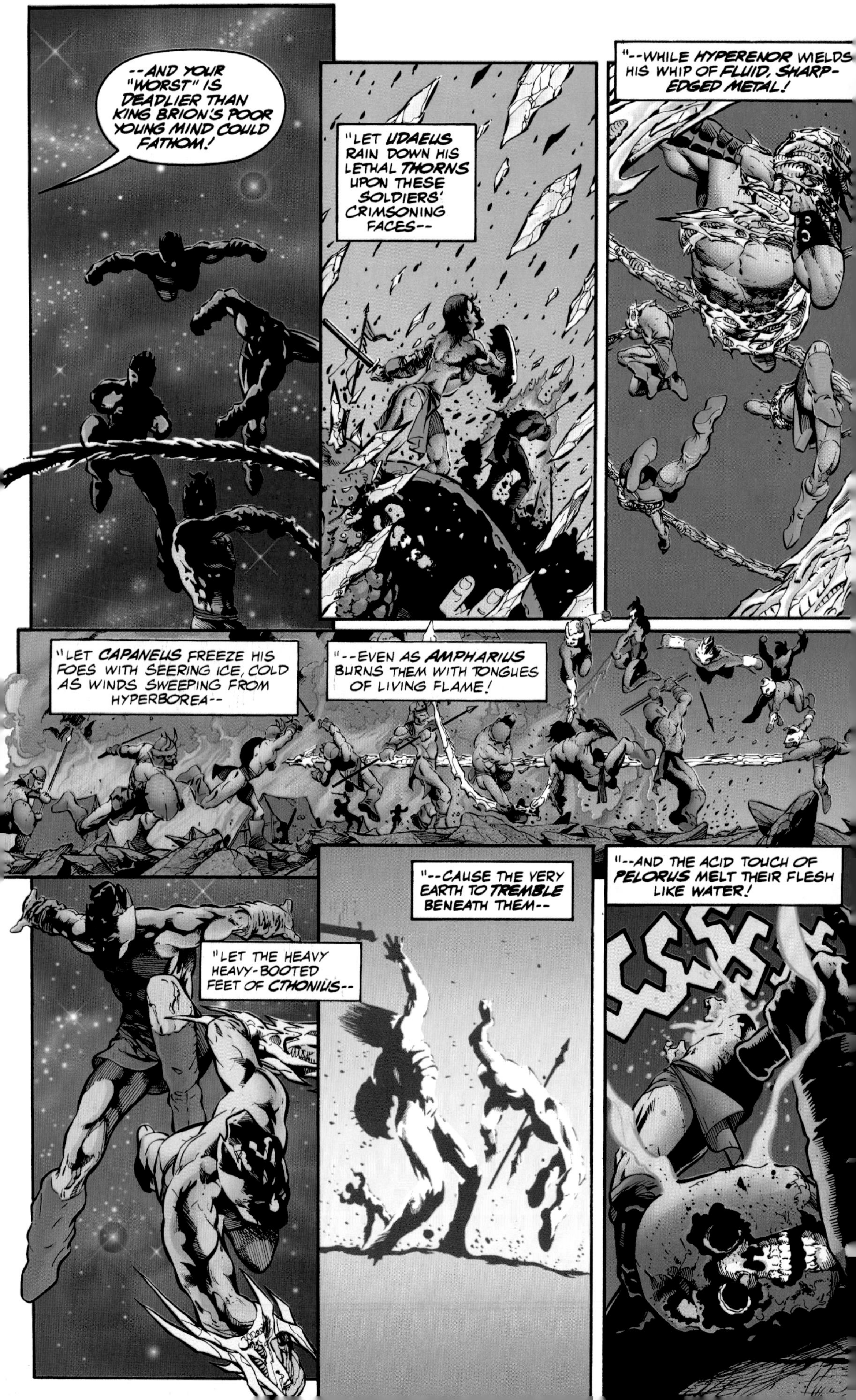
--AND YOUR "WORST" IS DEADLIER THAN KING BRION'S POOR YOUNG MIND COULD FATHOM!
"LET UDAEUS RAIN DOWN HIS LETHAL THORNS UPON THESE SOLDIERS' CRIMSONING FACES--
"--WHILE HYPERENOR WIELDS HIS WHIP OF FLUID, SHARP-EDGED METAL!
"LET CAPANEUS FREEZE HIS FOES WITH SEERING ICE, COLD AS WINDS SWEEPING FROM HYPERBOREA--
"--EVEN AS AMPHARIUS BURNS THEM WITH TONGUES OF LIVING FLAME!
"LET THE HEAVY HEAVY-BOOTED FEET OF CTHONIUS--
"--CAUSE THE VERY EARTH TO TREMBLE BENEATH THEM--
"--AND THE ACID TOUCH OF PELORUS MELT THEIR FLESH LIKE WATER!

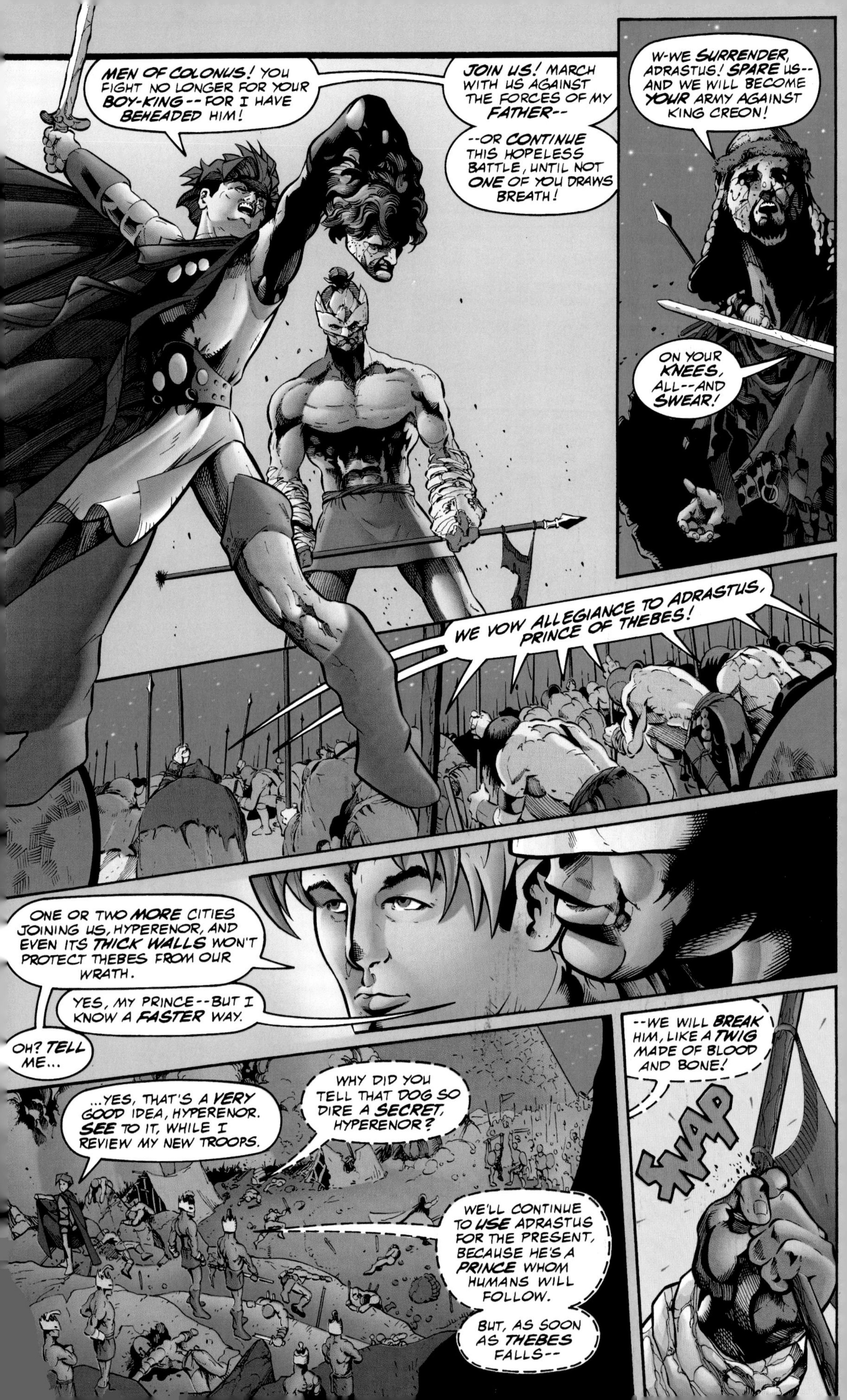
MEN OF COLONUS! YOU FIGHT NO LONGER FOR YOUR BOY-KING--FOR I HAVE BEHEADED HIM!
JOIN US! MARCH WITH US AGAINST THE FORCES OF MY FATHER--
--OR CONTINUE THIS HOPELESS BATTLE, UNTIL NOT ONE OF YOU DRAWS BREATH!
W-WE SURRENDER, ADRASTUS! SPARE US--AND WE WILL BECOME YOUR ARMY AGAINST KING CREON!
ON YOUR KNEES, ALL--AND SWEAR!
WE VOW ALLEGIANCE TO ADRASTUS, PRINCE OF THEBES!
ONE OR TWO MORE CITIES JOINING US, HYPERENOR, AND EVEN ITS THICK WALLS WON'T PROTECT THEBES FROM OUR WRATH.
YES, MY PRINCE--BUT I KNOW A FASTER WAY.
OH? TELL ME...
...YES, THAT'S A VERY GOOD IDEA, HYPERENOR. SEE TO IT, WHILE I REVIEW MY NEW TROOPS.
WHY DID YOU TELL THAT DOG SO DIRE A SECRET, HYPERENOR?
WE'LL CONTINUE TO USE ADRASTUS FOR THE PRESENT, BECAUSE HE'S A PRINCE WHOM HUMANS WILL FOLLOW.
BUT, AS SOON AS THEBES FALLS--
--WE WILL BREAK HIM, LIKE A TWIG MADE OF BLOOD AND BONE!
SNAP

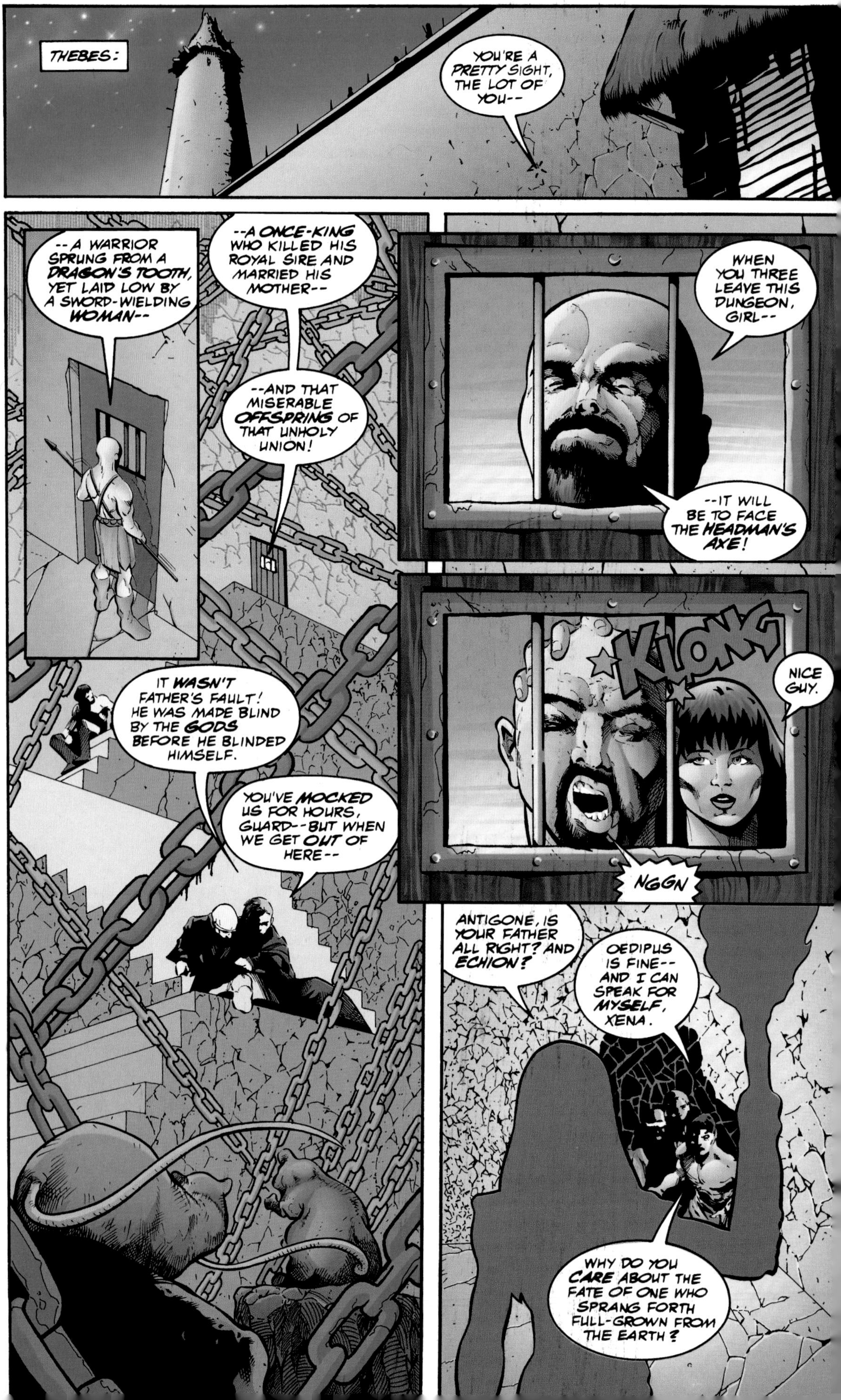
THEBES:
YOU'RE A PRETTY SIGHT, THE LOT OF YOU--
--A WARRIOR SPRUNG FROM A DRAGON'S TOOTH, YET LAID LOW BY A SWORD-WIELDING WOMAN--
--A ONCE-KING WHO KILLED HIS ROYAL SIRE AND MARRIED HIS MOTHER--
--AND THAT MISERABLE OFFSPRING OF THAT UNHOLY UNION!
IT WASN'T FATHER'S FAULT! HE WAS MADE BLIND BY THE GODS BEFORE HE BLINDED HIMSELF.
YOU'VE MOCKED US FOR HOURS, GUARD--BUT WHEN WE GET OUT OF HERE--
WHEN YOU THREE LEAVE THIS DUNGEON, GIRL--
--IT WILL BE TO FACE THE HEADMAN'S AXE!
KLONG
NICE GUY.
NGGN
ANTIGONE, IS YOUR FATHER ALL RIGHT? AND ECHION?
OEDIPUS IS FINE-- AND I CAN SPEAK FOR MYSELF, XENA.
WHY DO YOU CARE ABOUT THE FATE OF ONE WHO SPRANG FORTH FULL-GROWN FROM THE EARTH?

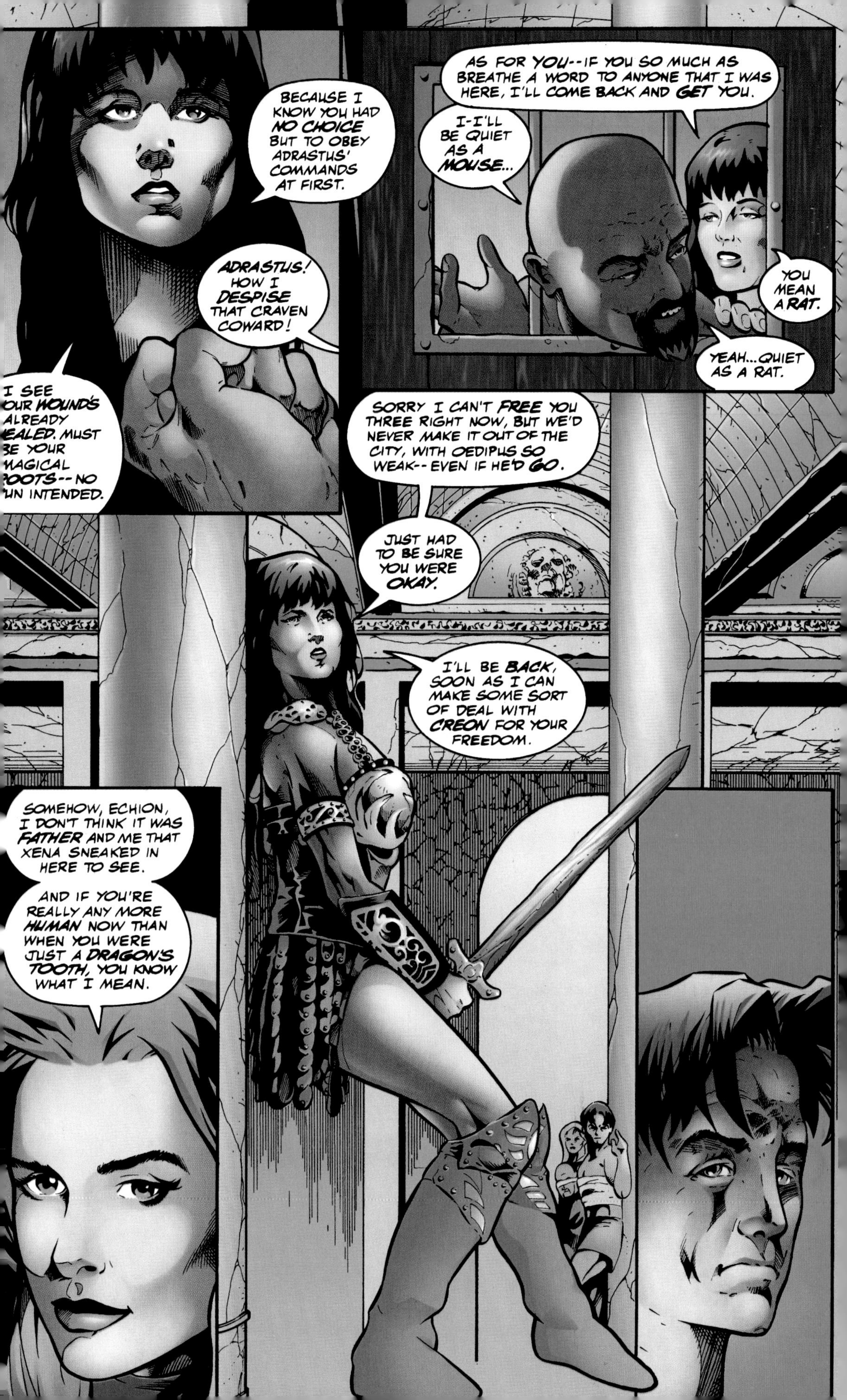
BECAUSE I KNOW YOU HAD NO CHOICE BUT TO OBEY ADRASTUS' COMMANDS AT FIRST.
ADRASTUS! HOW I DESPISE THAT CRAVEN COWARD!
I SEE YOUR WOUND'S ALREADY HEALED. MUST BE YOUR MAGICAL ROOTS-- NO PUN INTENDED.
AS FOR YOU--IF YOU SO MUCH AS BREATHE A WORD TO ANYONE THAT I WAS HERE, I'LL COME BACK AND GET YOU.
I-I'LL BE QUIET AS A MOUSE...
YOU MEAN A RAT.
YEAH... QUIET AS A RAT.
SORRY I CAN'T FREE YOU THREE RIGHT NOW, BUT WE'D NEVER MAKE IT OUT OF THE CITY, WITH OEDIPUS SO WEAK-- EVEN IF HE'D GO.
JUST HAD TO BE SURE YOU WERE OKAY.
I'LL BE BACK, SOON AS I CAN MAKE SOME SORT OF DEAL WITH CREON FOR YOUR FREEDOM.
SOMEHOW, ECHION, I DON'T THINK IT WAS FATHER AND ME THAT XENA SNEAKED IN HERE TO SEE.
AND IF YOU'RE REALLY ANY MORE HUMAN NOW THAN WHEN YOU WERE JUST A DRAGON'S TOOTH, YOU KNOW WHAT I MEAN.

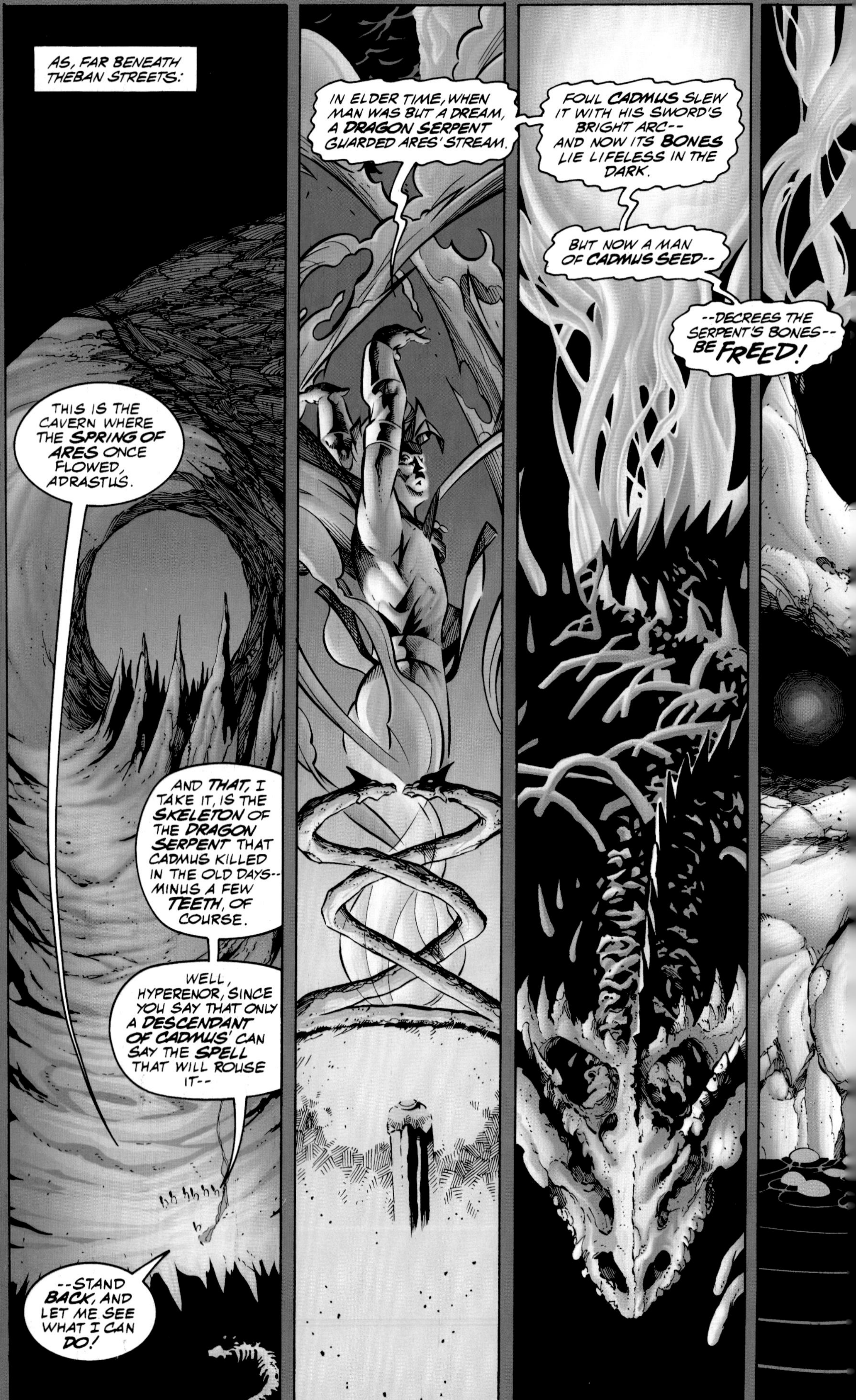
AS, FAR BENEATH THEBAN STREETS:
THIS IS THE CAVERN WHERE THE SPRING OF ARES ONCE FLOWED, ADRASTUS.
AND THAT, I TAKE IT, IS THE SKELETON OF THE DRAGON SERPENT THAT CADMUS KILLED IN THE OLD DAYS-- MINUS A FEW TEETH, OF COURSE.
WELL, HYPERENOR, SINCE YOU SAY THAT ONLY A DESCENDANT OF CADMUS' CAN SAY THE SPELL THAT WILL ROUSE IT--
--STAND BACK, AND LET ME SEE WHAT I CAN DO!
IN ELDER TIME, WHEN MAN WAS BUT A DREAM, A DRAGON SERPENT GUARDED ARES' STREAM.
FOUL CADMUS SLEW IT WITH HIS SWORD'S BRIGHT ARC-- AND NOW ITS BONES LIE LIFELESS IN THE DARK.
BUT NOW A MAN OF CADMUS SEED--
--DECREES THE SERPENT'S BONES-- BE FREED!

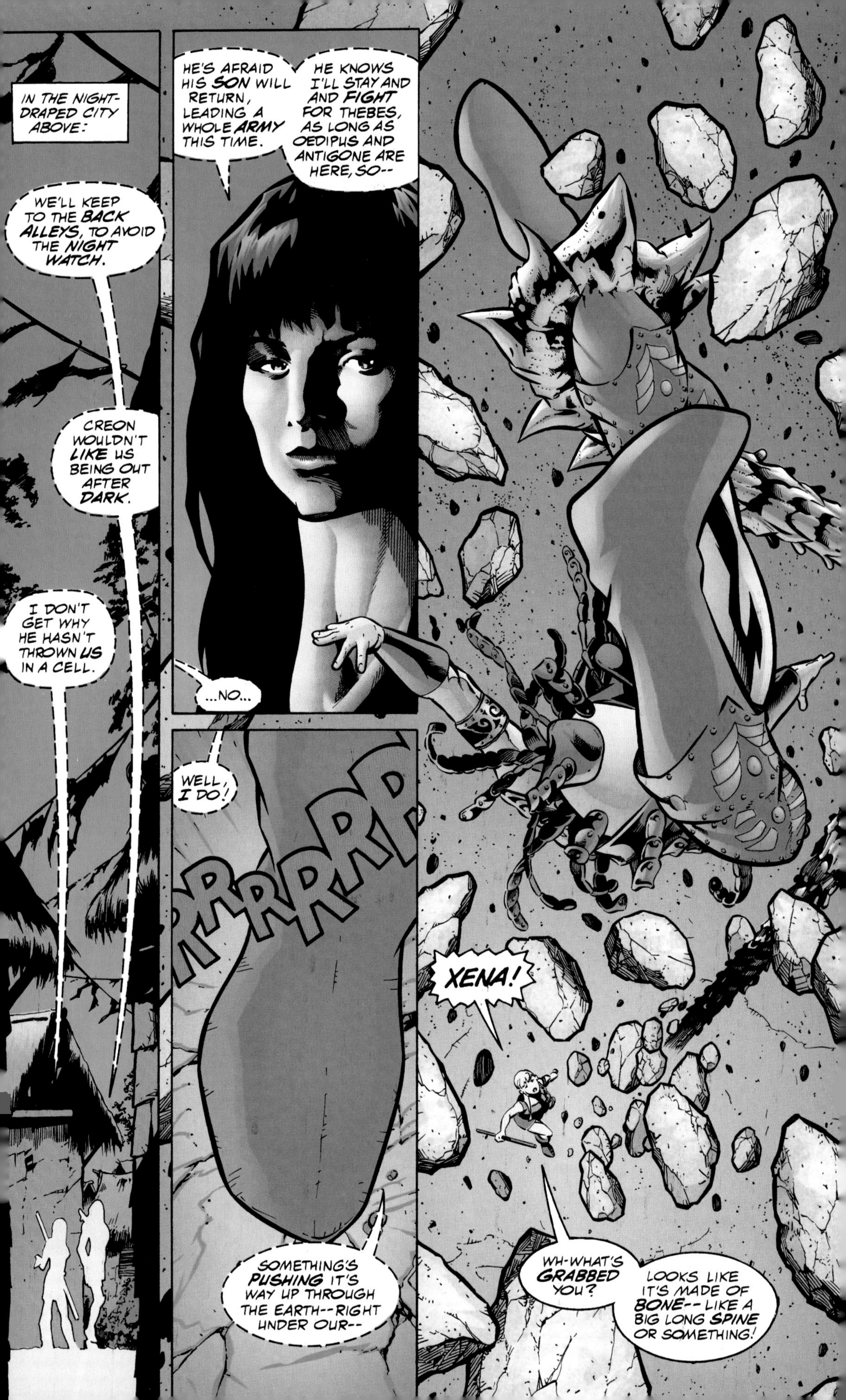
IN THE NIGHT-DRAPED CITY ABOVE:
WE'LL KEEP TO THE BACK ALLEYS, TO AVOID THE NIGHT WATCH.
CREON WOULDN'T LIKE US BEING OUT AFTER DARK.
I DON'T GET WHY HE HASN'T THROWN US IN A CELL.
HE'S AFRAID HIS SON WILL RETURN, LEADING A WHOLE ARMY THIS TIME.
HE KNOWS I'LL STAY AND AND FIGHT FOR THEBES, AS LONG AS OEDIPUS AND ANTIGONE ARE HERE, SO--
...NO...
WELL, I DO!
RRRRRP
SOMETHING'S PUSHING IT'S WAY UP THROUGH THE EARTH--RIGHT UNDER OUR--
XENA!
WH-WHAT'S GRABBED YOU?
LOOKS LIKE IT'S MADE OF BONE-- LIKE A BIG LONG SPINE OR SOMETHING!

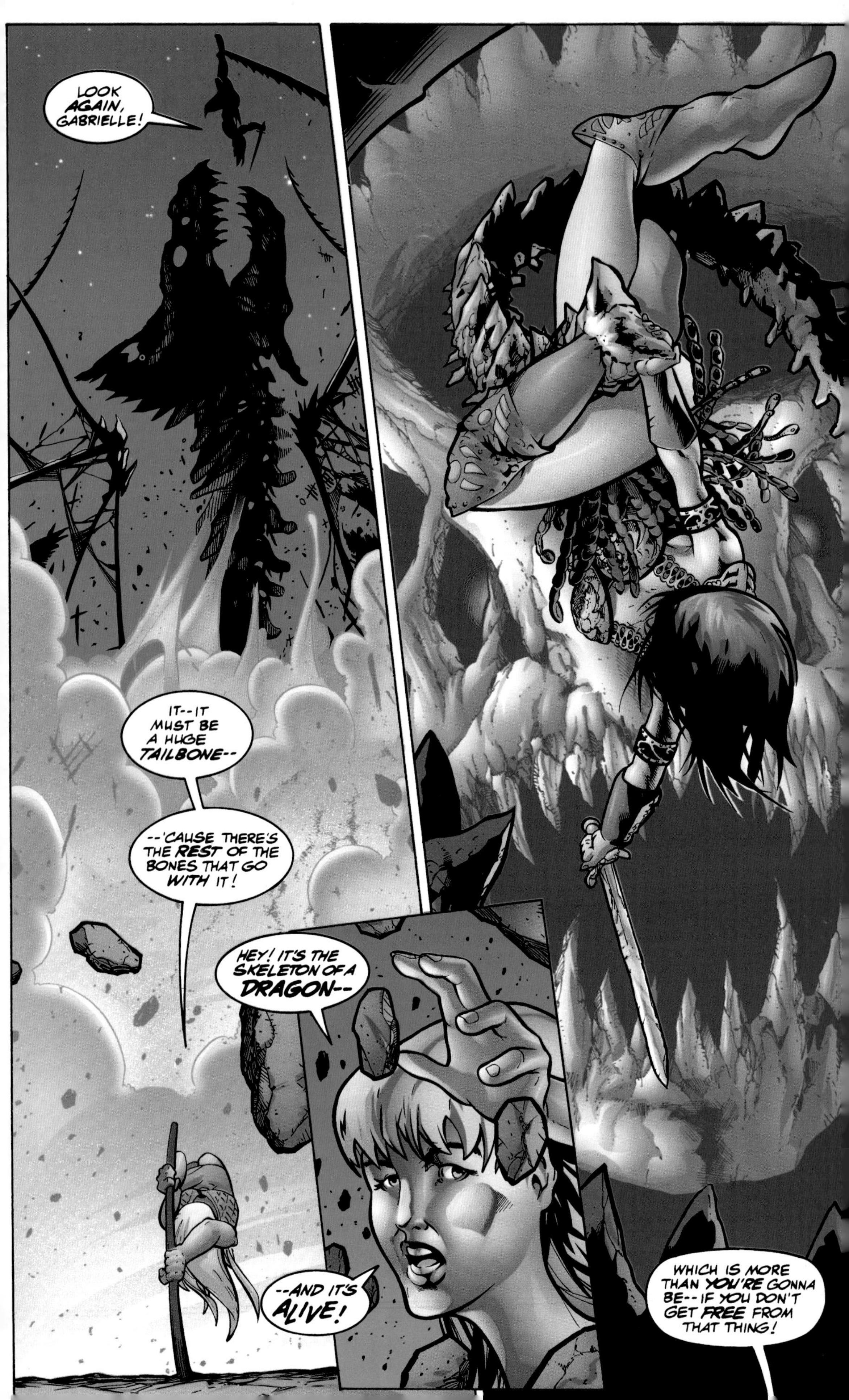
LOOK AGAIN, GABRIELLE!
IT--IT MUST BE A HUGE TAILBONE--
--'CAUSE THERE'S THE REST OF THE BONES THAT GO WITH IT!
HEY! IT'S THE SKELETON OF A DRAGON--
--AND IT'S ALIVE!
WHICH IS MORE THAN YOU'RE GONNA BE-- IF YOU DON'T GET FREE FROM THAT THING!

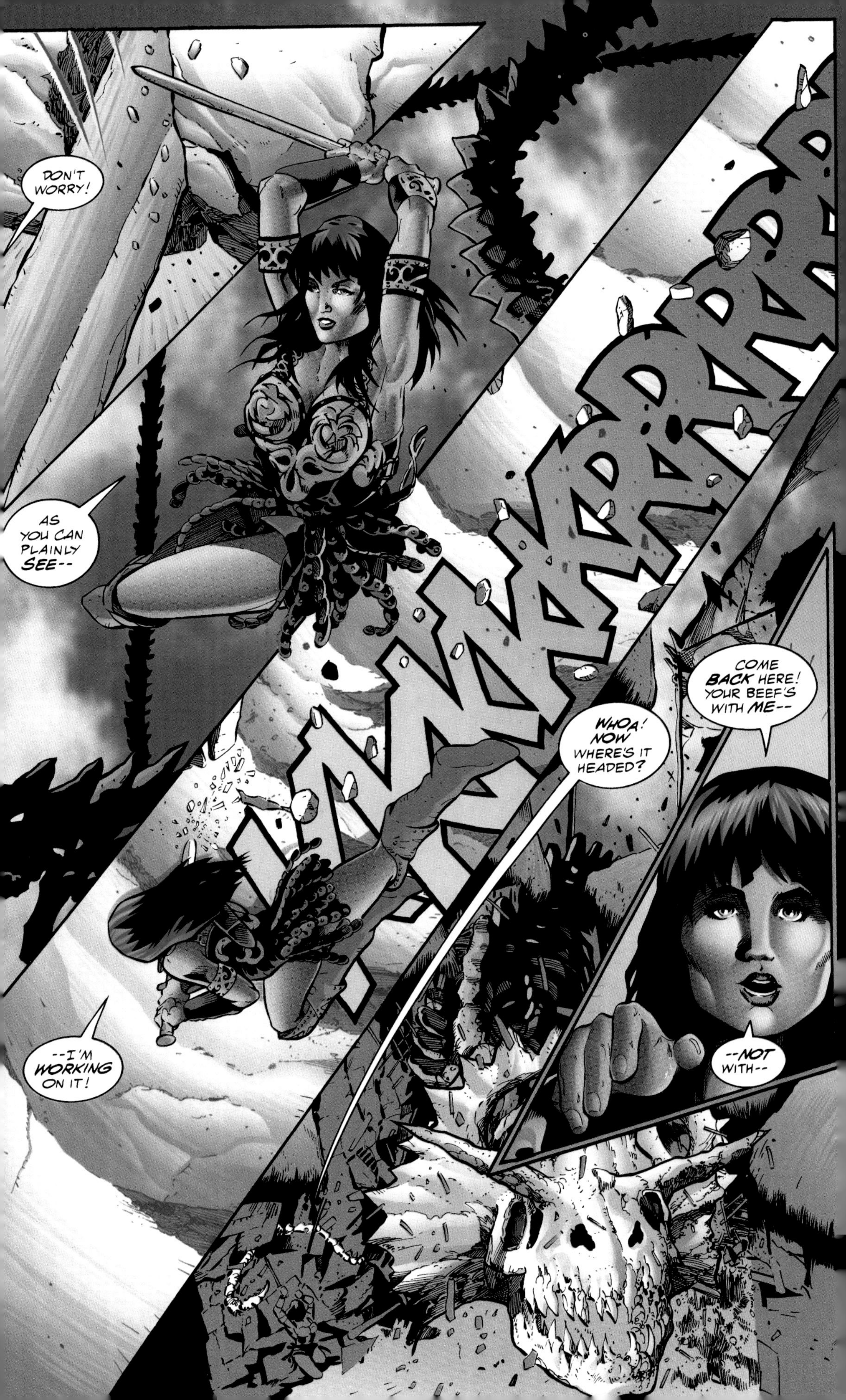
DON'T WORRY!
AS YOU CAN PLAINLY SEE--
--I'M WORKING ON IT!
WHOA! NOW WHERE'S IT HEADED?
COME BACK HERE! YOUR BEEF'S WITH ME--
--NOT WITH--

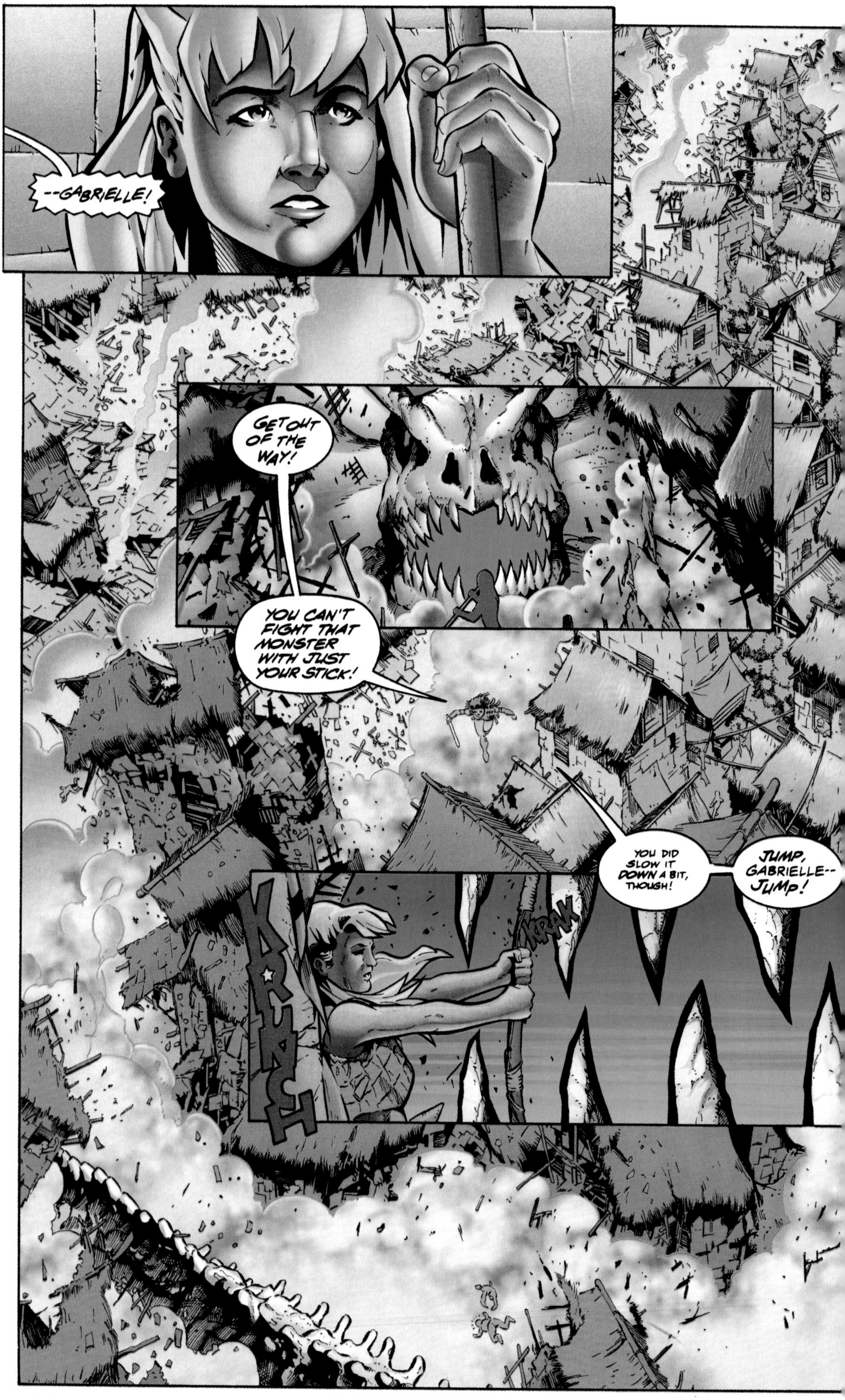
--GABRIELLE!
GET OUT OF THE WAY!
YOU CAN'T FIGHT THAT MONSTER WITH JUST YOUR STICK!
YOU DID SLOW IT DOWN A BIT, THOUGH!
JUMP, GABRIELLE--JUMP!
KRUNCH
KRAK

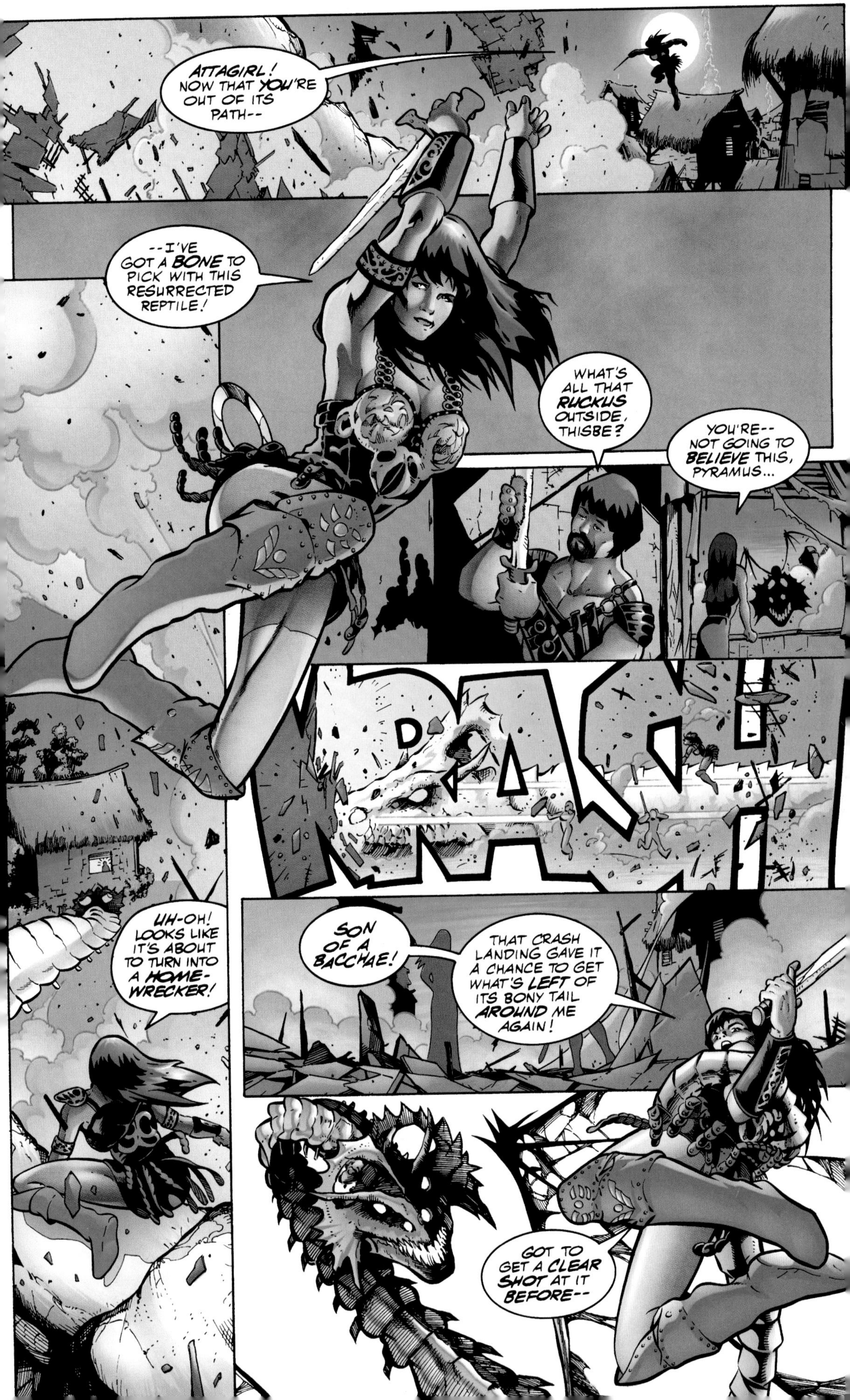

ATTAGIRL! NOW THAT YOU'RE OUT OF ITS PATH--
--I'VE GOT A BONE TO PICK WITH THIS RESURRECTED REPTILE!
WHAT'S ALL THAT RUCKUS OUTSIDE, THISBE?
YOU'RE--NOT GOING TO BELIEVE THIS, PYRAMUS...
UH-OH! LOOKS LIKE IT'S ABOUT TO TURN INTO A HOME-WRECKER!
SON OF A BACCHAE!
THAT CRASH LANDING GAVE IT A CHANCE TO GET WHAT'S LEFT OF ITS BONY TAIL AROUND ME AGAIN!
GOT TO GET A CLEAR SHOT AT IT BEFORE--

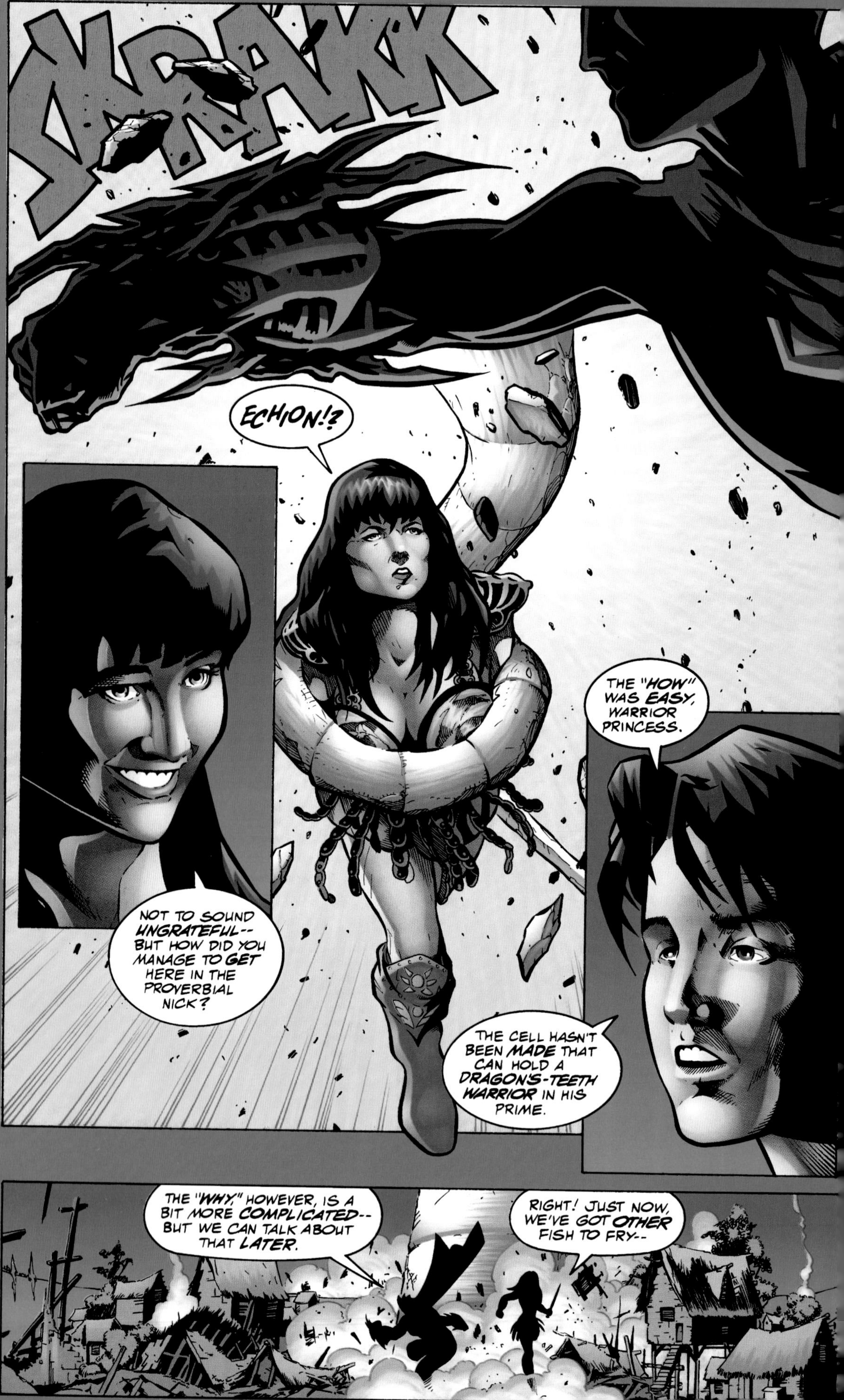
KRAKK
ECHION!?
NOT TO SOUND UNGRATEFUL-- BUT HOW DID YOU MANAGE TO GET HERE IN THE PROVERBIAL NICK?
THE "HOW" WAS EASY, WARRIOR PRINCESS.
THE CELL HASN'T BEEN MADE THAT CAN HOLD A DRAGON'S-TEETH WARRIOR IN HIS PRIME.
THE "WHY," HOWEVER, IS A BIT MORE COMPLICATED-- BUT WE CAN TALK ABOUT THAT LATER.
RIGHT! JUST NOW, WE'VE GOT OTHER FISH TO FRY--

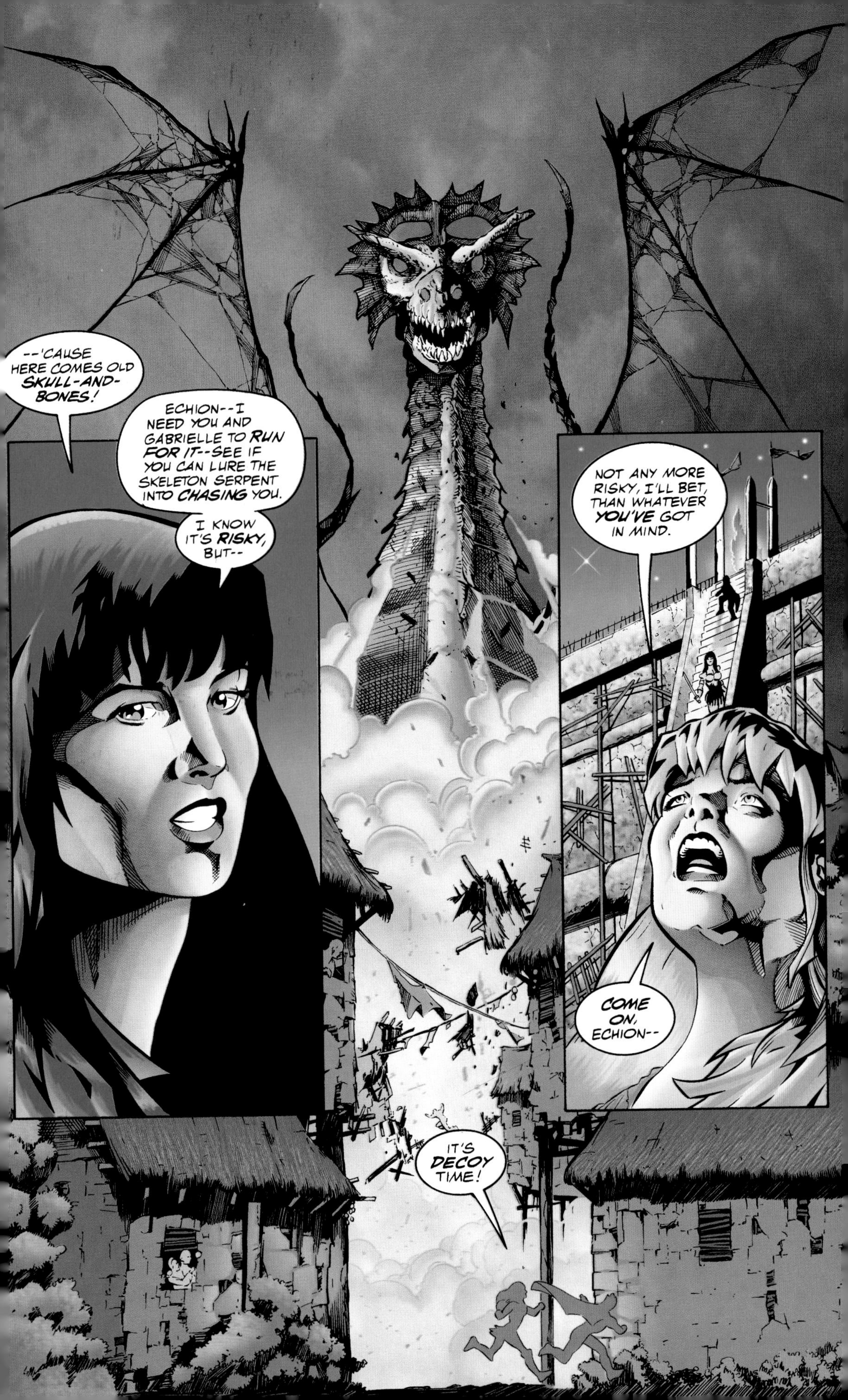
--'CAUSE HERE COMES OLD SKULL-AND-BONES!
ECHION--I NEED YOU AND GABRIELLE TO RUN FOR IT--SEE IF YOU CAN LURE THE SKELETON SERPENT INTO CHASING YOU.
I KNOW IT'S RISKY, BUT--
NOT ANY MORE RISKY, I'LL BET, THAN WHATEVER YOU'VE GOT IN MIND.
COME ON, ECHION--
IT'S DECOY TIME!

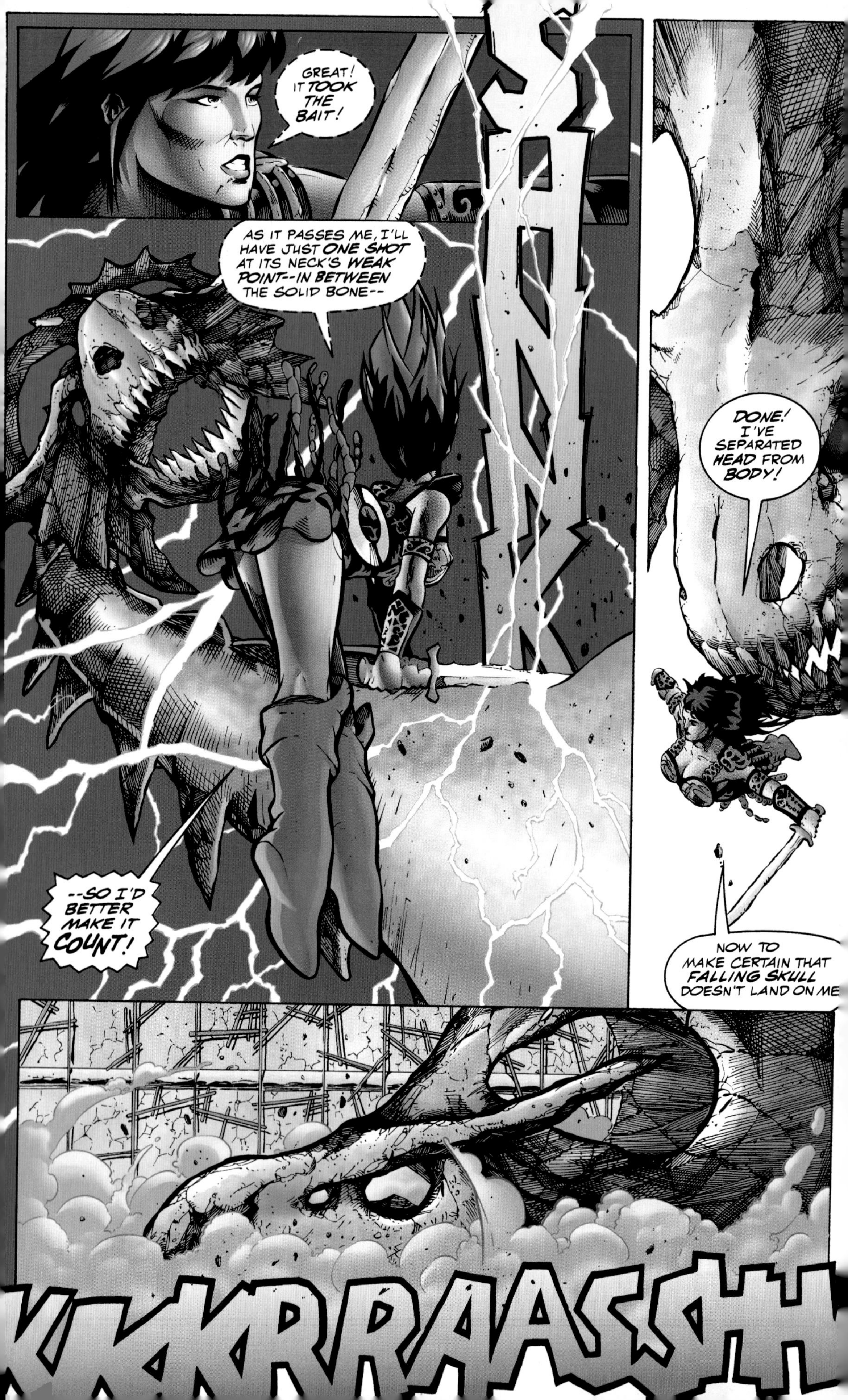
GREAT! IT TOOK THE BAIT!
AS IT PASSES ME, I'LL HAVE JUST ONE SHOT AT ITS NECK'S WEAK POINT--IN BETWEEN THE SOLID BONE--
--SO I'D BETTER MAKE IT COUNT!
DONE! I'VE SEPARATED HEAD FROM BODY!
NOW TO MAKE CERTAIN THAT FALLING SKULL DOESN'T LAND ON ME
KKKRRAASCH

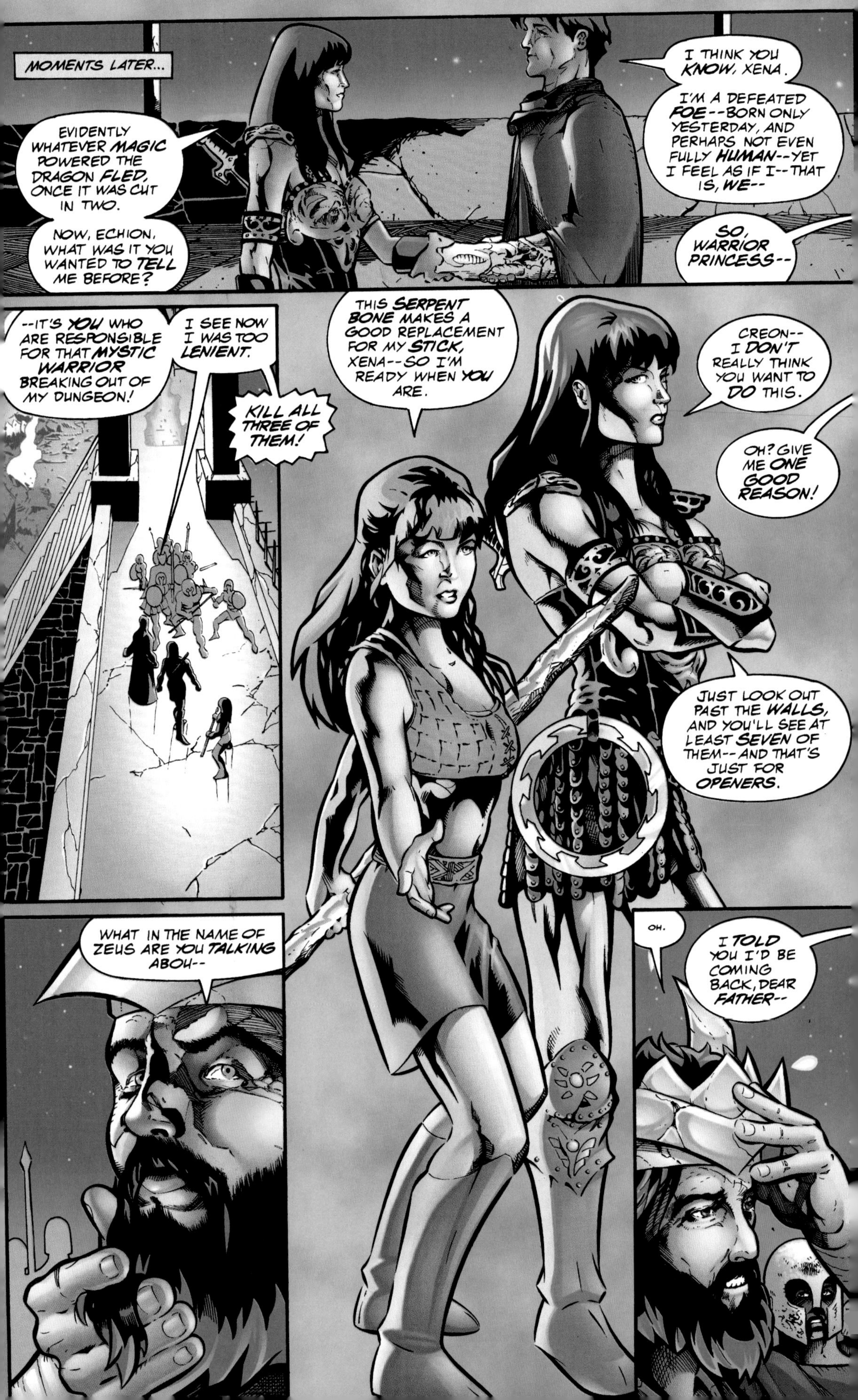
MOMENTS LATER...
EVIDENTLY WHATEVER MAGIC POWERED THE DRAGON FLED, ONCE IT WAS CUT IN TWO.
NOW, ECHION, WHAT WAS IT YOU WANTED TO TELL ME BEFORE?
I THINK YOU KNOW, XENA.
I'M A DEFEATED FOE--BORN ONLY YESTERDAY, AND PERHAPS NOT EVEN FULLY HUMAN--YET I FEEL AS IF I--THAT IS, WE--
SO, WARRIOR PRINCESS--
--IT'S YOU WHO ARE RESPONSIBLE FOR THAT MYSTIC WARRIOR BREAKING OUT OF MY DUNGEON!
I SEE NOW I WAS TOO LENIENT.
KILL ALL THREE OF THEM!
THIS SERPENT BONE MAKES A GOOD REPLACEMENT FOR MY STICK, XENA--SO I'M READY WHEN YOU ARE.
CREON--I DON'T REALLY THINK YOU WANT TO DO THIS.
OH? GIVE ME ONE GOOD REASON!
JUST LOOK OUT PAST THE WALLS, AND YOU'LL SEE AT LEAST SEVEN OF THEM--AND THAT'S JUST FOR OPENERS.
WHAT IN THE NAME OF ZEUS ARE YOU TALKING ABOU--
OH.
I TOLD YOU I'D BE COMING BACK, DEAR FATHER--

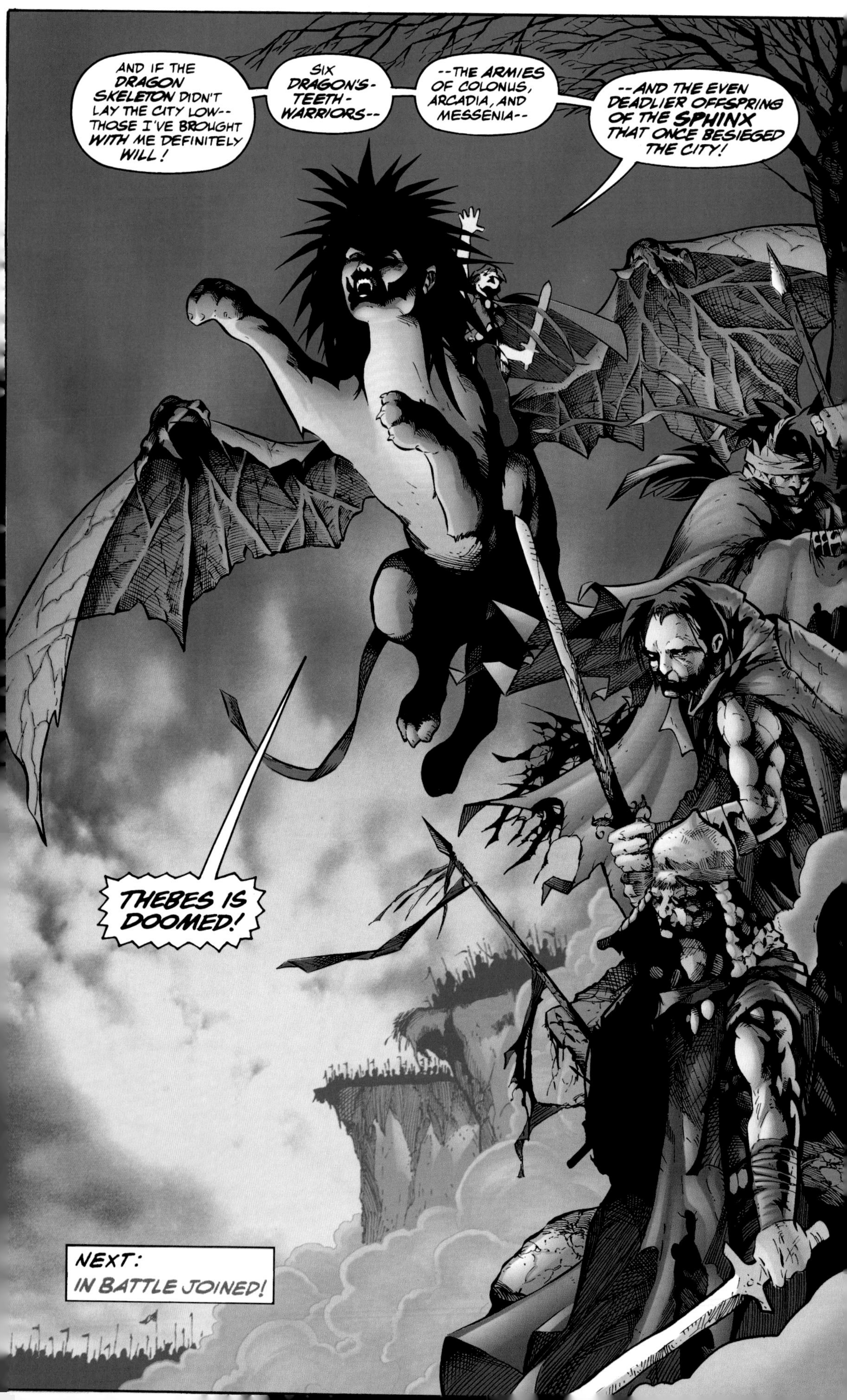
AND IF THE DRAGON SKELETON DIDN'T LAY THE CITY LOW-- THOSE I'VE BROUGHT WITH ME DEFINITELY WILL!
SIX DRAGON'S-TEETH-WARRIORS--
--THE ARMIES OF COLONUS, ARCADIA, AND MESSENIA--
--AND THE EVEN DEADLIER OFFSPRING OF THE SPHINX THAT ONCE BESIEGED THE CITY!
THEBES IS DOOMED!
NEXT: IN BATTLE JOINED!

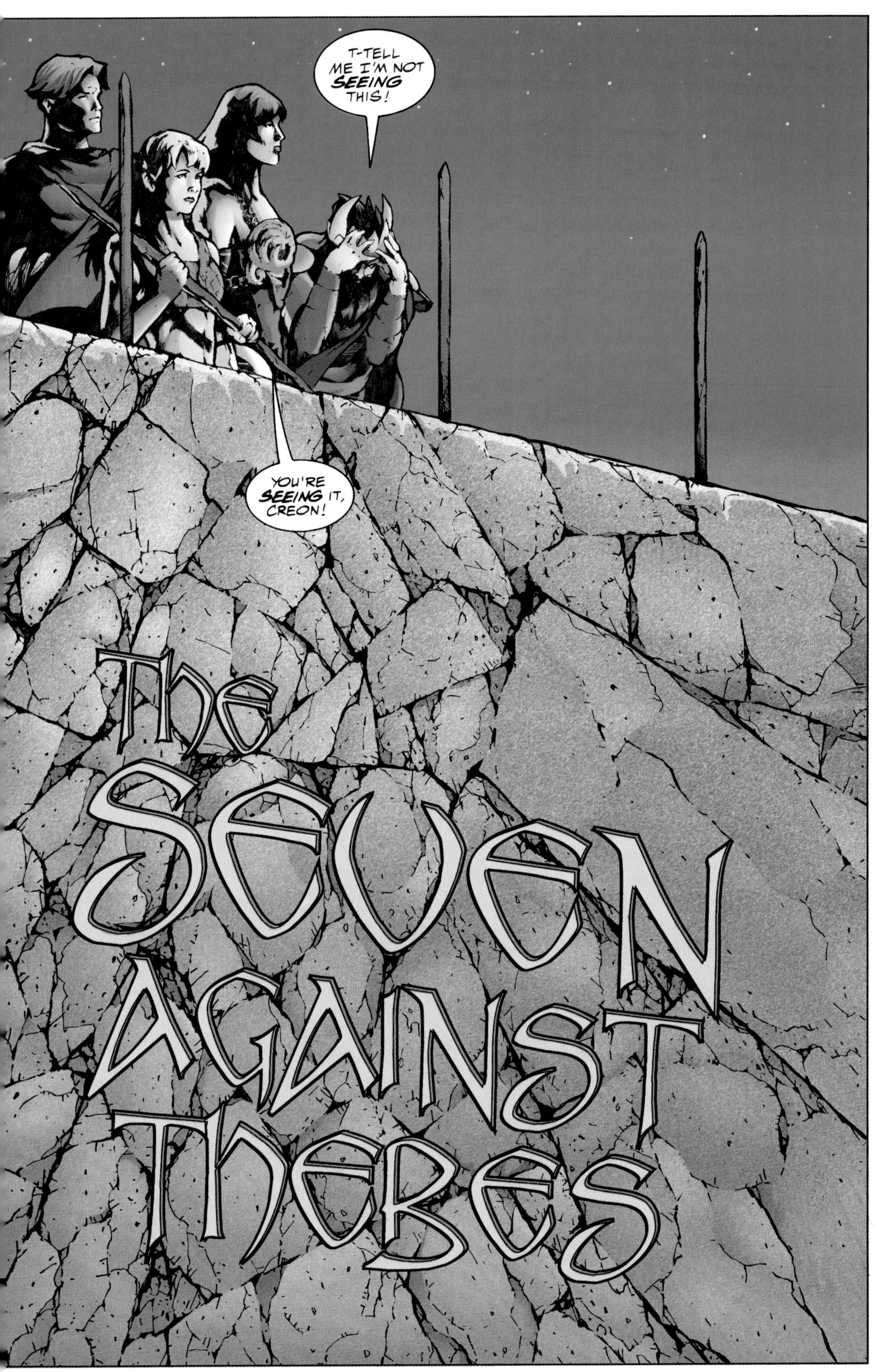
T-TELL ME I'M NOT SEEING THIS!
YOU'RE SEEING IT, CREON!
The Seven Against Thebes

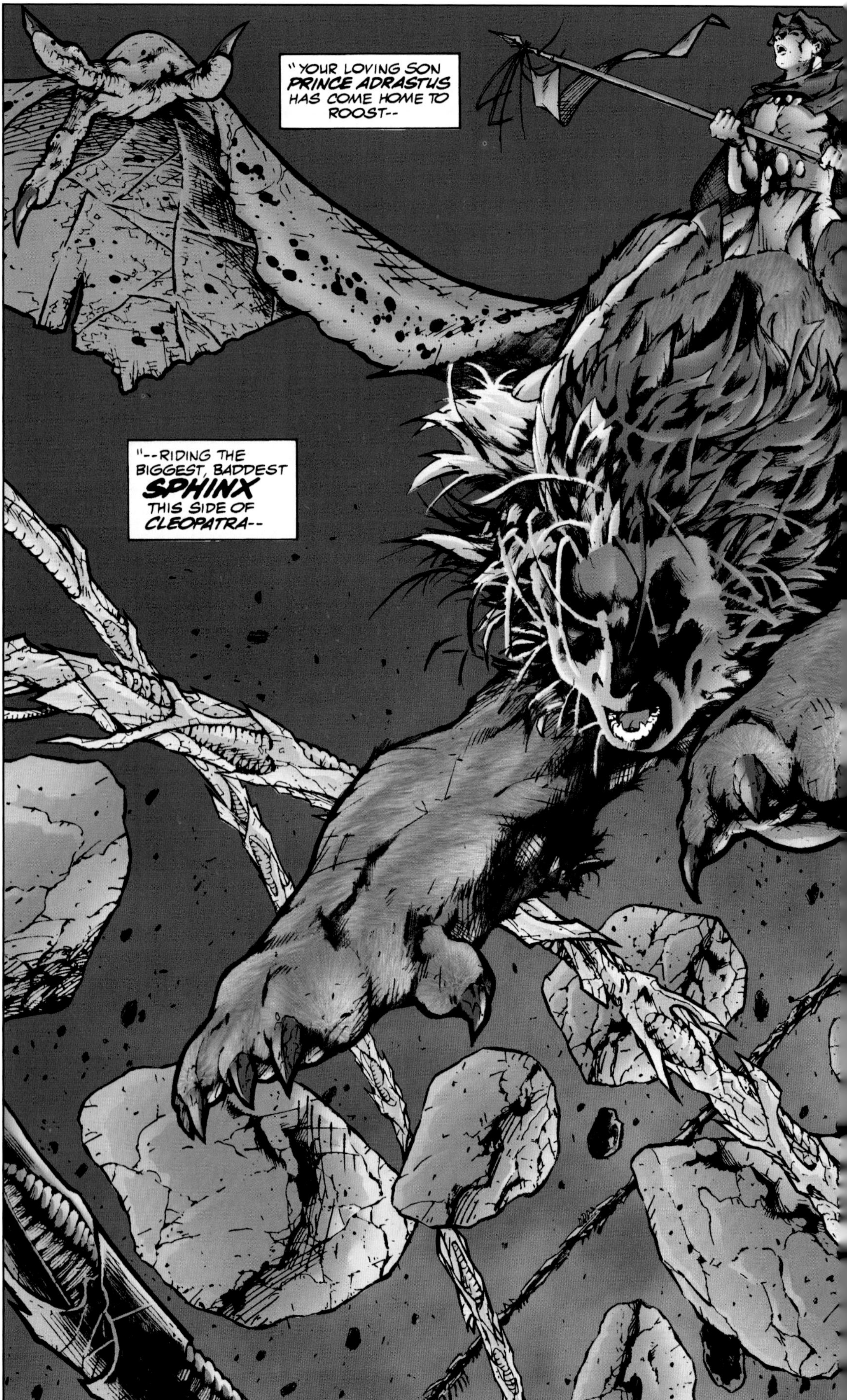
"YOUR LOVING SON PRINCE ADRASTUS HAS COME HOME TO ROOST--
"--RIDING THE BIGGEST, BADDEST SPHINX THIS SIDE OF CLEOPATRA--

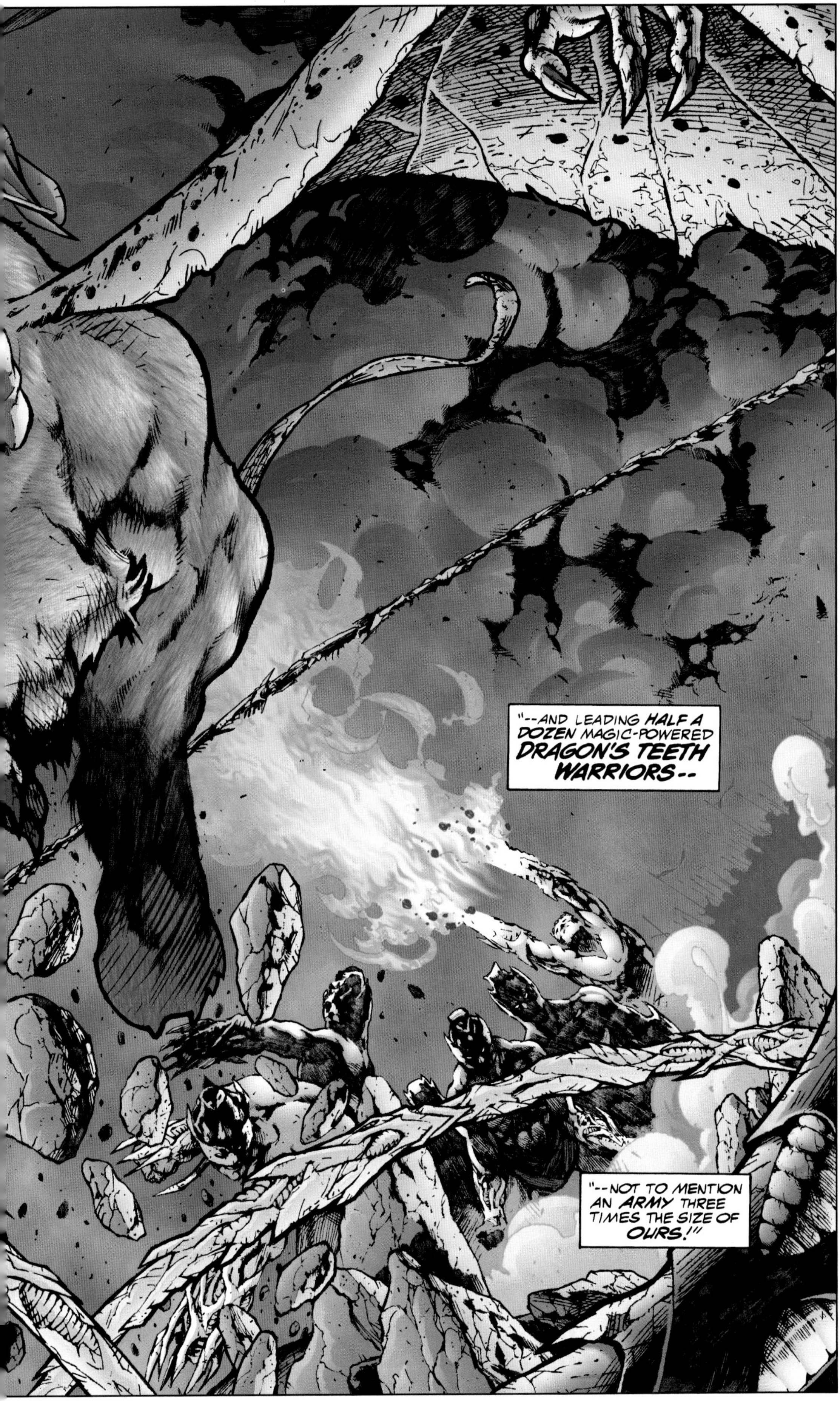
"--AND LEADING HALF A DOZEN MAGIC-POWERED DRAGON'S TEETH WARRIORS--
"--NOT TO MENTION AN ARMY THREE TIMES THE SIZE OF OURS!"

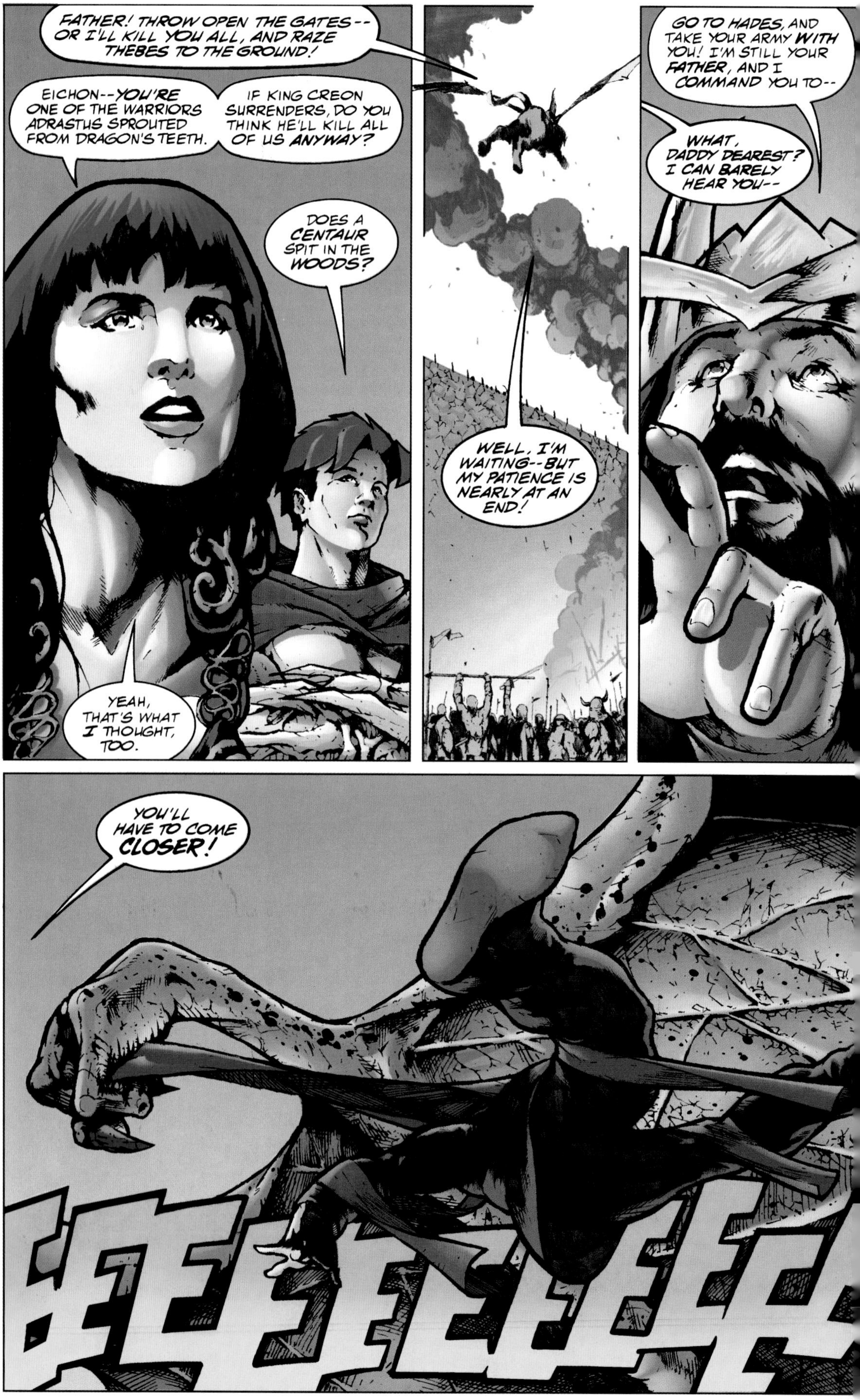
FATHER! THROW OPEN THE GATES-- OR I'LL KILL YOU ALL, AND RAZE THEBES TO THE GROUND!
EICHON--YOU'RE ONE OF THE WARRIORS ADRASTUS SPROUTED FROM DRAGON'S TEETH.
IF KING CREON SURRENDERS, DO YOU THINK HE'LL KILL ALL OF US ANYWAY?
DOES A CENTAUR SPIT IN THE WOODS?
YEAH, THAT'S WHAT I THOUGHT, TOO.
WELL, I'M WAITING--BUT MY PATIENCE IS NEARLY AT AN END!
GO TO HADES, AND TAKE YOUR ARMY WITH YOU! I'M STILL YOUR FATHER, AND I COMMAND YOU TO--
WHAT, DADDY DEAREST? I CAN BARELY HEAR YOU--
YOU'LL HAVE TO COME CLOSER!
EEEEEA

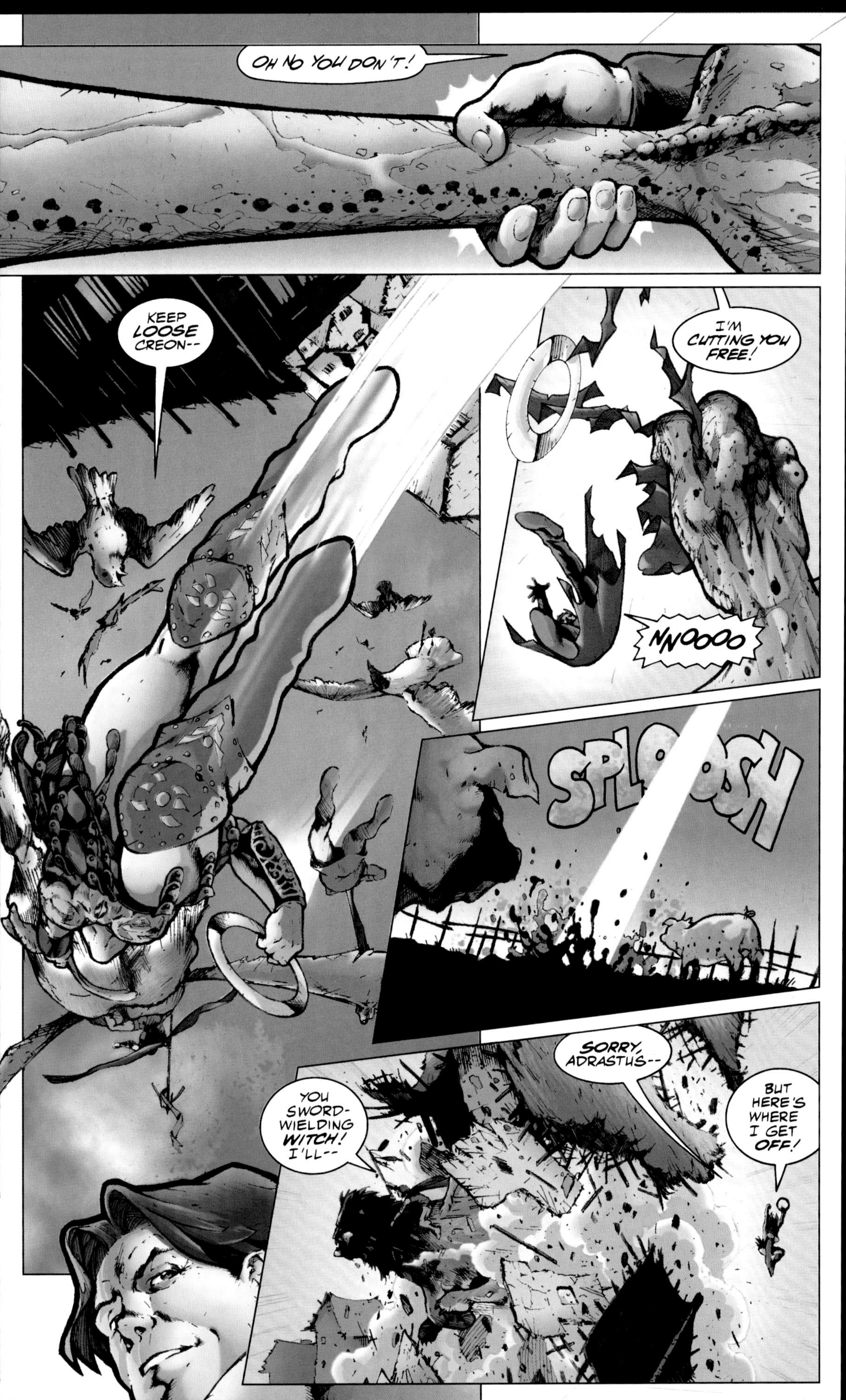

OH NO YOU DON'T!
KEEP LOOSE CREON--
I'M CUTTING YOU FREE!
NNOOOO
SPLOOSH
SORRY, ADRASTUS--
YOU SWORD-WIELDING WITCH! I'LL--
BUT HERE'S WHERE I GET OFF!

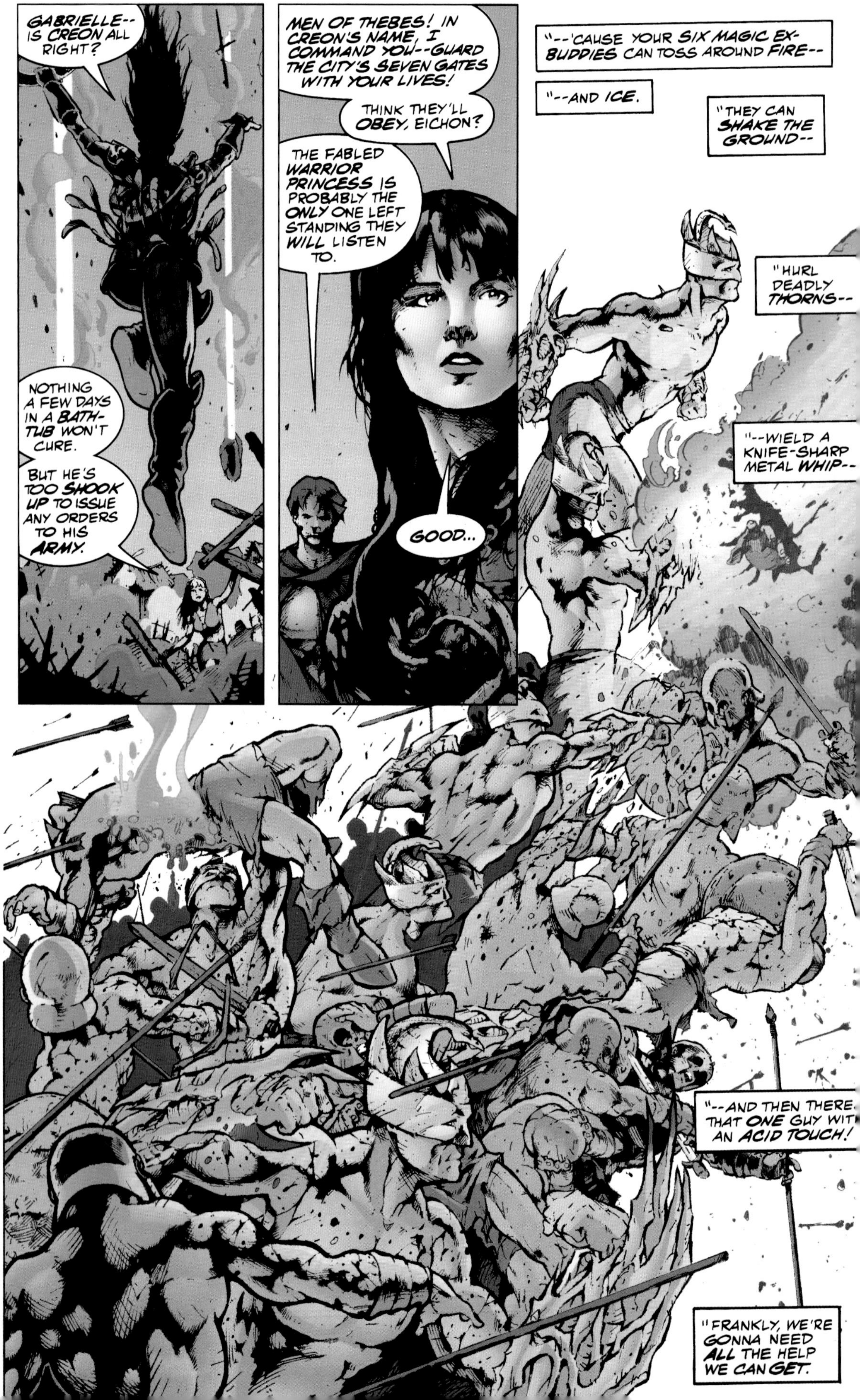
GABRIELLE-- IS CREON ALL RIGHT?
NOTHING A FEW DAYS IN A BATH-TUB WON'T CURE.
BUT HE'S TOO SHOOK UP TO ISSUE ANY ORDERS TO HIS ARMY.
MEN OF THEBES! IN CREON'S NAME, I COMMAND YOU--GUARD THE CITY'S SEVEN GATES WITH YOUR LIVES!
THINK THEY'LL OBEY, EICHON?
THE FABLED WARRIOR PRINCESS IS PROBABLY THE ONLY ONE LEFT STANDING THEY WILL LISTEN TO.
GOOD...
"--'CAUSE YOUR SIX MAGIC EX-BUDDIES CAN TOSS AROUND FIRE--
"--AND ICE.
"THEY CAN SHAKE THE GROUND--
"HURL DEADLY THORNS--
"--WIELD A KNIFE-SHARP METAL WHIP--
"--AND THEN THERE'S THAT ONE GUY WITH AN ACID TOUCH!
"FRANKLY, WE'RE GONNA NEED ALL THE HELP WE CAN GET.

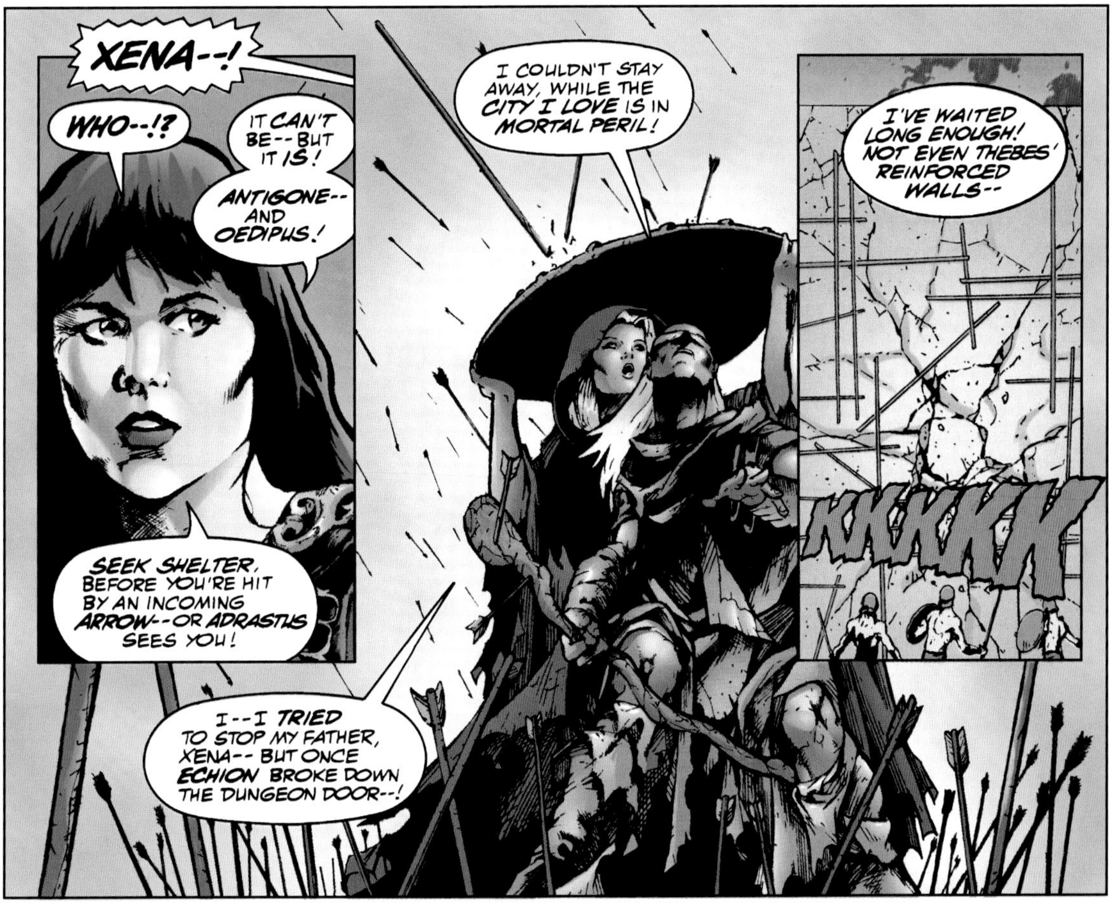
XENA--!
WHO--!?
IT CAN'T BE--BUT IT IS!
ANTIGONE--AND OEDIPUS!
SEEK SHELTER, BEFORE YOU'RE HIT BY AN INCOMING ARROW--OR ADRASTUS SEES YOU!
I COULDN'T STAY AWAY, WHILE THE CITY I LOVE IS IN MORTAL PERIL!
I--I TRIED TO STOP MY FATHER, XENA-- BUT ONCE ECHION BROKE DOWN THE DUNGEON DOOR--!
I'VE WAITED LONG ENOUGH! NOT EVEN THEBES' REINFORCED WALLS--
KKKKK
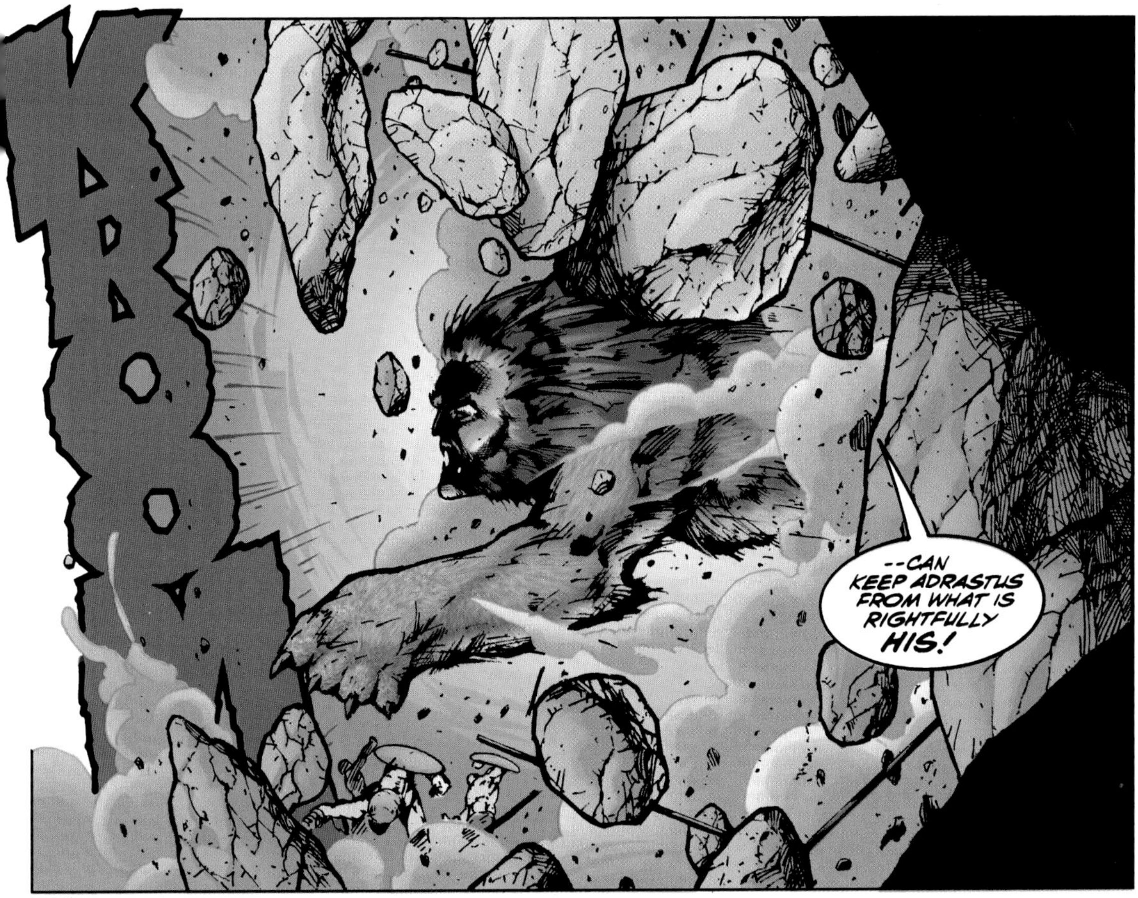
--CAN KEEP ADRASTUS FROM WHAT IS RIGHTFULLY HIS!

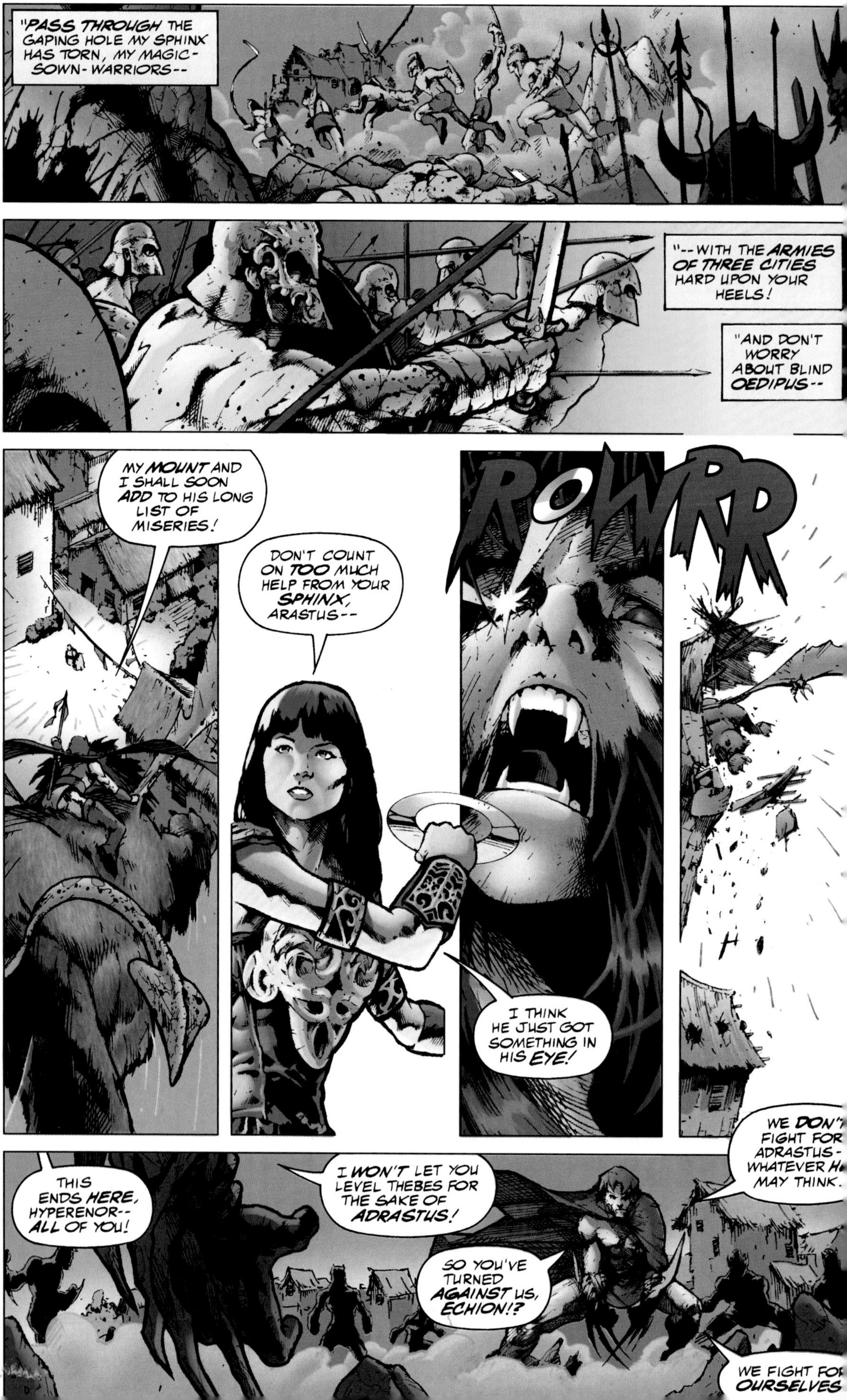
"PASS THROUGH THE GAPING HOLE MY SPHINX HAS TORN, MY MAGIC-SOWN-WARRIORS--
"--WITH THE ARMIES OF THREE CITIES HARD UPON YOUR HEELS!
"AND DON'T WORRY ABOUT BLIND OEDIPUS--
MY MOUNT AND I SHALL SOON ADD TO HIS LONG LIST OF MISERIES!
DON'T COUNT ON TOO MUCH HELP FROM YOUR SPHINX, ARASTUS--
ROWRR
I THINK HE JUST GOT SOMETHING IN HIS EYE!
THIS ENDS HERE, HYPERENOR-- ALL OF YOU!
I WON'T LET YOU LEVEL THEBES FOR THE SAKE OF ADRASTUS!
SO YOU'VE TURNED AGAINST US, ECHION!?
WE DON'T FIGHT FOR ADRASTUS-- WHATEVER HE MAY THINK.
WE FIGHT FOR OURSELVES

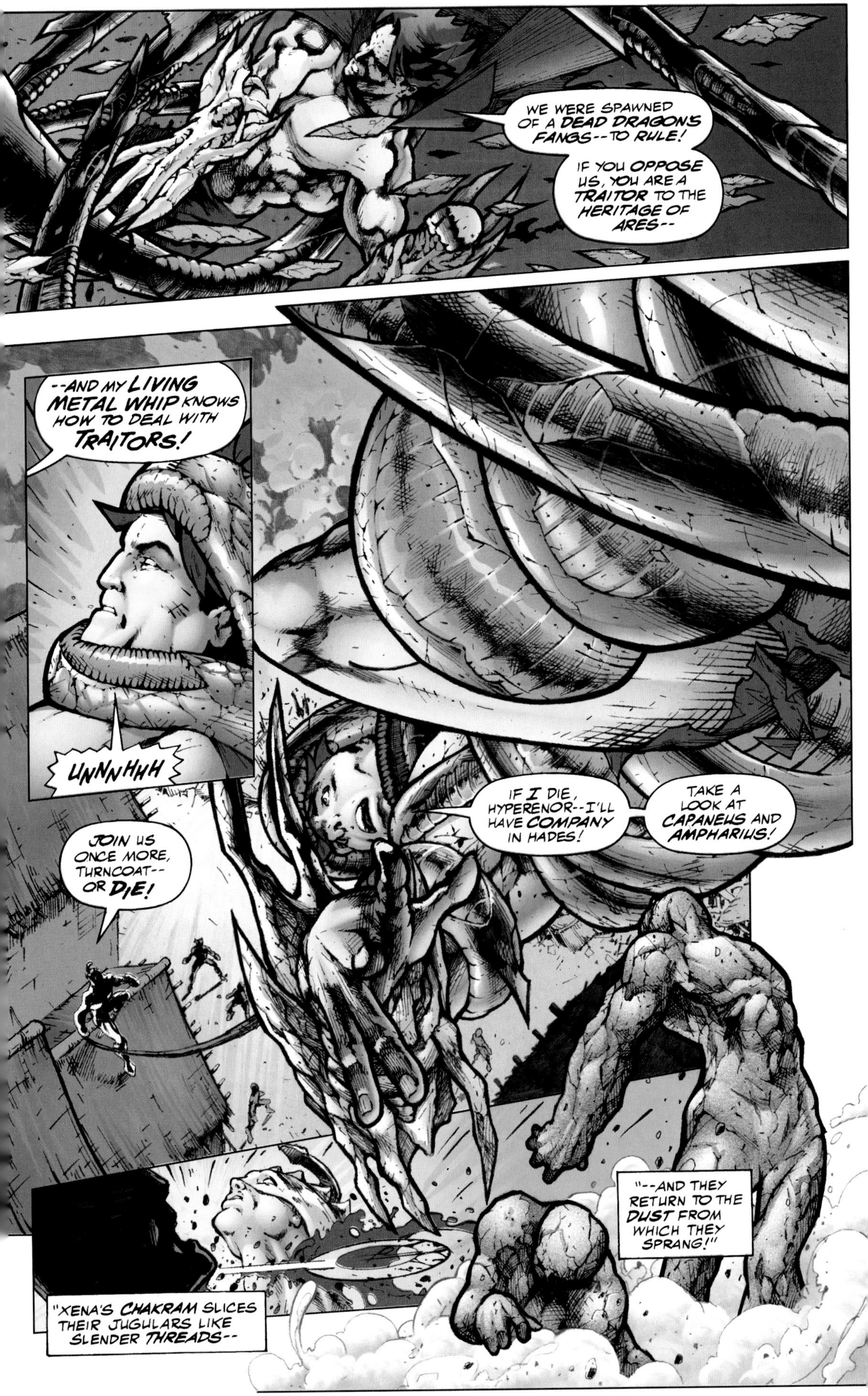
WE WERE SPAWNED OF A DEAD DRAGON'S FANGS--TO RULE!
IF YOU OPPOSE US, YOU ARE A TRAITOR TO THE HERITAGE OF ARES--
--AND MY LIVING METAL WHIP KNOWS HOW TO DEAL WITH TRAITORS!
UNNNHHH
JOIN US ONCE MORE, TURNCOAT-- OR DIE!
IF I DIE, HYPERENOR--I'LL HAVE COMPANY IN HADES!
TAKE A LOOK AT CAPANEUS AND AMPHARIUS!
"XENA'S CHAKRAM SLICES THEIR JUGULARS LIKE SLENDER THREADS--
"--AND THEY RETURN TO THE DUST FROM WHICH THEY SPRANG!"

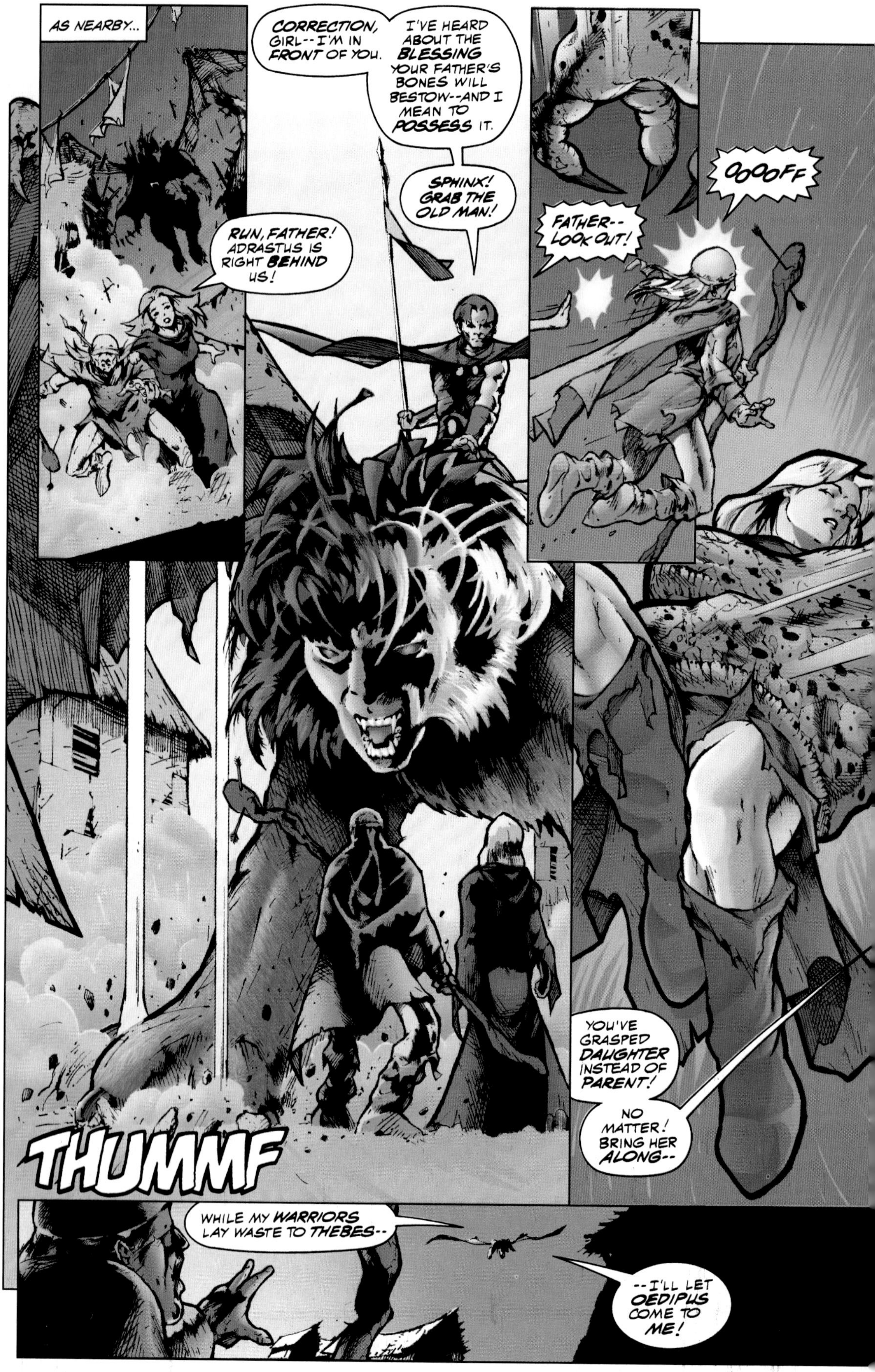
AS NEARBY...
RUN, FATHER! ADRASTUS IS RIGHT BEHIND US!
CORRECTION, GIRL--I'M IN FRONT OF YOU.
I'VE HEARD ABOUT THE BLESSING YOUR FATHER'S BONES WILL BESTOW--AND I MEAN TO POSSESS IT.
SPHINX! GRAB THE OLD MAN!
FATHER-- LOOK OUT!
OOOOFF
THUMMF
YOU'VE GRASPED DAUGHTER INSTEAD OF PARENT!
NO MATTER! BRING HER ALONG--
WHILE MY WARRIORS LAY WASTE TO THEBES--
--I'LL LET OEDIPUS COME TO ME!

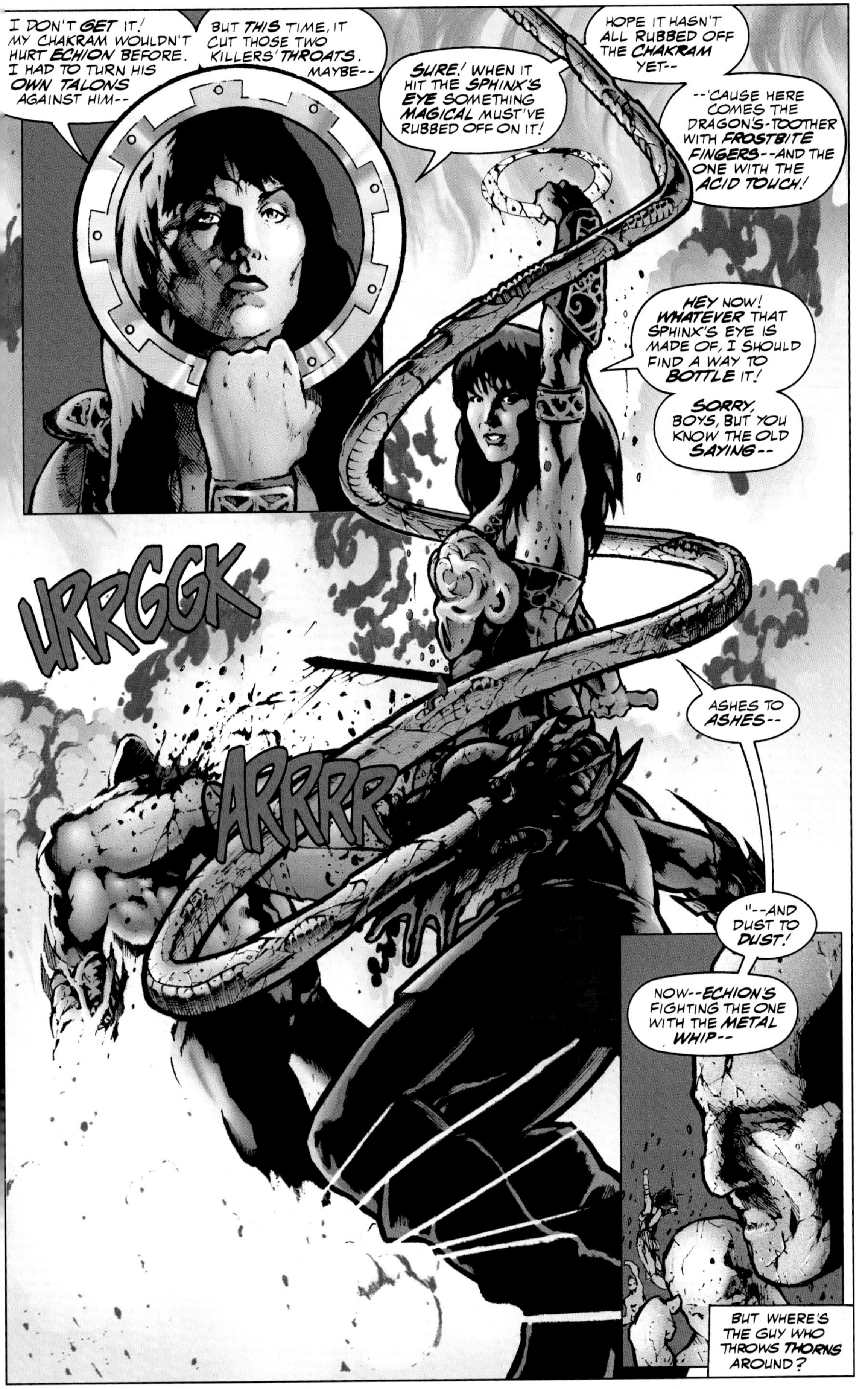
I DON'T GET IT! MY CHAKRAM WOULDN'T HURT ECHION BEFORE. I HAD TO TURN HIS OWN TALONS AGAINST HIM--
BUT THIS TIME, IT CUT THOSE TWO KILLERS' THROATS. MAYBE--
SURE! WHEN IT HIT THE SPHINX'S EYE SOMETHING MAGICAL MUST'VE RUBBED OFF ON IT!
HOPE IT HASN'T ALL RUBBED OFF THE CHAKRAM YET--
--'CAUSE HERE COMES THE DRAGON'S-TOOTHER WITH FROSTBITE FINGERS--AND THE ONE WITH THE ACID TOUCH!
HEY NOW! WHATEVER THAT SPHINX'S EYE IS MADE OF, I SHOULD FIND A WAY TO BOTTLE IT!
SORRY, BOYS, BUT YOU KNOW THE OLD SAYING--
URRGGK
ARRRR
ASHES TO ASHES--
"--AND DUST TO DUST!
NOW--ECHION'S FIGHTING THE ONE WITH THE METAL WHIP--
BUT WHERE'S THE GUY WHO THROWS THORNS AROUND?

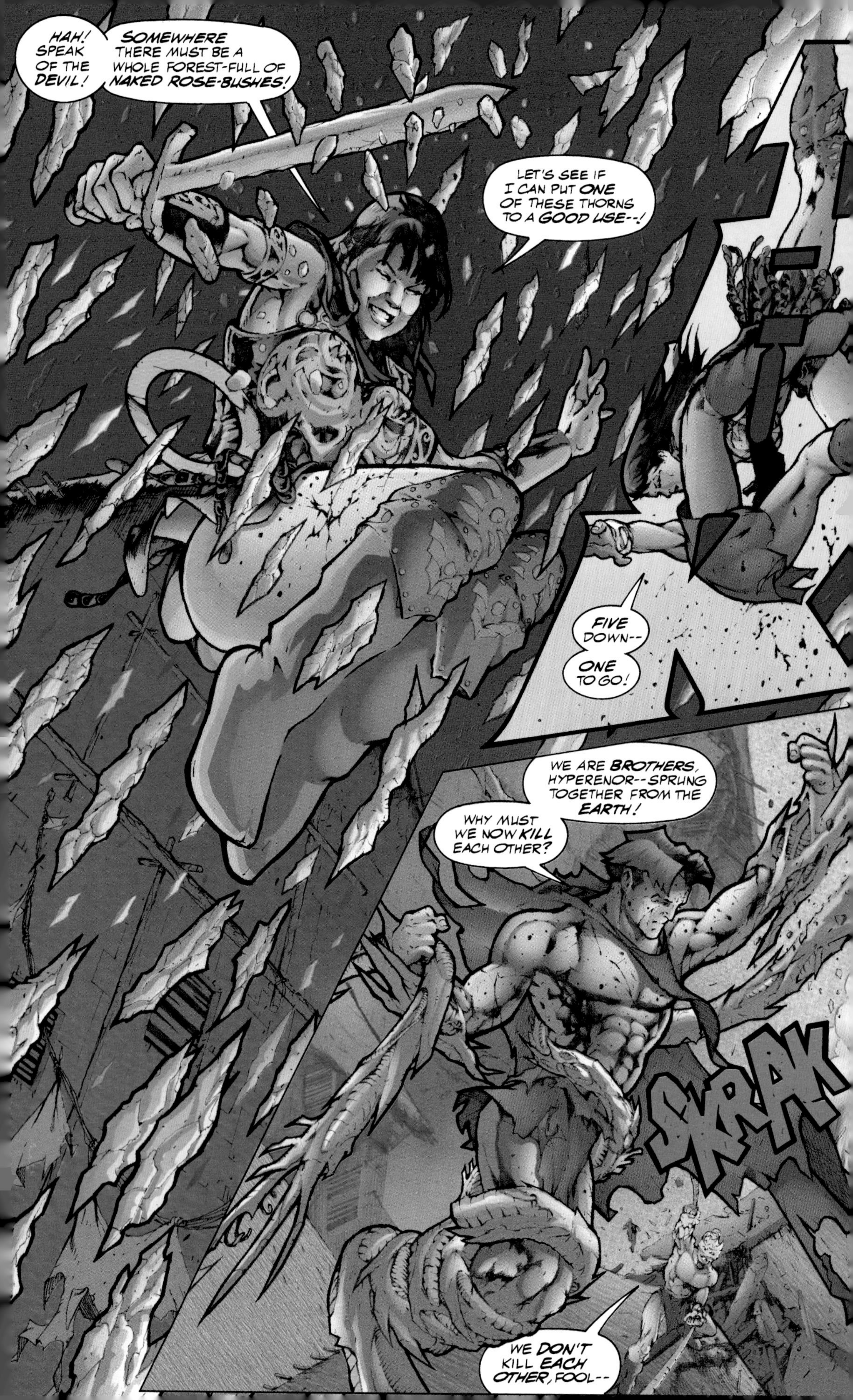

HAH! SPEAK OF THE DEVIL!
SOMEWHERE THERE MUST BE A WHOLE FOREST-FULL OF NAKED ROSE-BUSHES!
LET'S SEE IF I CAN PUT ONE OF THESE THORNS TO A GOOD USE--!
FIVE DOWN--
ONE TO GO!
WE ARE BROTHERS, HYPERENOR--SPRUNG TOGETHER FROM THE EARTH!
WHY MUST WE NOW KILL EACH OTHER?
SKRAK
WE DON'T KILL EACH OTHER, FOOL--

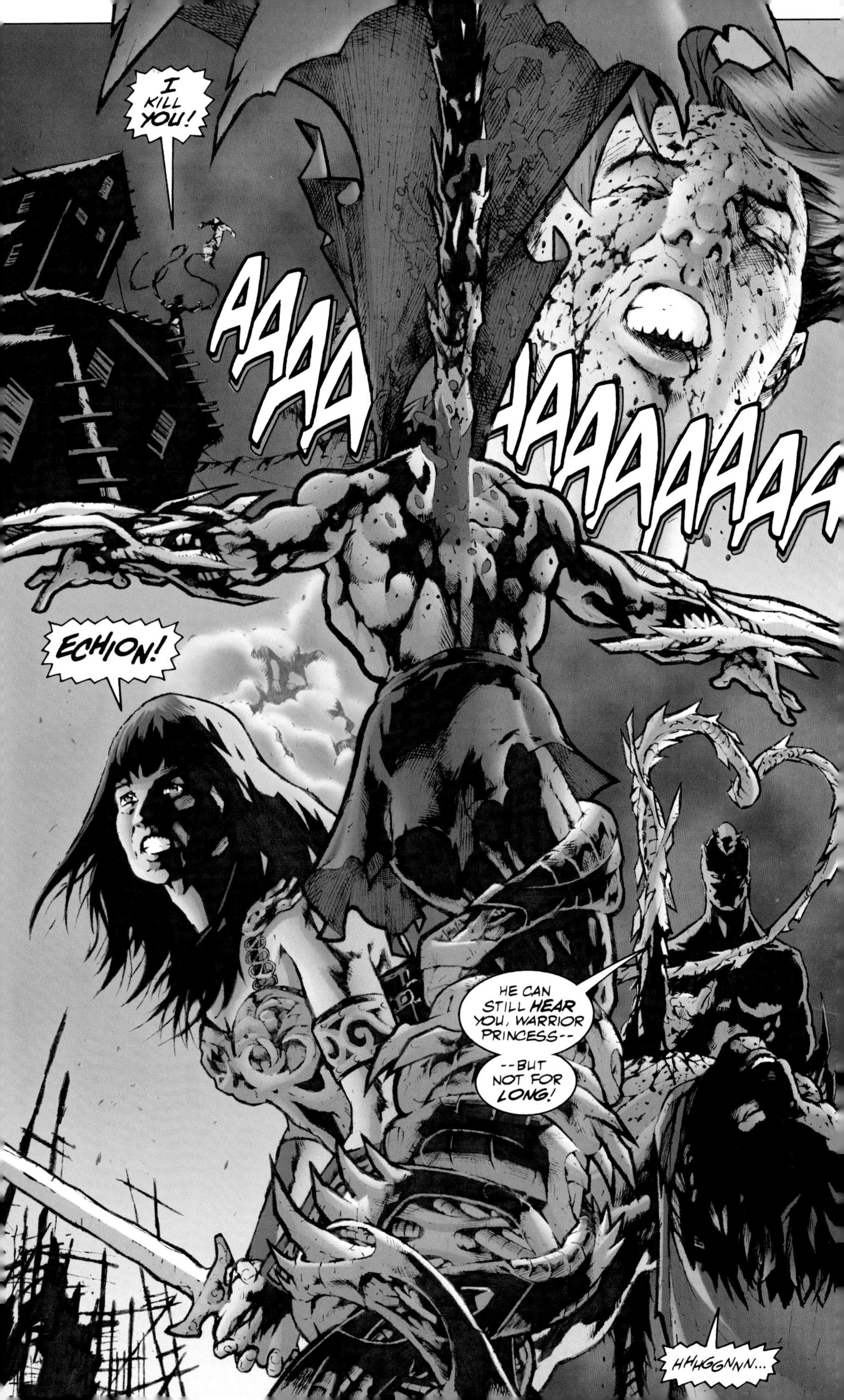

I KILL YOU!
AAAAAAAAAAAAAAAA
ECHION!
HE CAN STILL HEAR YOU, WARRIOR PRINCESS--
--BUT NOT FOR LONG!
HHHGGNNN...

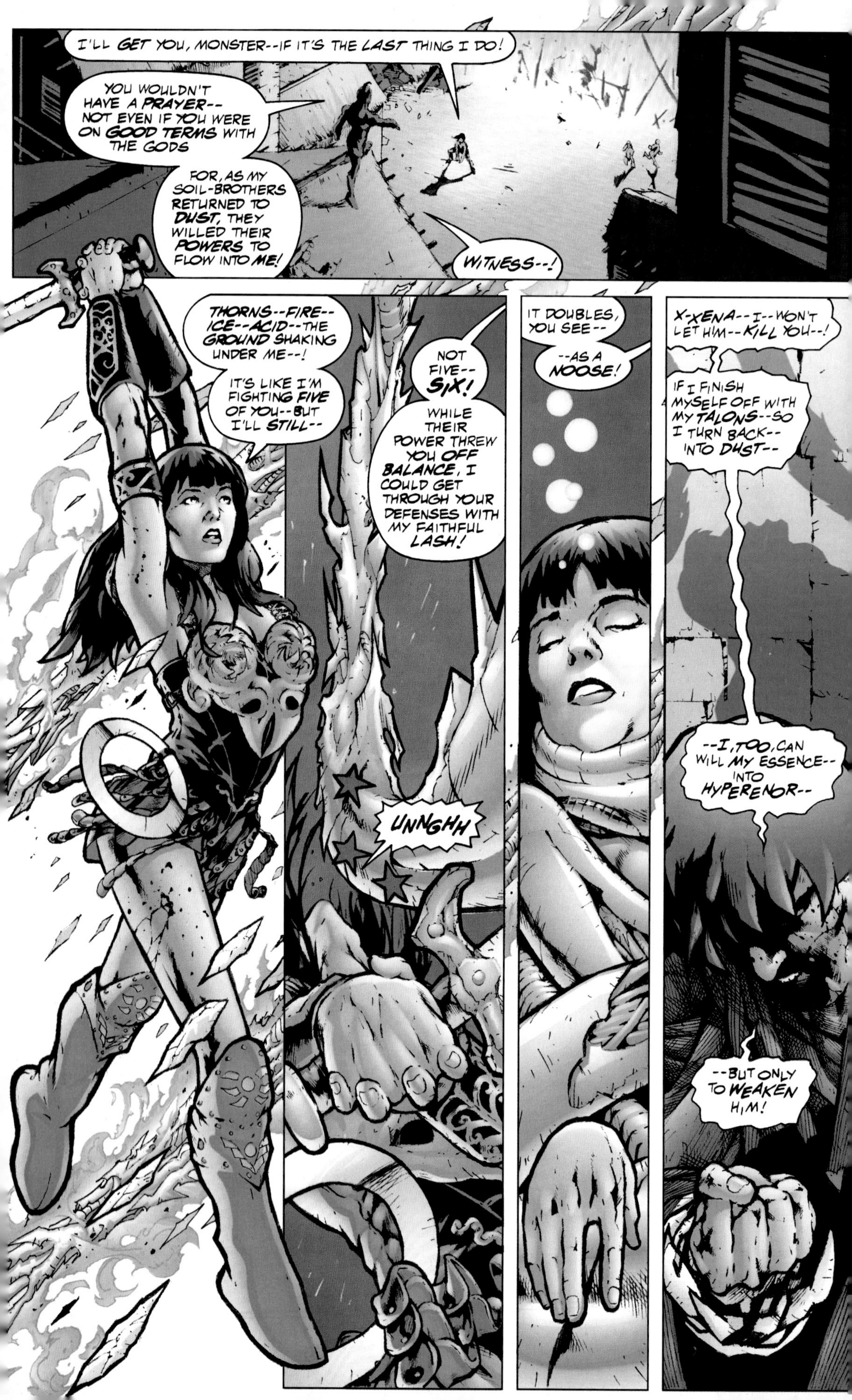
I'LL GET YOU, MONSTER--IF IT'S THE LAST THING I DO!
YOU WOULDN'T HAVE A PRAYER-- NOT EVEN IF YOU WERE ON GOOD TERMS WITH THE GODS
FOR, AS MY SOIL-BROTHERS RETURNED TO DUST, THEY WILLED THEIR POWERS TO FLOW INTO ME!
WITNESS--!
THORNS--FIRE--ICE--ACID--THE GROUND SHAKING UNDER ME--!
IT'S LIKE I'M FIGHTING FIVE OF YOU--BUT I'LL STILL--
NOT FIVE--SIX!
WHILE THEIR POWER THREW YOU OFF BALANCE, I COULD GET THROUGH YOUR DEFENSES WITH MY FAITHFUL LASH!
UNNGHH
IT DOUBLES, YOU SEE--
--AS A NOOSE!
X-XENA--I--WON'T LET HIM--KILL YOU--!
IF I FINISH MYSELF OFF WITH MY TALONS--SO I TURN BACK--INTO DUST--
--I, TOO, CAN WILL MY ESSENCE--INTO HYPERENOR--
--BUT ONLY TO WEAKEN HIM!

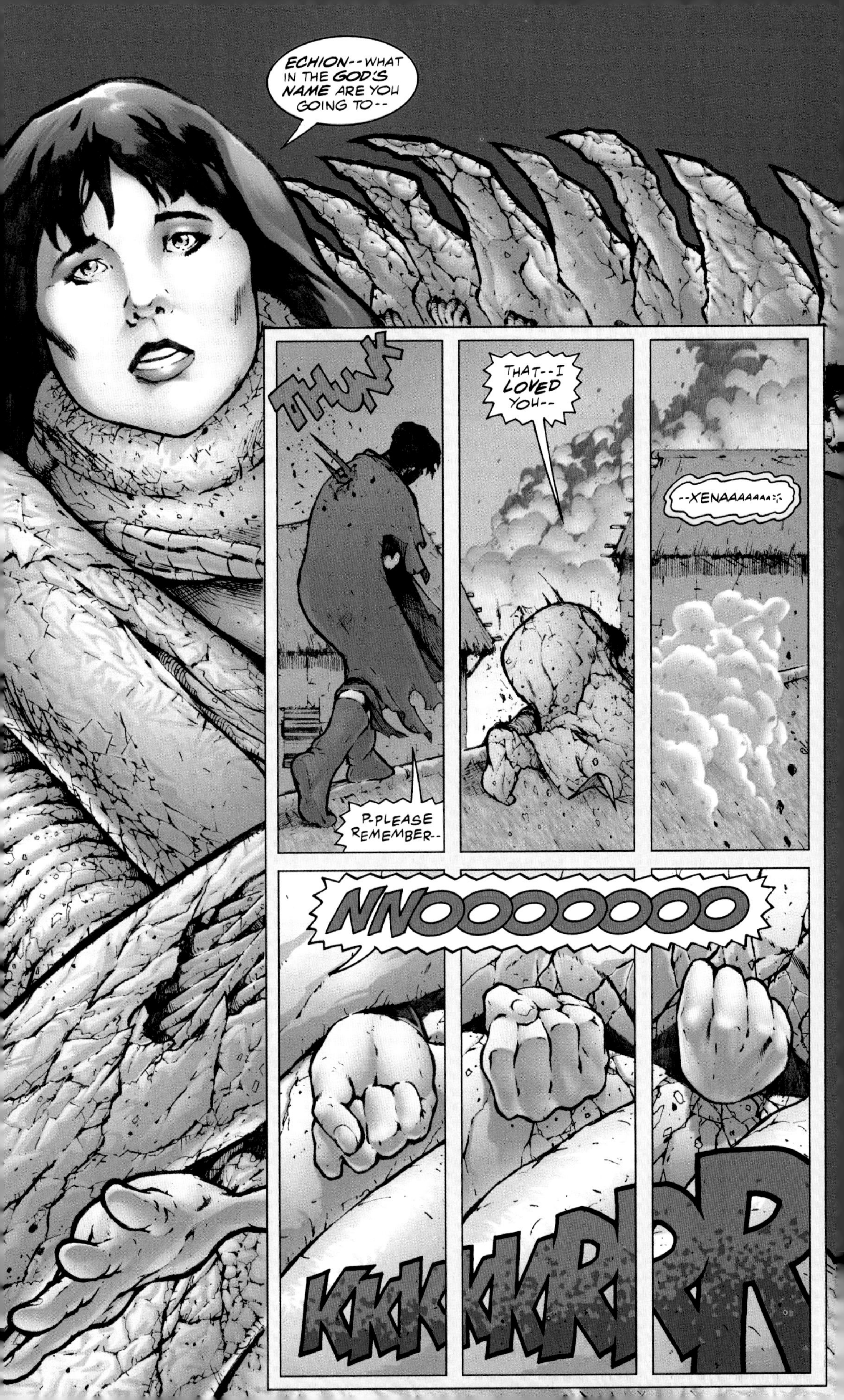
ECHION--WHAT IN THE GOD'S NAME ARE YOU GOING TO--
THUNK
P-PLEASE REMEMBER--
THAT--I LOVED YOU--
--XENAAAAAAA
NNOOOOOOOOO
KKKKKRRR

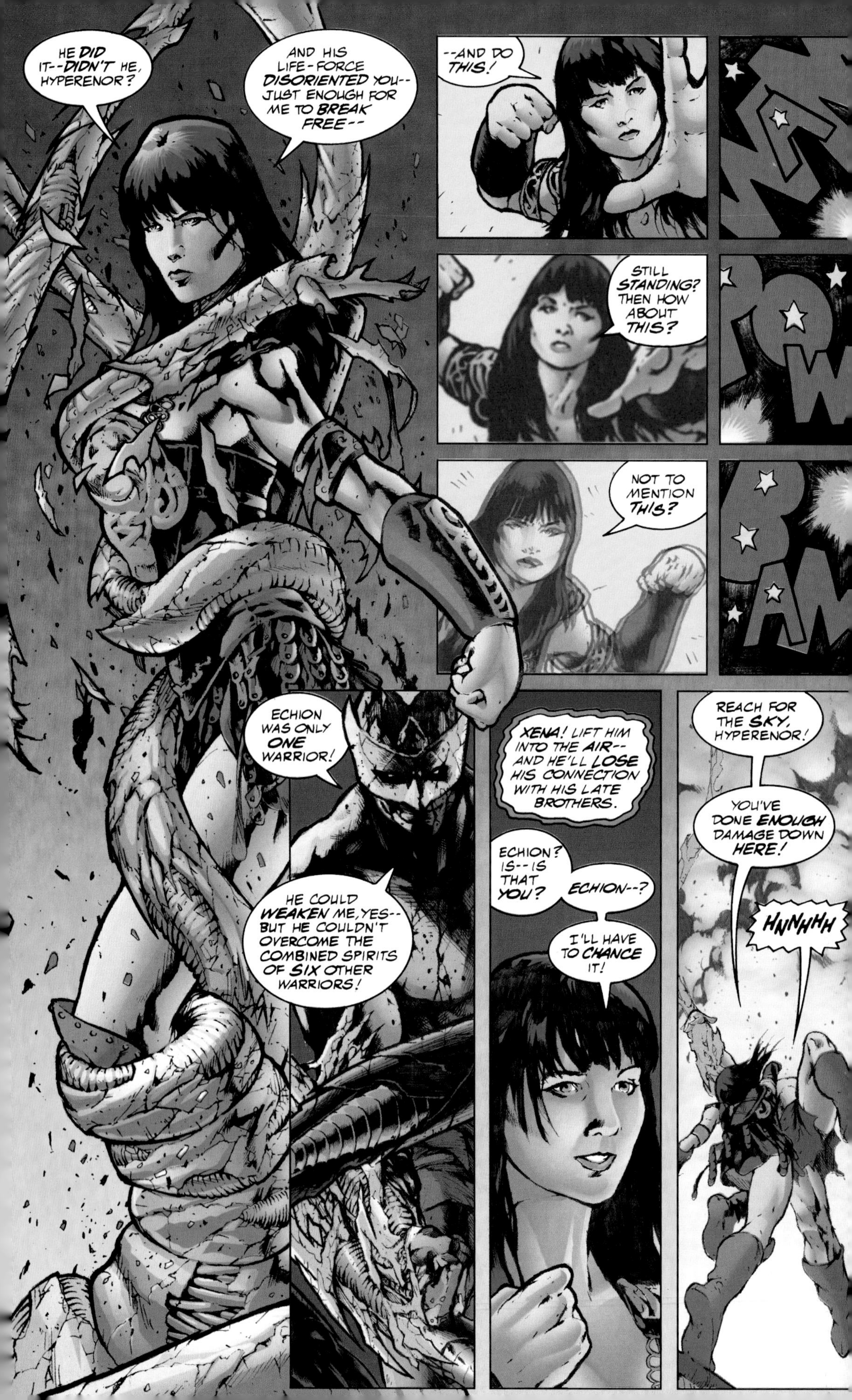
HE DID IT--DIDN'T HE, HYPERENOR?
AND HIS LIFE-FORCE DISORIENTED YOU-- JUST ENOUGH FOR ME TO BREAK FREE--
--AND DO THIS!
STILL STANDING? THEN HOW ABOUT THIS?
NOT TO MENTION THIS?
ECHION WAS ONLY ONE WARRIOR!
HE COULD WEAKEN ME, YES-- BUT HE COULDN'T OVERCOME THE COMBINED SPIRITS OF SIX OTHER WARRIORS!
XENA! LIFT HIM INTO THE AIR-- AND HE'LL LOSE HIS CONNECTION WITH HIS LATE BROTHERS.
ECHION? IS--IS THAT YOU?
ECHION--?
I'LL HAVE TO CHANCE IT!
REACH FOR THE SKY, HYPERENOR!
YOU'VE DONE ENOUGH DAMAGE DOWN HERE!
HNNHHH

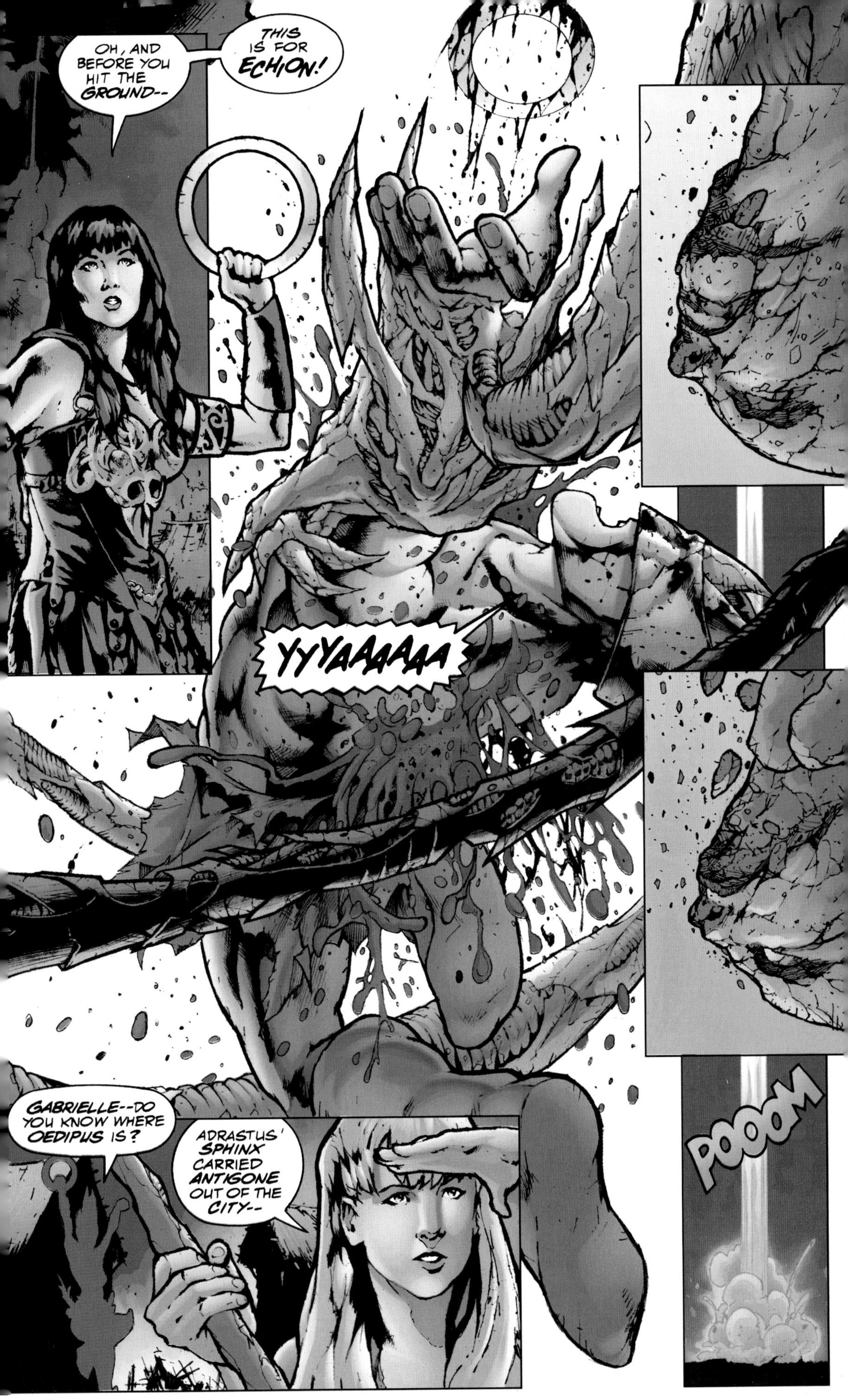

OH, AND BEFORE YOU HIT THE GROUND--
THIS IS FOR ECHION!
YYYAAAAAA
GABRIELLE--DO YOU KNOW WHERE OEDIPUS IS?
ADRASTUS' SPHINX CARRIED ANTIGONE OUT OF THE CITY--
POOOM

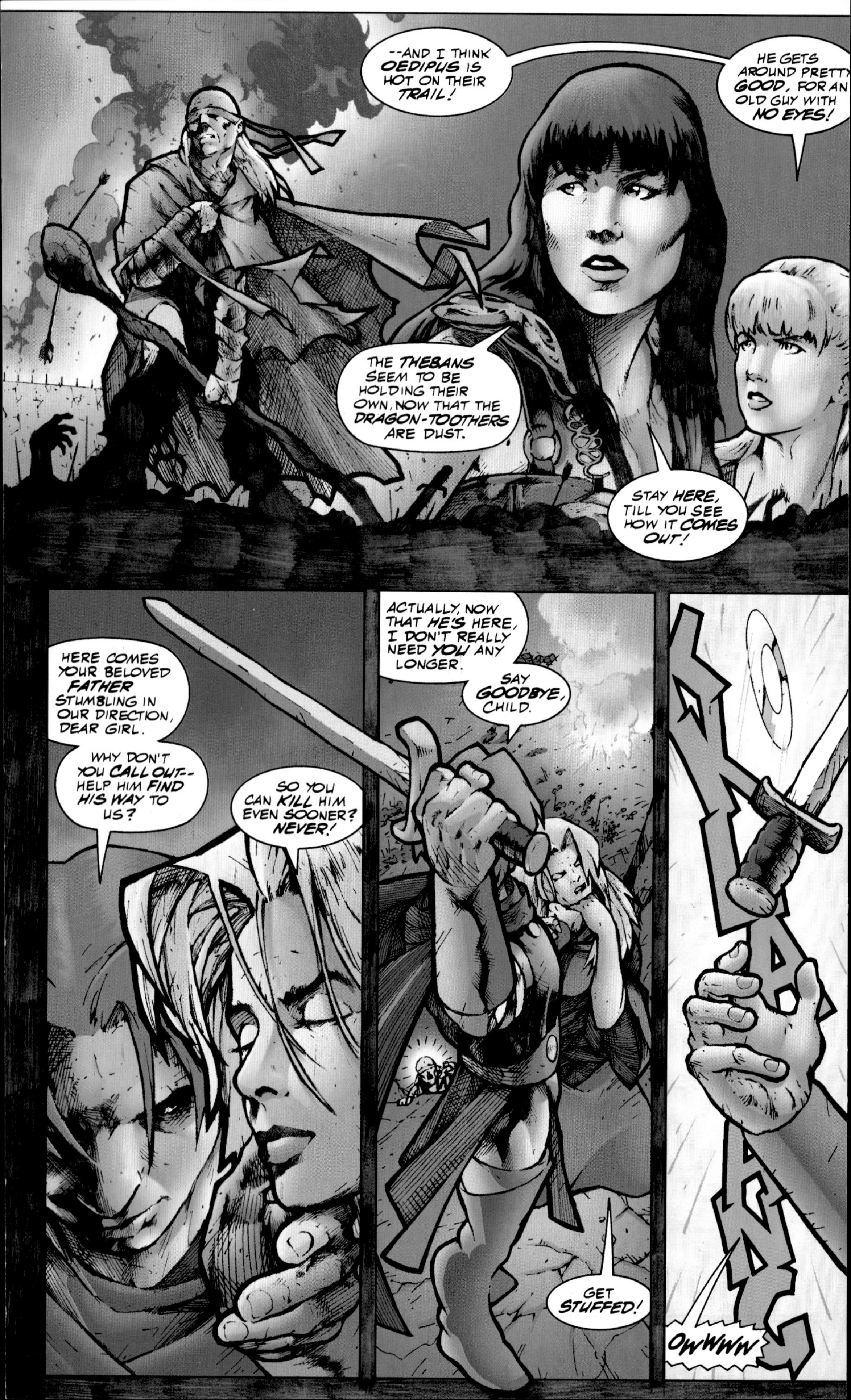
--AND I THINK OEDIPUS IS HOT ON THEIR TRAIL!
HE GETS AROUND PRETTY GOOD, FOR AN OLD GUY WITH NO EYES!
THE THEBANS SEEM TO BE HOLDING THEIR OWN, NOW THAT THE DRAGON-TOOTHERS ARE DUST.
STAY HERE, TILL YOU SEE HOW IT COMES OUT!
HERE COMES YOUR BELOVED FATHER STUMBLING IN OUR DIRECTION, DEAR GIRL.
WHY DON'T YOU CALL OUT--HELP HIM FIND HIS WAY TO US?
SO YOU CAN KILL HIM EVEN SOONER? NEVER!
ACTUALLY, NOW THAT HE'S HERE, I DON'T REALLY NEED YOU ANY LONGER.
SAY GOODBYE, CHILD.
GET STUFFED!
OWWWW

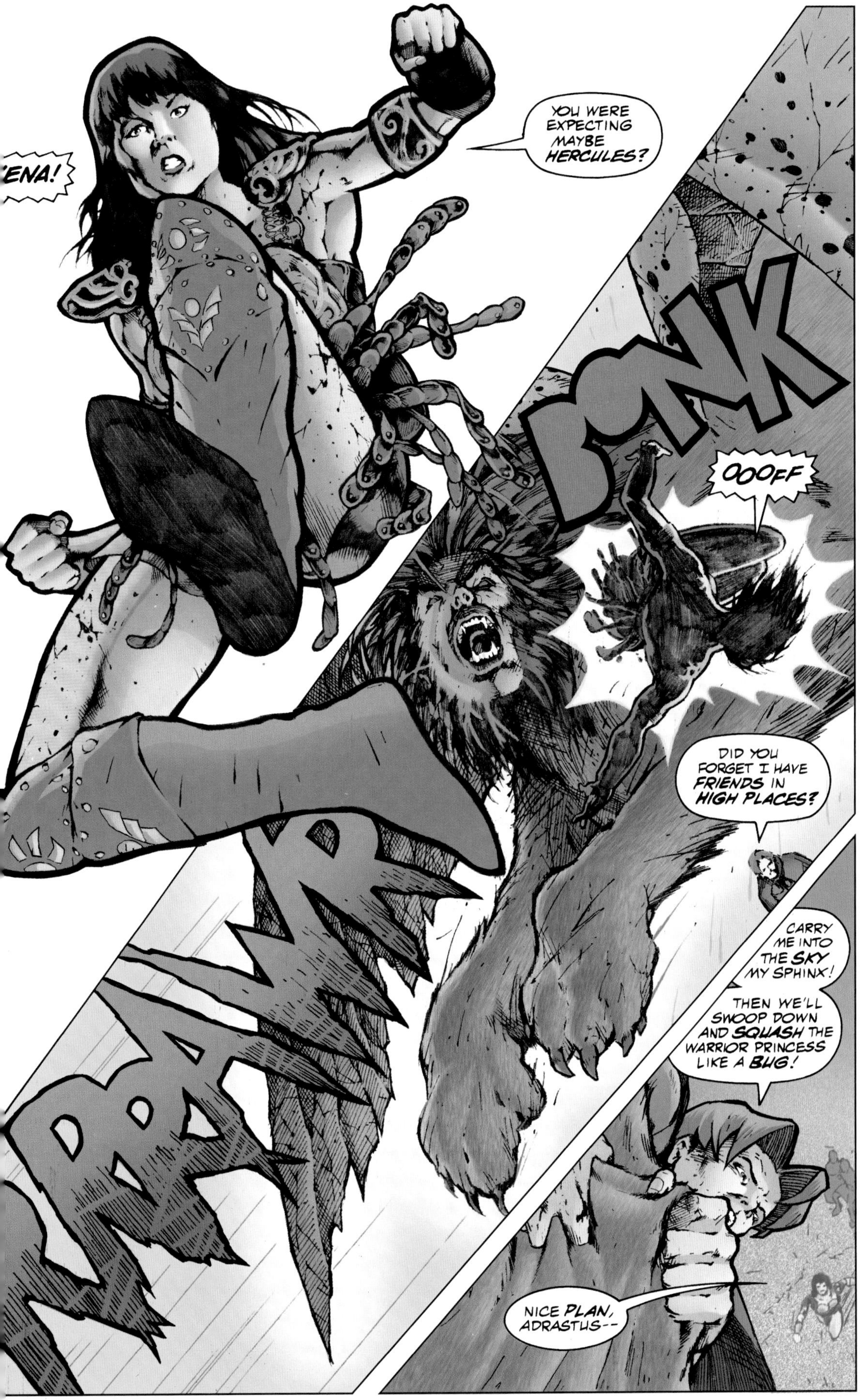
ENA!
YOU WERE EXPECTING MAYBE HERCULES?
BONK
OOOFF
DID YOU FORGET I HAVE FRIENDS IN HIGH PLACES?
CARRY ME INTO THE SKY MY SPHINX!
THEN WE'LL SWOOP DOWN AND SQUASH THE WARRIOR PRINCESS LIKE A BUG!
NICE PLAN, ADRASTUS--

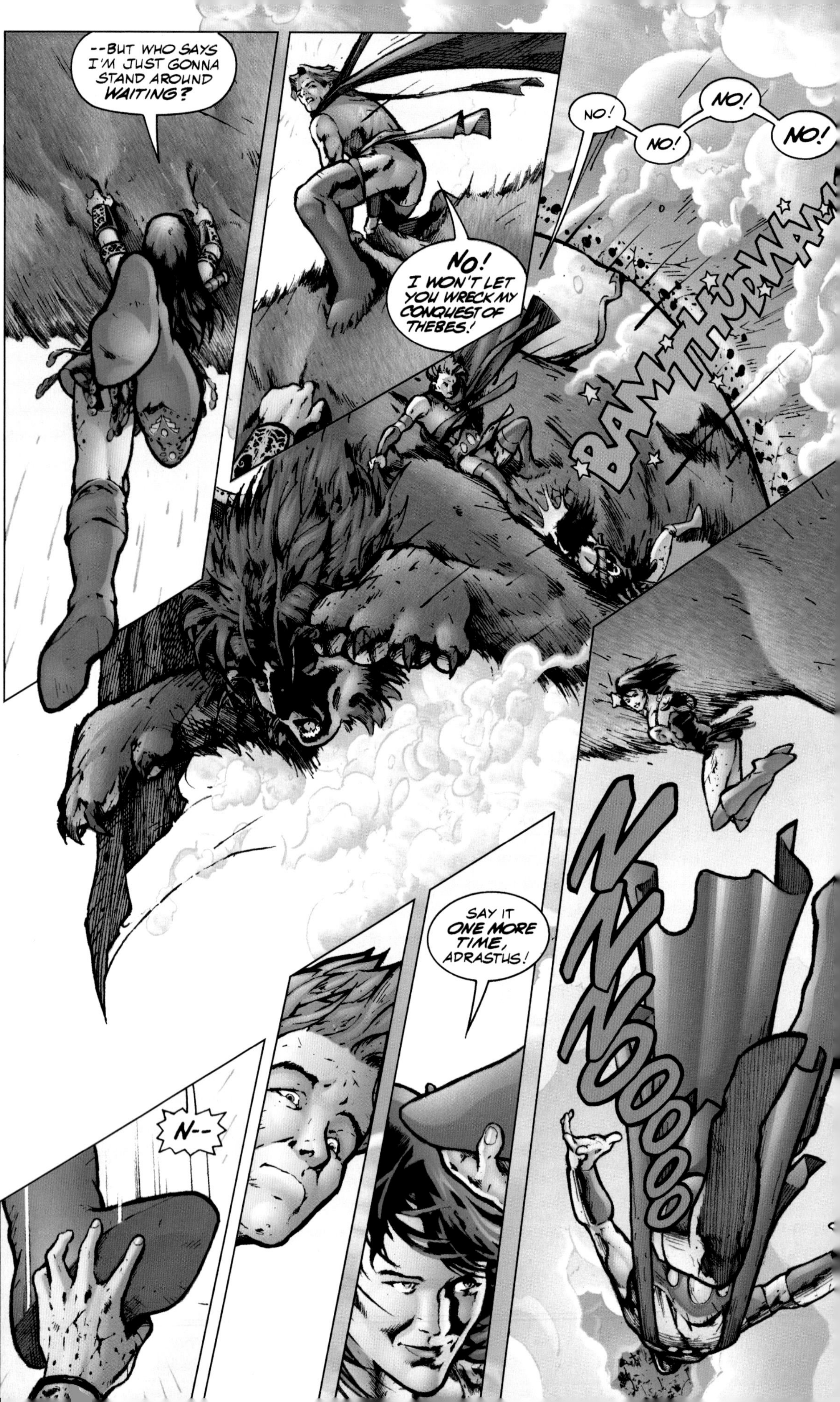
--BUT WHO SAYS I'M JUST GONNA STAND AROUND WAITING?
NO! I WON'T LET YOU WRECK MY CONQUEST OF THEBES!
NO! NO! NO! NO!
BAMTHUDWAM
N--
SAY IT ONE MORE TIME, ADRASTUS!
NNNOOOOO

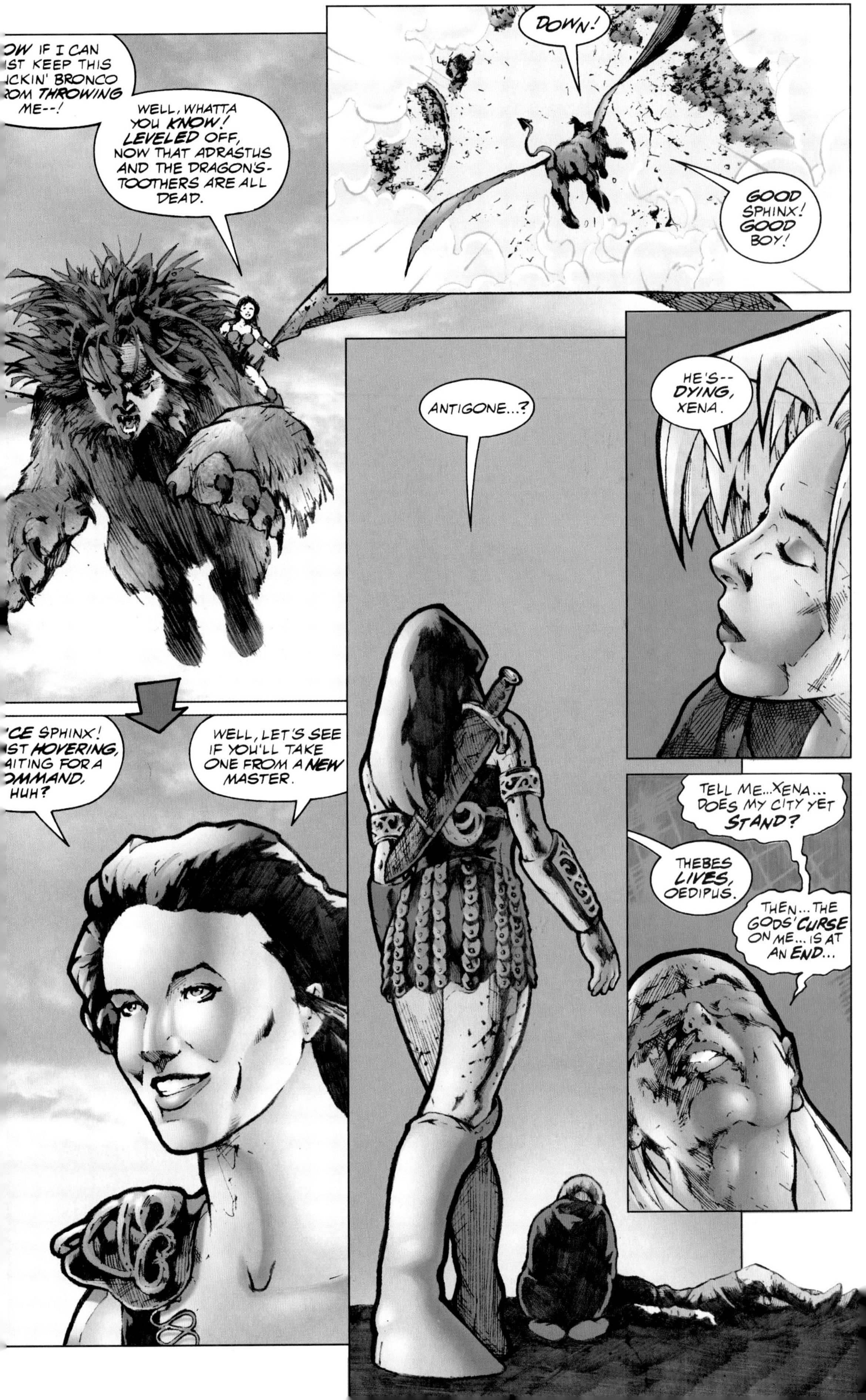

OW IF I CAN
IST KEEP THIS
ICKIN' BRONCO
ROM THROWING
ME--!
WELL, WHATTA YOU KNOW! LEVELED OFF, NOW THAT ADRASTUS AND THE DRAGON'S-TOOTHERS ARE ALL DEAD.
DOWN!
GOOD SPHINX! GOOD BOY!
'CE SPHINX!
IST HOVERING,
AITING FOR A
OMMAND,
HUH?
WELL, LET'S SEE IF YOU'LL TAKE ONE FROM A NEW MASTER.
ANTIGONE...?
HE'S-- DYING, XENA.
TELL ME...XENA... DOES MY CITY YET STAND?
THEBES LIVES, OEDIPUS.
THEN... THE GODS' CURSE ON ME... IS AT AN END...

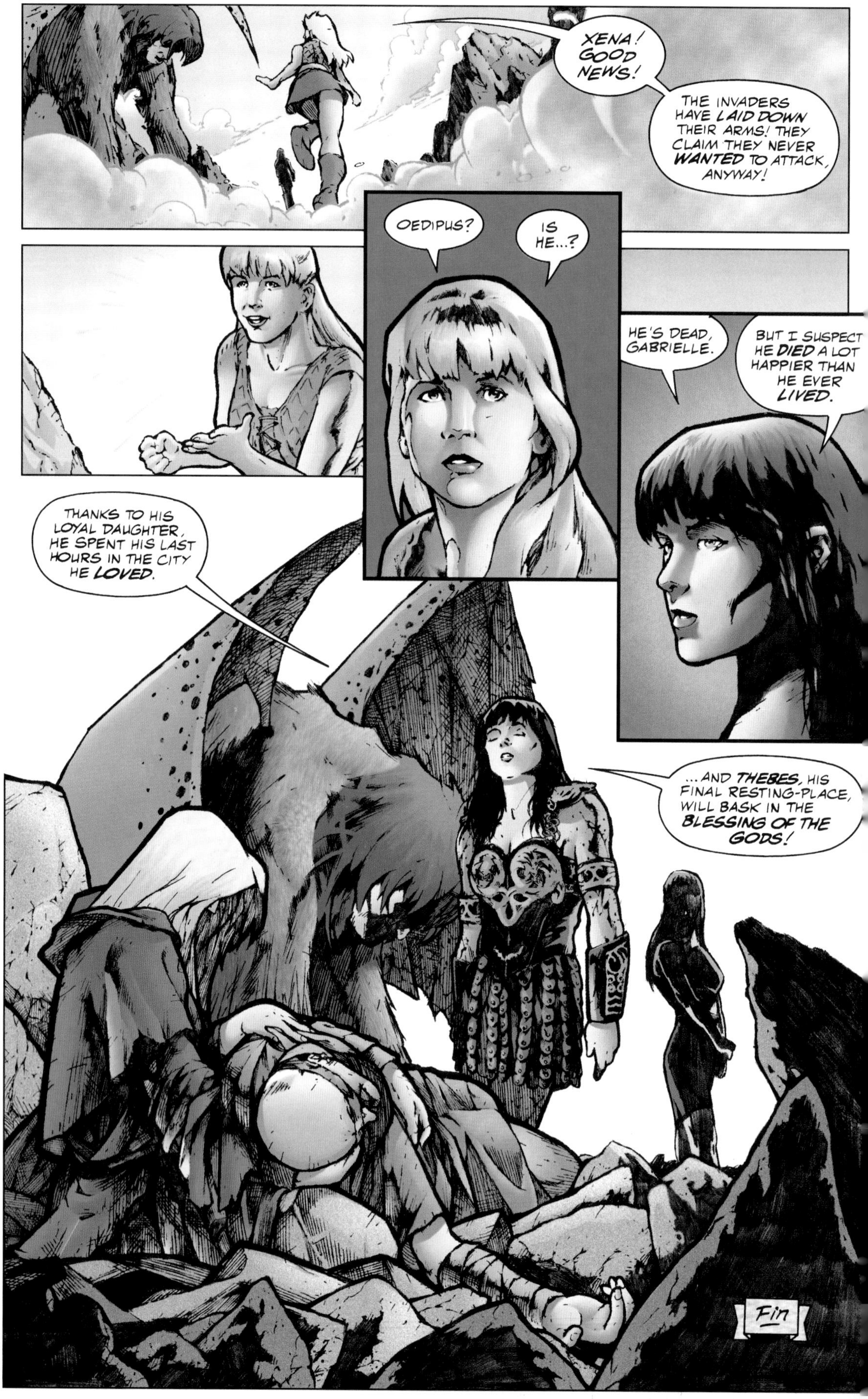
XENA! GOOD NEWS!
THE INVADERS HAVE LAID DOWN THEIR ARMS! THEY CLAIM THEY NEVER WANTED TO ATTACK, ANYWAY!
OEDIPUS?
IS HE...?
HE'S DEAD, GABRIELLE.
BUT I SUSPECT HE DIED A LOT HAPPIER THAN HE EVER LIVED.
THANKS TO HIS LOYAL DAUGHTER, HE SPENT HIS LAST HOURS IN THE CITY HE LOVED.
...AND THEBES, HIS FINAL RESTING-PLACE, WILL BASK IN THE BLESSING OF THE GODS!
Fin

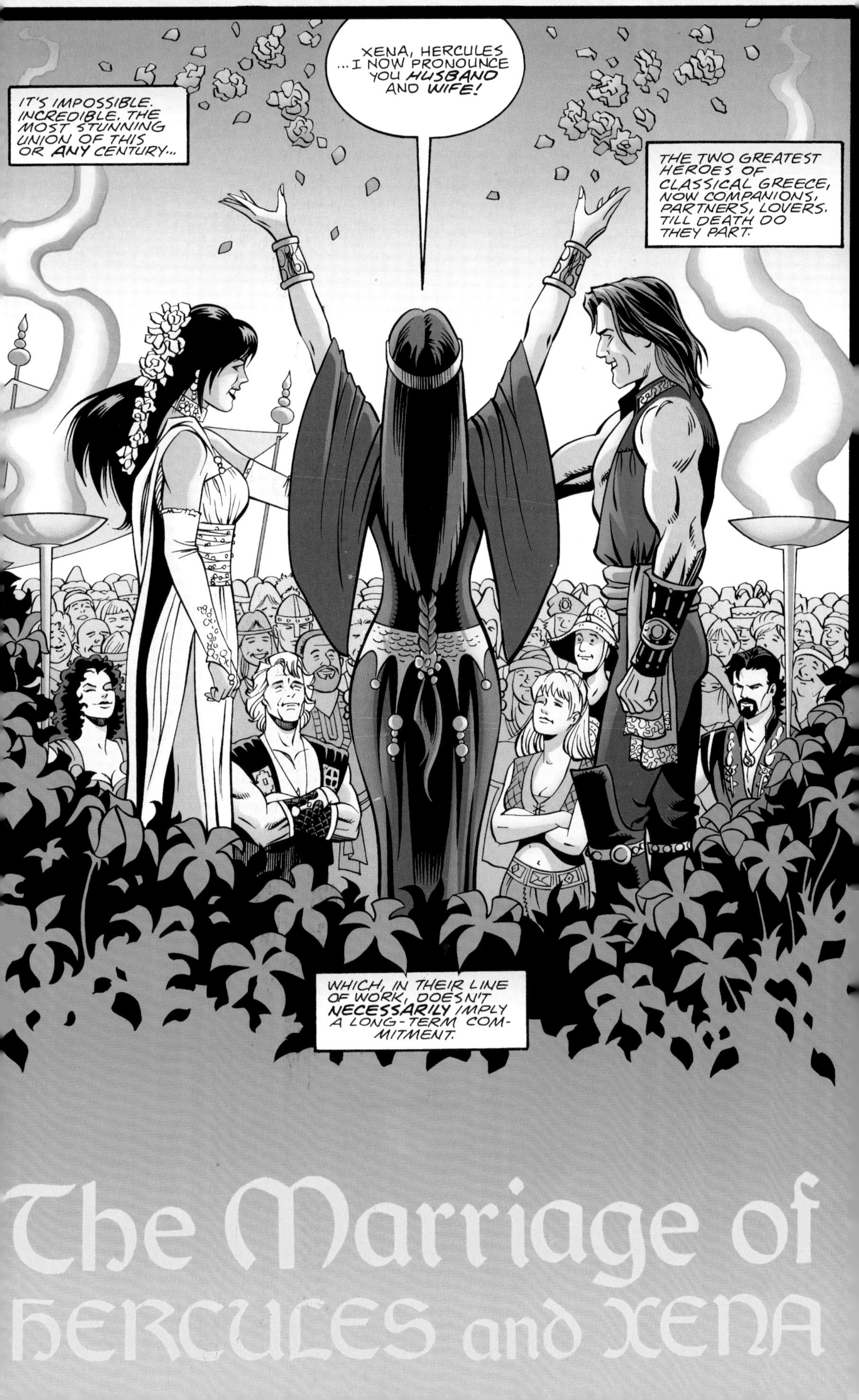
IT'S IMPOSSIBLE. INCREDIBLE. THE MOST STUNNING UNION OF THIS OR ANY CENTURY...
XENA, HERCULES ...I NOW PRONOUNCE YOU HUSBAND AND WIFE!
THE TWO GREATEST HEROES OF CLASSICAL GREECE, NOW COMPANIONS, PARTNERS, LOVERS. TILL DEATH DO THEY PART.
WHICH, IN THEIR LINE OF WORK, DOESN'T NECESSARILY IMPLY A LONG-TERM COM-MITMENT.

The Marriage of HERCULES and XENA

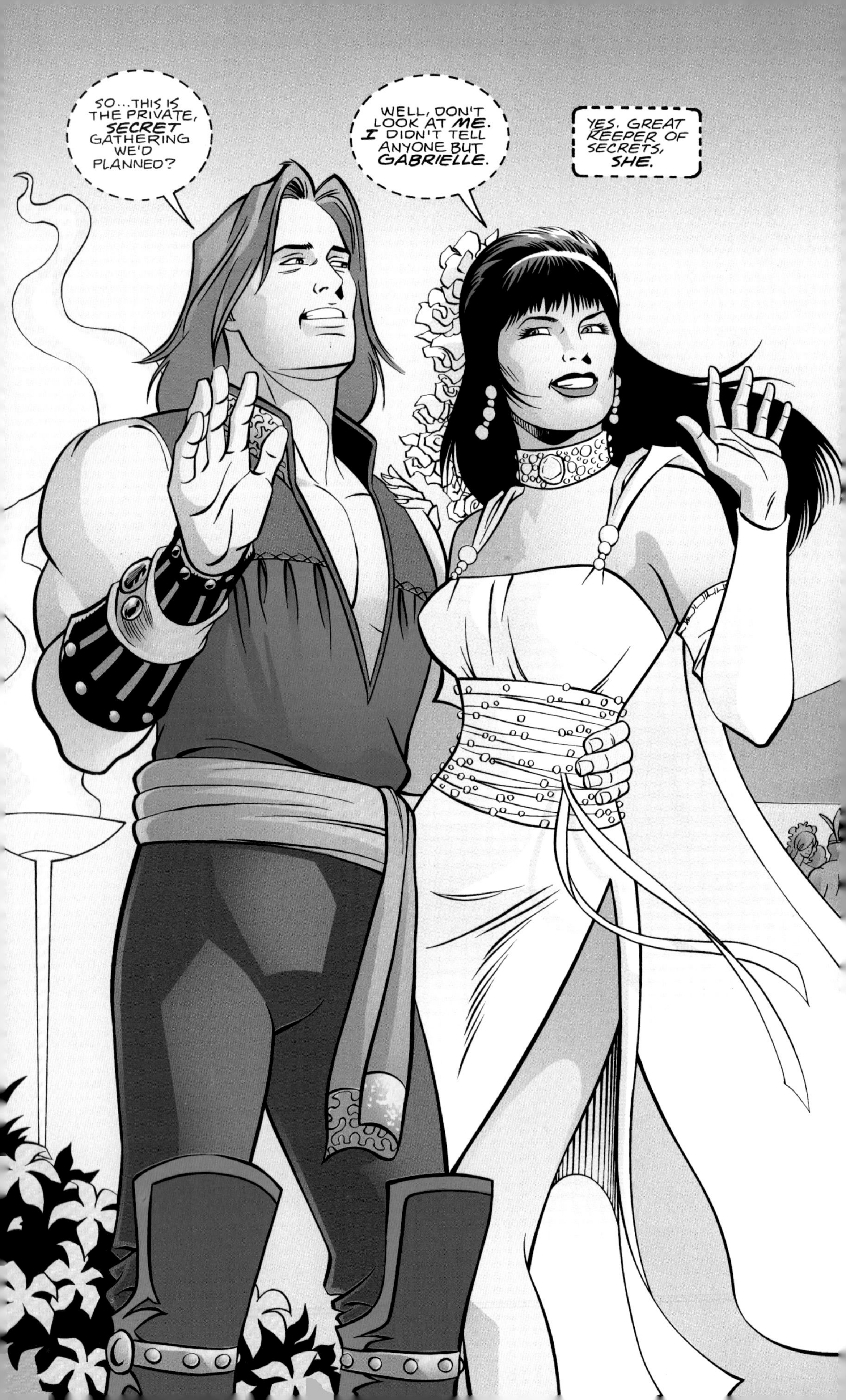
SO... THIS IS THE PRIVATE, SECRET GATHERING WE'D PLANNED?
WELL, DON'T LOOK AT ME. I DIDN'T TELL ANYONE BUT GABRIELLE.
YES. GREAT KEEPER OF SECRETS, SHE.

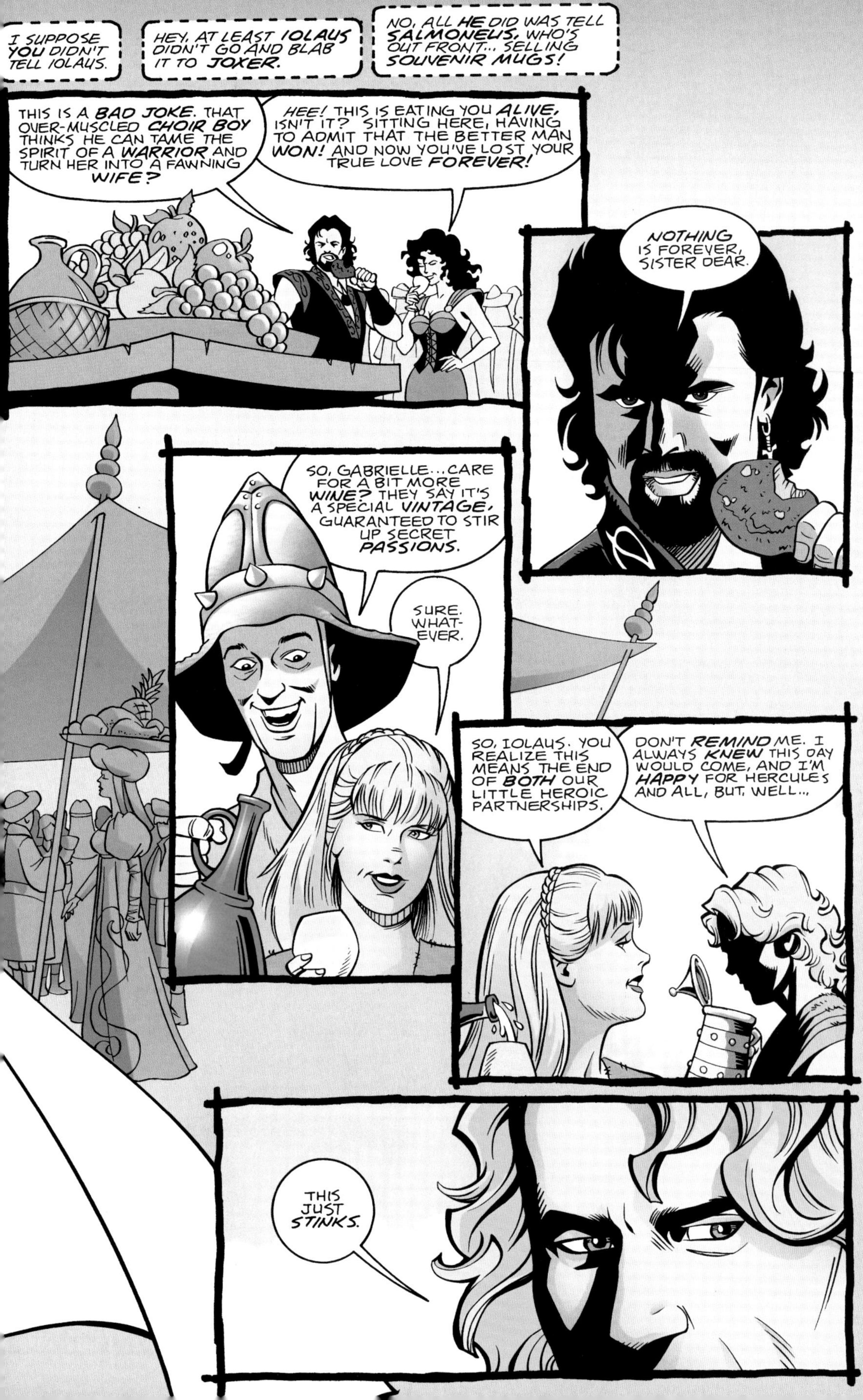
I SUPPOSE YOU DIDN'T TELL IOLAUS.
HEY, AT LEAST IOLAUS DIDN'T GO AND BLAB IT TO JOXER.
NO, ALL HE DID WAS TELL SALMONEUS, WHO'S OUT FRONT... SELLING SOUVENIR MUGS!
THIS IS A BAD JOKE. THAT OVER-MUSCLED CHOIR BOY THINKS HE CAN TAME THE SPIRIT OF A WARRIOR AND TURN HER INTO A FAWNING WIFE?
HEE! THIS IS EATING YOU ALIVE, ISN'T IT? SITTING HERE, HAVING TO ADMIT THAT THE BETTER MAN WON! AND NOW YOU'VE LOST YOUR TRUE LOVE FOREVER!
NOTHING IS FOREVER, SISTER DEAR.
SO, GABRIELLE... CARE FOR A BIT MORE WINE? THEY SAY IT'S A SPECIAL VINTAGE, GUARANTEED TO STIR UP SECRET PASSIONS.
SURE. WHAT-EVER.
SO, IOLAUS. YOU REALIZE THIS MEANS THE END OF BOTH OUR LITTLE HEROIC PARTNERSHIPS.
DON'T REMIND ME. I ALWAYS KNEW THIS DAY WOULD COME, AND I'M HAPPY FOR HERCULES AND ALL, BUT, WELL...
THIS JUST STINKS.

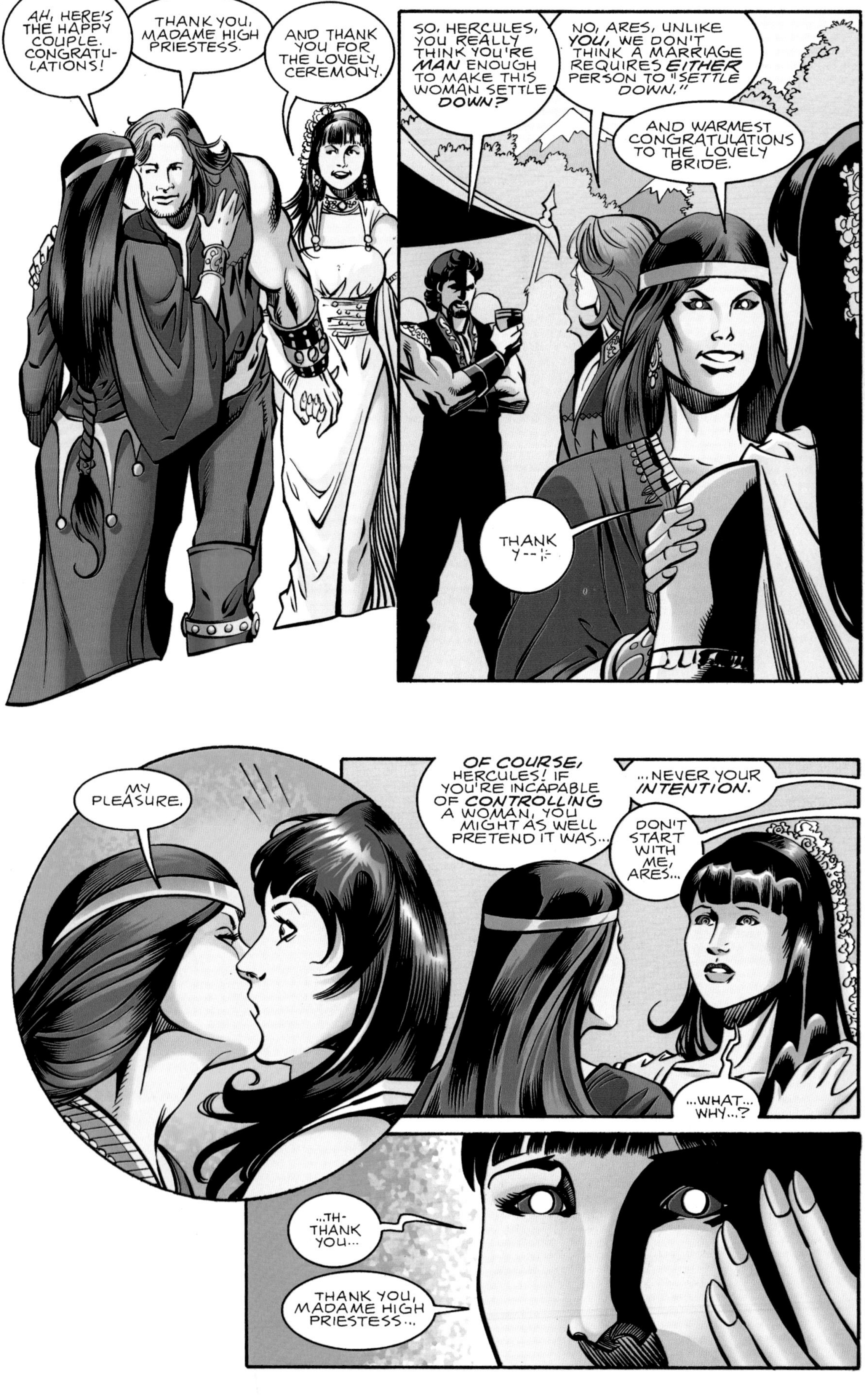
AH, HERE'S THE HAPPY COUPLE. CONGRATULATIONS!
THANK YOU, MADAME HIGH PRIESTESS.
AND THANK YOU FOR THE LOVELY CEREMONY.
SO, HERCULES, YOU REALLY THINK YOU'RE MAN ENOUGH TO MAKE THIS WOMAN SETTLE DOWN?
NO, ARES, UNLIKE YOU, WE DON'T THINK A MARRIAGE REQUIRES EITHER PERSON TO "SETTLE DOWN."
AND WARMEST CONGRATULATIONS TO THE LOVELY BRIDE.
THANK Y--!
MY PLEASURE.
OF COURSE, HERCULES! IF YOU'RE INCAPABLE OF CONTROLLING A WOMAN, YOU MIGHT AS WELL PRETEND IT WAS...
...NEVER YOUR INTENTION.
DON'T START WITH ME, ARES...
...WHAT... WHY...?
...TH-THANK YOU...
THANK YOU, MADAME HIGH PRIESTESS...

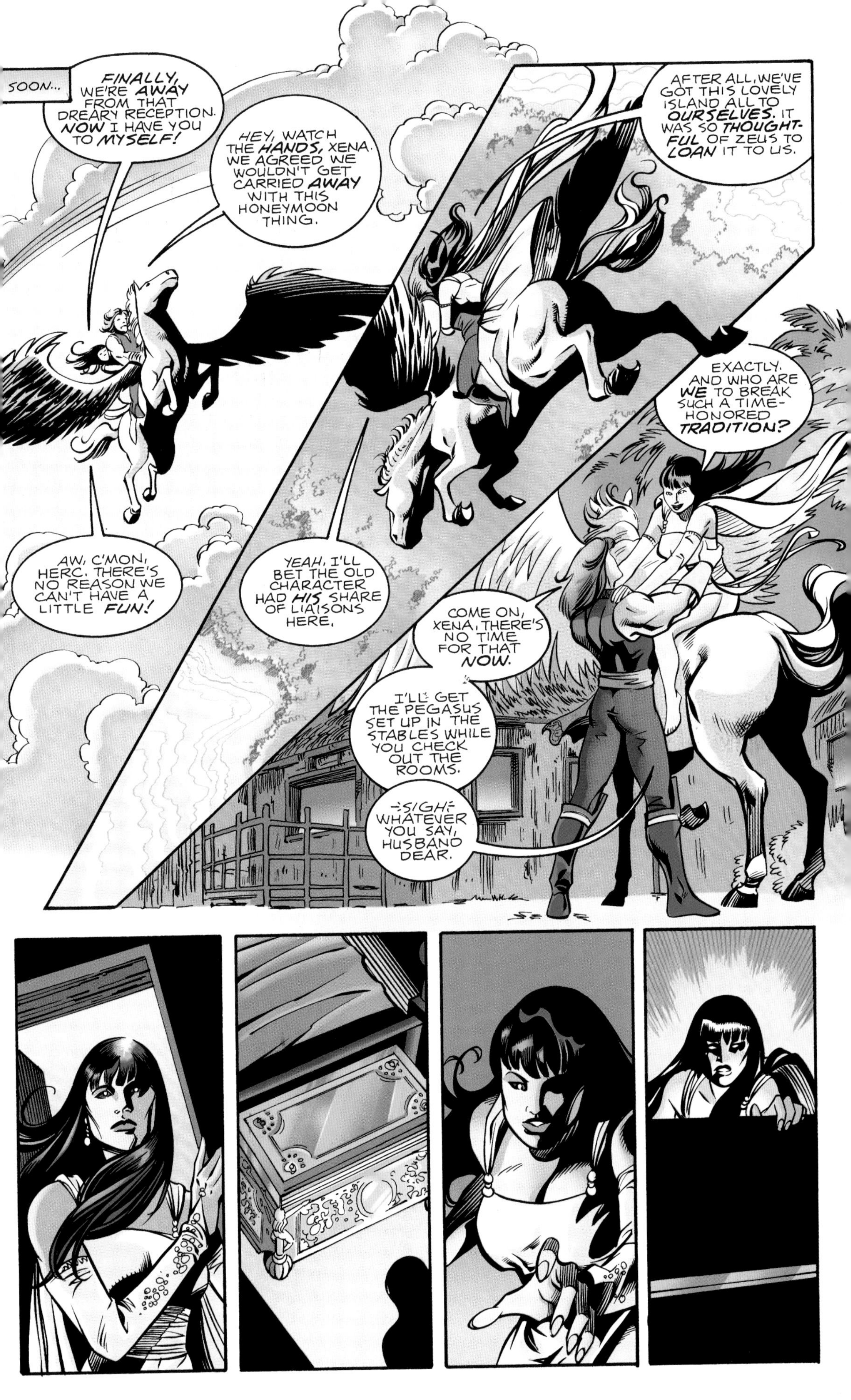
SOON...
FINALLY, WE'RE AWAY FROM THAT DREARY RECEPTION. NOW I HAVE YOU TO MYSELF!
HEY, WATCH THE HANDS, XENA. WE AGREED WE WOULDN'T GET CARRIED AWAY WITH THIS HONEYMOON THING.
AW, C'MON, HERC. THERE'S NO REASON WE CAN'T HAVE A LITTLE FUN!
AFTER ALL, WE'VE GOT THIS LOVELY ISLAND ALL TO OURSELVES. IT WAS SO THOUGHTFUL OF ZEUS TO LOAN IT TO US.
YEAH, I'LL BET THE OLD CHARACTER HAD HIS SHARE OF LIAISONS HERE.
EXACTLY. AND WHO ARE WE TO BREAK SUCH A TIME-HONORED TRADITION?
COME ON, XENA, THERE'S NO TIME FOR THAT NOW.
I'LL GET THE PEGASUS SET UP IN THE STABLES WHILE YOU CHECK OUT THE ROOMS.
-SIGH- WHATEVER YOU SAY, HUSBAND DEAR.

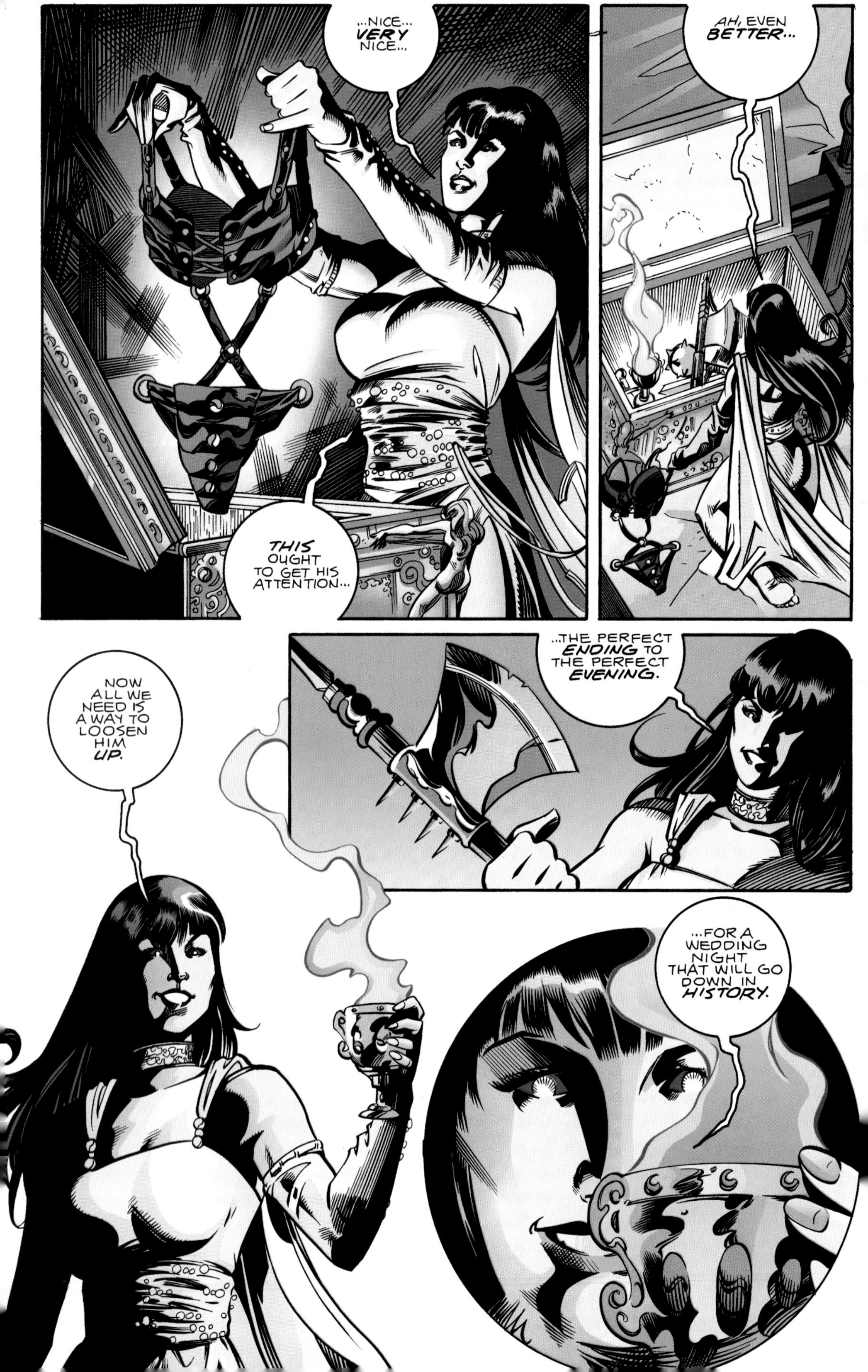
...NICE... VERY NICE...
THIS OUGHT TO GET HIS ATTENTION...
AH, EVEN BETTER...
NOW ALL WE NEED IS A WAY TO LOOSEN HIM UP.
...THE PERFECT ENDING TO THE PERFECT EVENING.
...FOR A WEDDING NIGHT THAT WILL GO DOWN IN HISTORY.

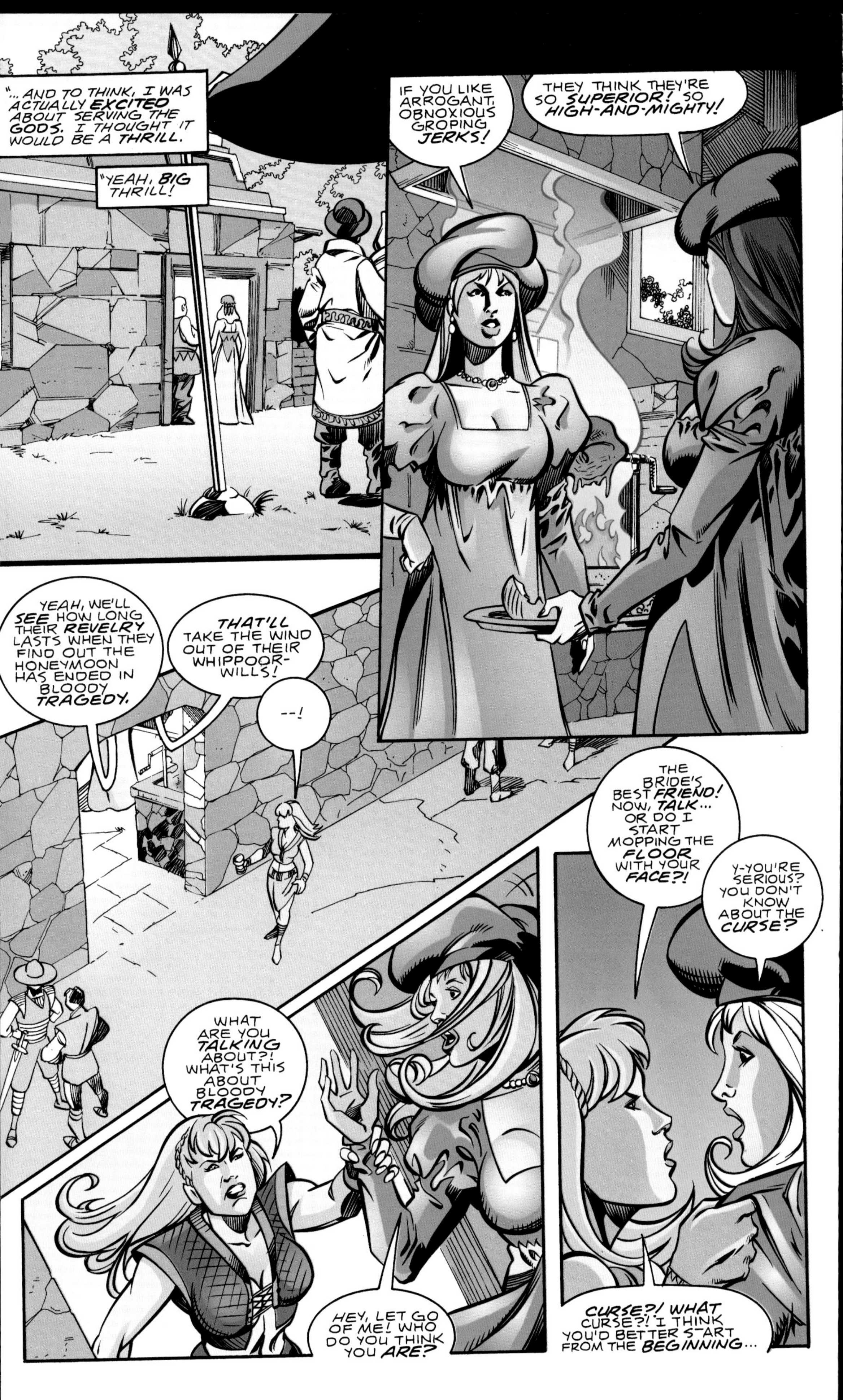
"...AND TO THINK, I WAS ACTUALLY EXCITED ABOUT SERVING THE GODS. I THOUGHT IT WOULD BE A THRILL.
"YEAH, BIG THRILL!
IF YOU LIKE ARROGANT, OBNOXIOUS GROPING JERKS!
THEY THINK THEY'RE SO SUPERIOR! SO HIGH-AND-MIGHTY!
YEAH, WE'LL SEE HOW LONG THEIR REVELRY LASTS WHEN THEY FIND OUT THE HONEYMOON HAS ENDED IN BLOODY TRAGEDY.
THAT'LL TAKE THE WIND OUT OF THEIR WHIPPOOR-WILLS!
--!
WHAT ARE YOU TALKING ABOUT?! WHAT'S THIS ABOUT BLOODY TRAGEDY?
HEY, LET GO OF ME! WHO DO YOU THINK YOU ARE?
THE BRIDE'S BEST FRIEND! NOW, TALK... OR DO I START MOPPING THE FLOOR WITH YOUR FACE?!
Y-YOU'RE SERIOUS? YOU DON'T KNOW ABOUT THE CURSE?
CURSE?! WHAT CURSE?! I THINK YOU'D BETTER START FROM THE BEGINNING...

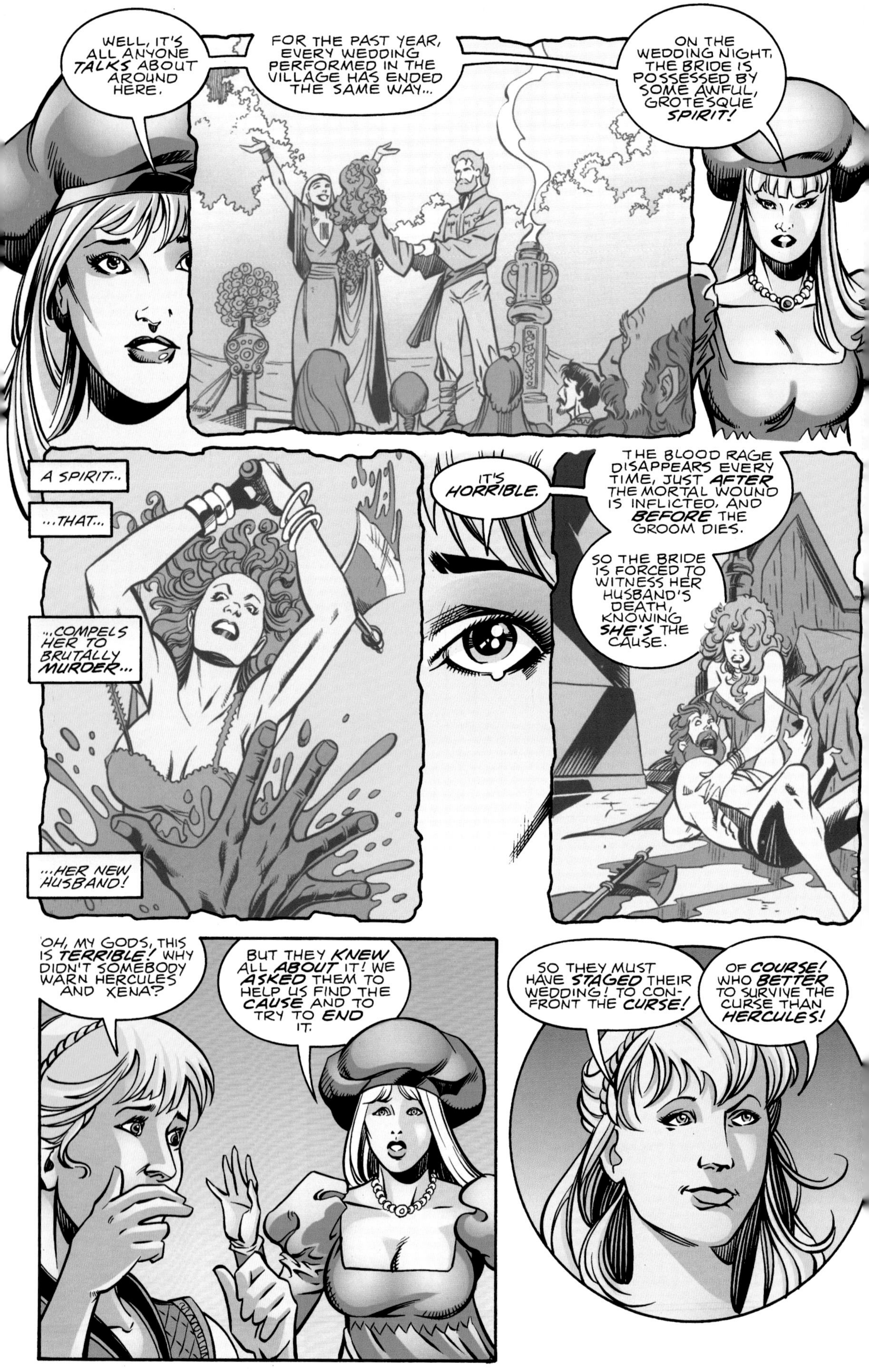
WELL, IT'S ALL ANYONE TALKS ABOUT AROUND HERE.
FOR THE PAST YEAR, EVERY WEDDING PERFORMED IN THE VILLAGE HAS ENDED THE SAME WAY...
ON THE WEDDING NIGHT, THE BRIDE IS POSSESSED BY SOME AWFUL, GROTESQUE SPIRIT!
A SPIRIT...
...THAT...
...COMPELS HER TO BRUTALLY MURDER...
...HER NEW HUSBAND!
IT'S HORRIBLE.
THE BLOOD RAGE DISAPPEARS EVERY TIME, JUST AFTER THE MORTAL WOUND IS INFLICTED, AND BEFORE THE GROOM DIES.
SO THE BRIDE IS FORCED TO WITNESS HER HUSBAND'S DEATH, KNOWING SHE'S THE CAUSE.
OH, MY GODS, THIS IS TERRIBLE! WHY DIDN'T SOMEBODY WARN HERCULES AND XENA?
BUT THEY KNEW ALL ABOUT IT! WE ASKED THEM TO HELP US FIND THE CAUSE AND TO TRY TO END IT.
SO THEY MUST HAVE STAGED THEIR WEDDING! TO CONFRONT THE CURSE!
OF COURSE! WHO BETTER TO SURVIVE THE CURSE THAN HERCULES!

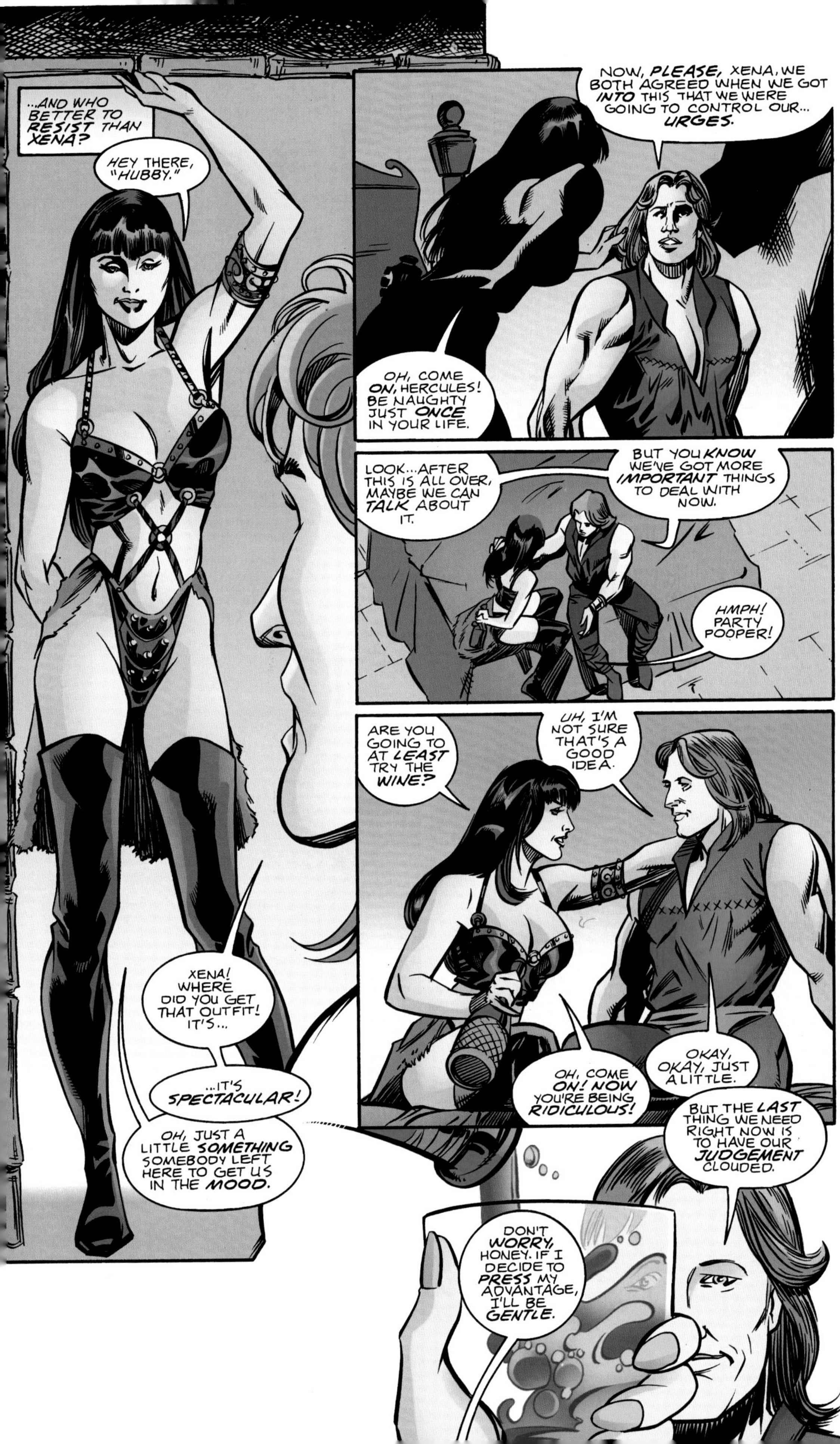
...AND WHO BETTER TO RESIST THAN XENA?
HEY THERE, "HUBBY."
XENA! WHERE DID YOU GET THAT OUTFIT! IT'S...
...IT'S SPECTACULAR!
OH, JUST A LITTLE SOMETHING SOMEBODY LEFT HERE TO GET US IN THE MOOD.
NOW, PLEASE, XENA, WE BOTH AGREED WHEN WE GOT INTO THIS THAT WE WERE GOING TO CONTROL OUR... URGES.
OH, COME ON, HERCULES! BE NAUGHTY JUST ONCE IN YOUR LIFE.
LOOK... AFTER THIS IS ALL OVER, MAYBE WE CAN TALK ABOUT IT.
BUT YOU KNOW WE'VE GOT MORE IMPORTANT THINGS TO DEAL WITH NOW.
HMPH! PARTY POOPER!
ARE YOU GOING TO AT LEAST TRY THE WINE?
UH, I'M NOT SURE THAT'S A GOOD IDEA.
OH, COME ON! NOW YOU'RE BEING RIDICULOUS!
OKAY, OKAY, JUST A LITTLE.
BUT THE LAST THING WE NEED RIGHT NOW IS TO HAVE OUR JUDGEMENT CLOUDED.
DON'T WORRY, HONEY. IF I DECIDE TO PRESS MY ADVANTAGE, I'LL BE GENTLE.

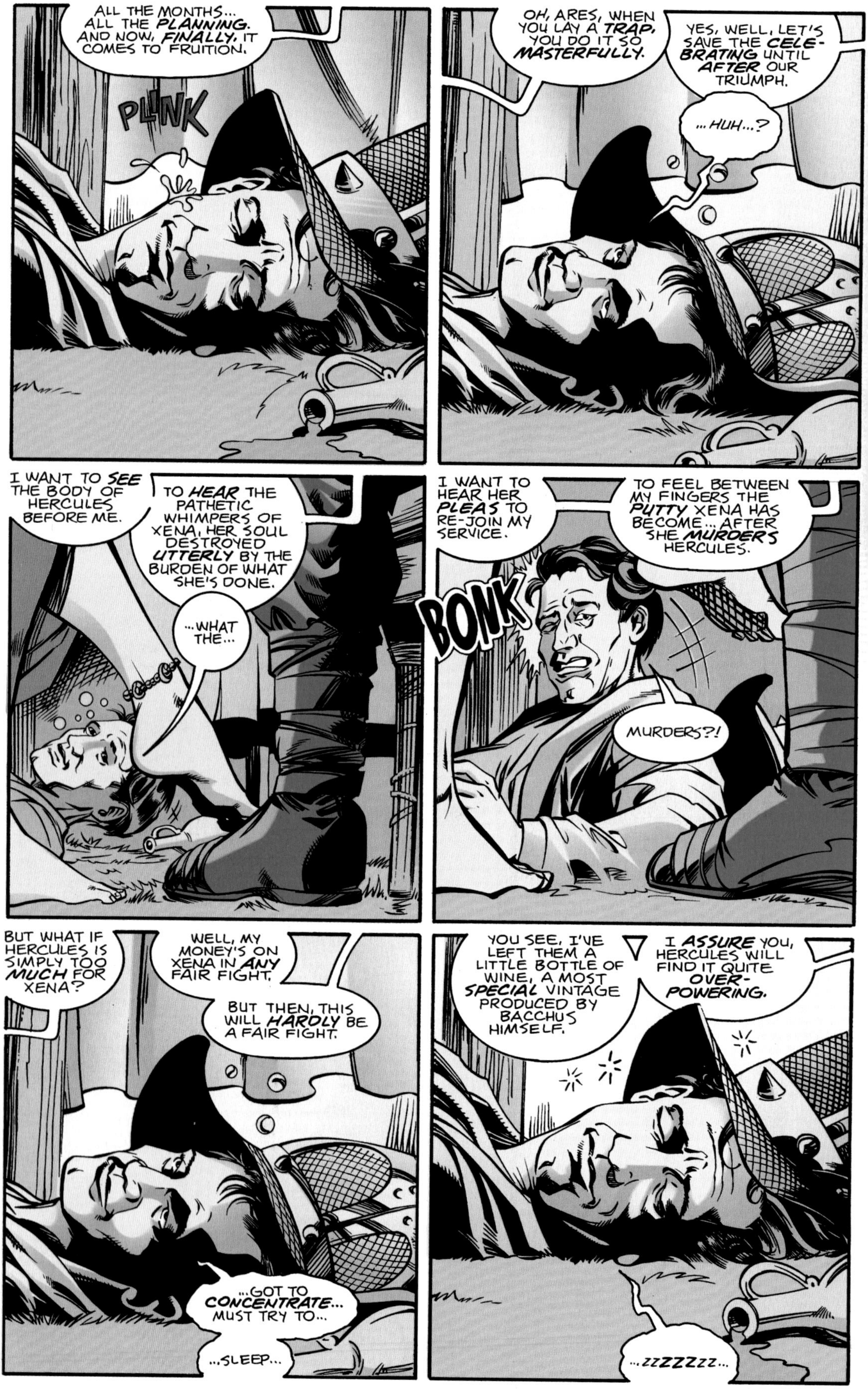
ALL THE MONTHS... ALL THE PLANNING. AND NOW, FINALLY, IT COMES TO FRUITION.
PLINK
OH, ARES, WHEN YOU LAY A TRAP, YOU DO IT SO MASTERFULLY.
YES, WELL, LET'S SAVE THE CELE-BRATING UNTIL AFTER OUR TRIUMPH.
...HUH...?
I WANT TO SEE THE BODY OF HERCULES BEFORE ME.
TO HEAR THE PATHETIC WHIMPERS OF XENA, HER SOUL DESTROYED UTTERLY BY THE BURDEN OF WHAT SHE'S DONE.
...WHAT THE...
I WANT TO HEAR HER PLEAS TO RE-JOIN MY SERVICE.
TO FEEL BETWEEN MY FINGERS THE PUTTY XENA HAS BECOME... AFTER SHE MURDERS HERCULES.
BONK
MURDERS?!
BUT WHAT IF HERCULES IS SIMPLY TOO MUCH FOR XENA?
WELL, MY MONEY'S ON XENA IN ANY FAIR FIGHT.
BUT THEN, THIS WILL HARDLY BE A FAIR FIGHT.
...GOT TO CONCENTRATE... MUST TRY TO...
...SLEEP...
YOU SEE, I'VE LEFT THEM A LITTLE BOTTLE OF WINE, A MOST SPECIAL VINTAGE PRODUCED BY BACCHUS HIMSELF.
I ASSURE YOU, HERCULES WILL FIND IT QUITE OVER-POWERING.
...zzZZZzz...

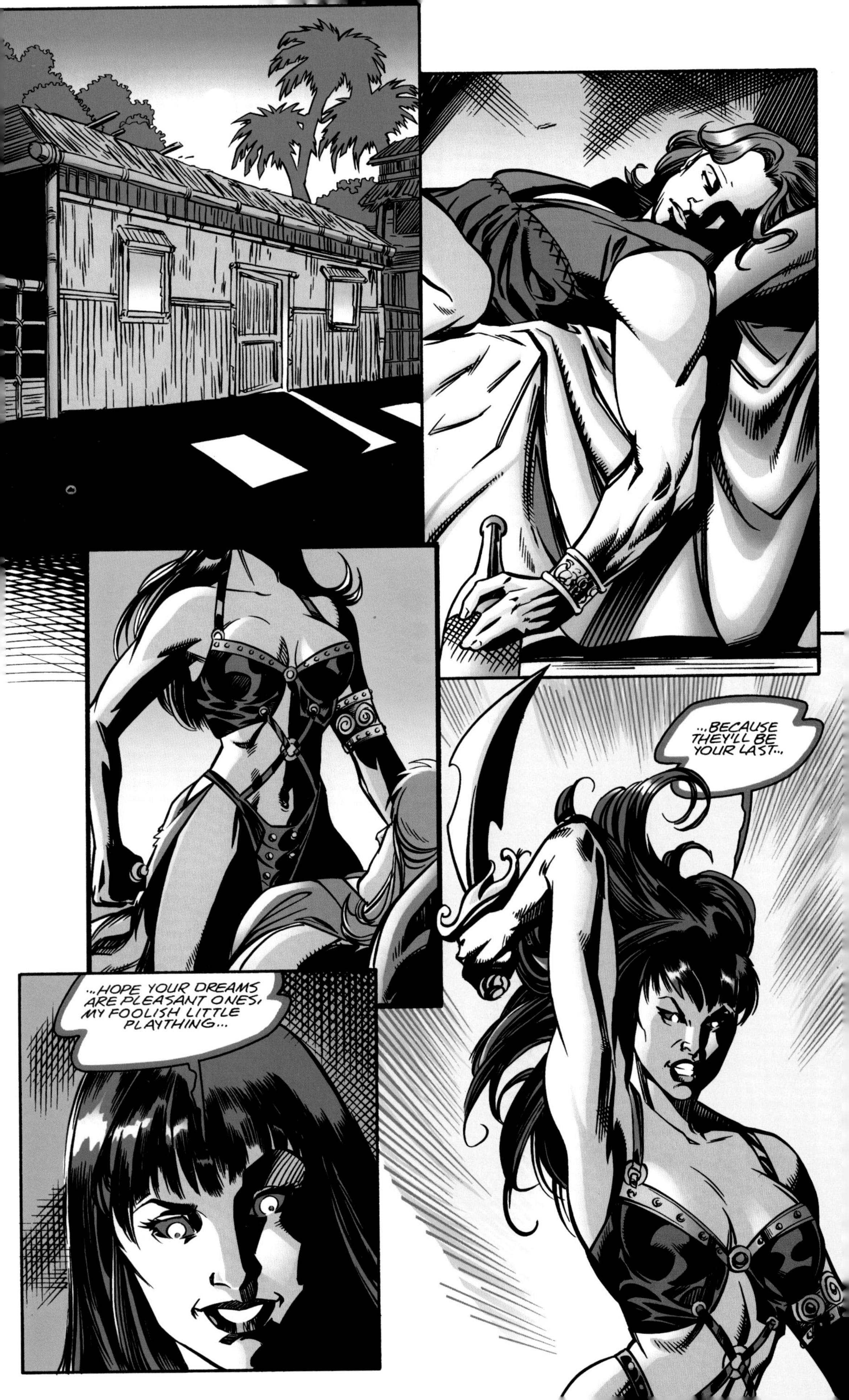
...HOPE YOUR DREAMS ARE PLEASANT ONES, MY FOOLISH LITTLE PLAYTHING...
...BECAUSE THEY'LL BE YOUR LAST...

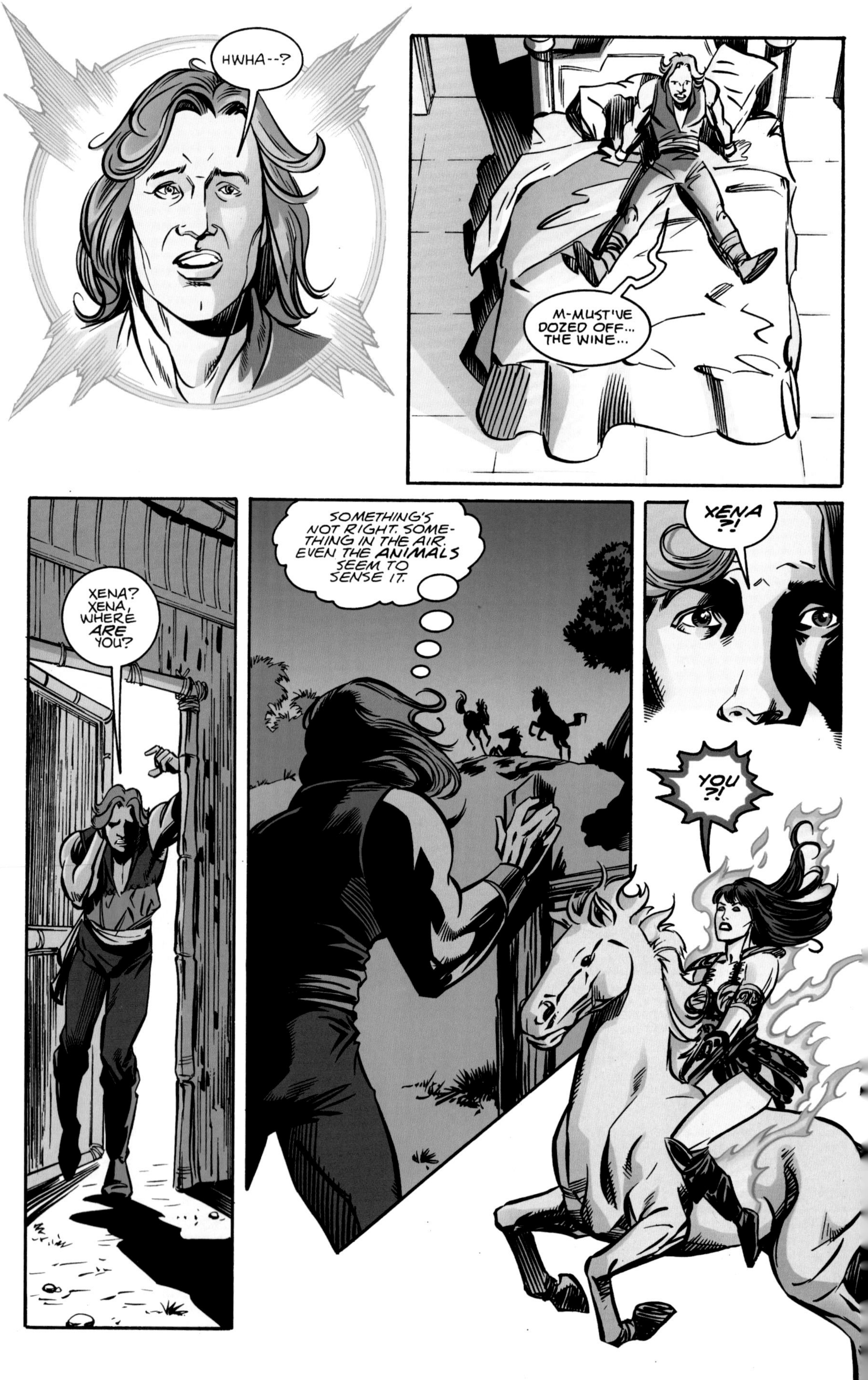
HWHA--?
M-MUST'VE DOZED OFF... THE WINE...
XENA? XENA, WHERE *ARE* YOU?
SOMETHING'S NOT RIGHT. SOMETHING IN THE AIR. EVEN THE *ANIMALS* SEEM TO SENSE IT.
XENA ?!
YOU ?!

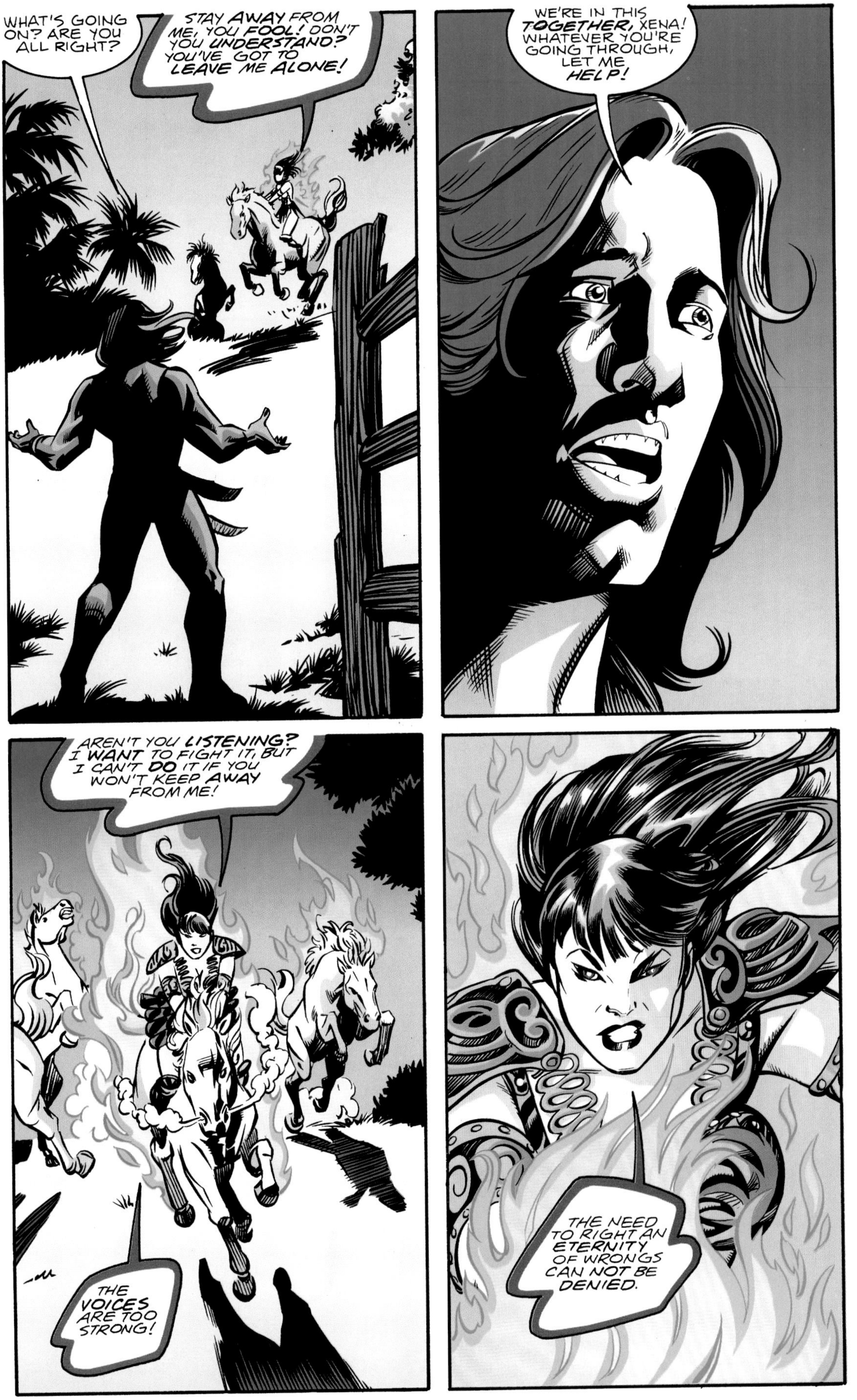
WHAT'S GOING ON? ARE YOU ALL RIGHT?
STAY AWAY FROM ME, YOU FOOL! DON'T YOU UNDERSTAND? YOU'VE GOT TO LEAVE ME ALONE!
WE'RE IN THIS TOGETHER, XENA! WHATEVER YOU'RE GOING THROUGH, LET ME HELP!
AREN'T YOU LISTENING? I WANT TO FIGHT IT, BUT I CAN'T DO IT IF YOU WON'T KEEP AWAY FROM ME!
THE VOICES ARE TOO STRONG!
THE NEED TO RIGHT AN ETERNITY OF WRONGS CAN NOT BE DENIED.

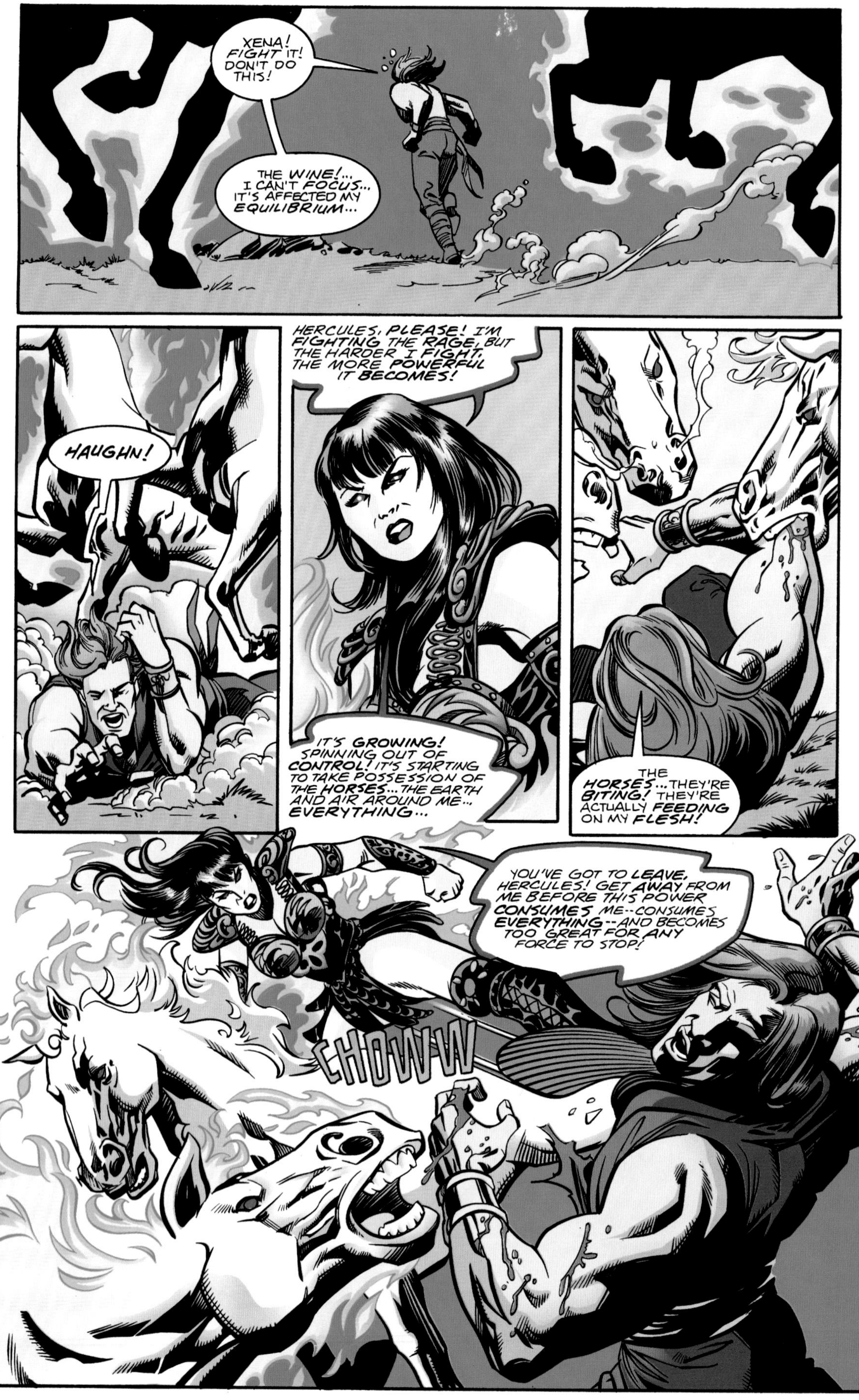
XENA! FIGHT IT! DON'T DO THIS!
THE WINE!... I CAN'T FOCUS... IT'S AFFECTED MY EQUILIBRIUM...
HAUGHN!
HERCULES, PLEASE! I'M FIGHTING THE RAGE, BUT THE HARDER I FIGHT, THE MORE POWERFUL IT BECOMES!
IT'S GROWING! SPINNING OUT OF CONTROL! IT'S STARTING TO TAKE POSSESSION OF THE HORSES... THE EARTH AND AIR AROUND ME... EVERYTHING...
THE HORSES... THEY'RE BITING! THEY'RE ACTUALLY FEEDING ON MY FLESH!
YOU'VE GOT TO LEAVE, HERCULES! GET AWAY FROM ME BEFORE THIS POWER CONSUMES ME--CONSUMES EVERYTHING--AND BECOMES TOO GREAT FOR ANY FORCE TO STOP!
CHOWW

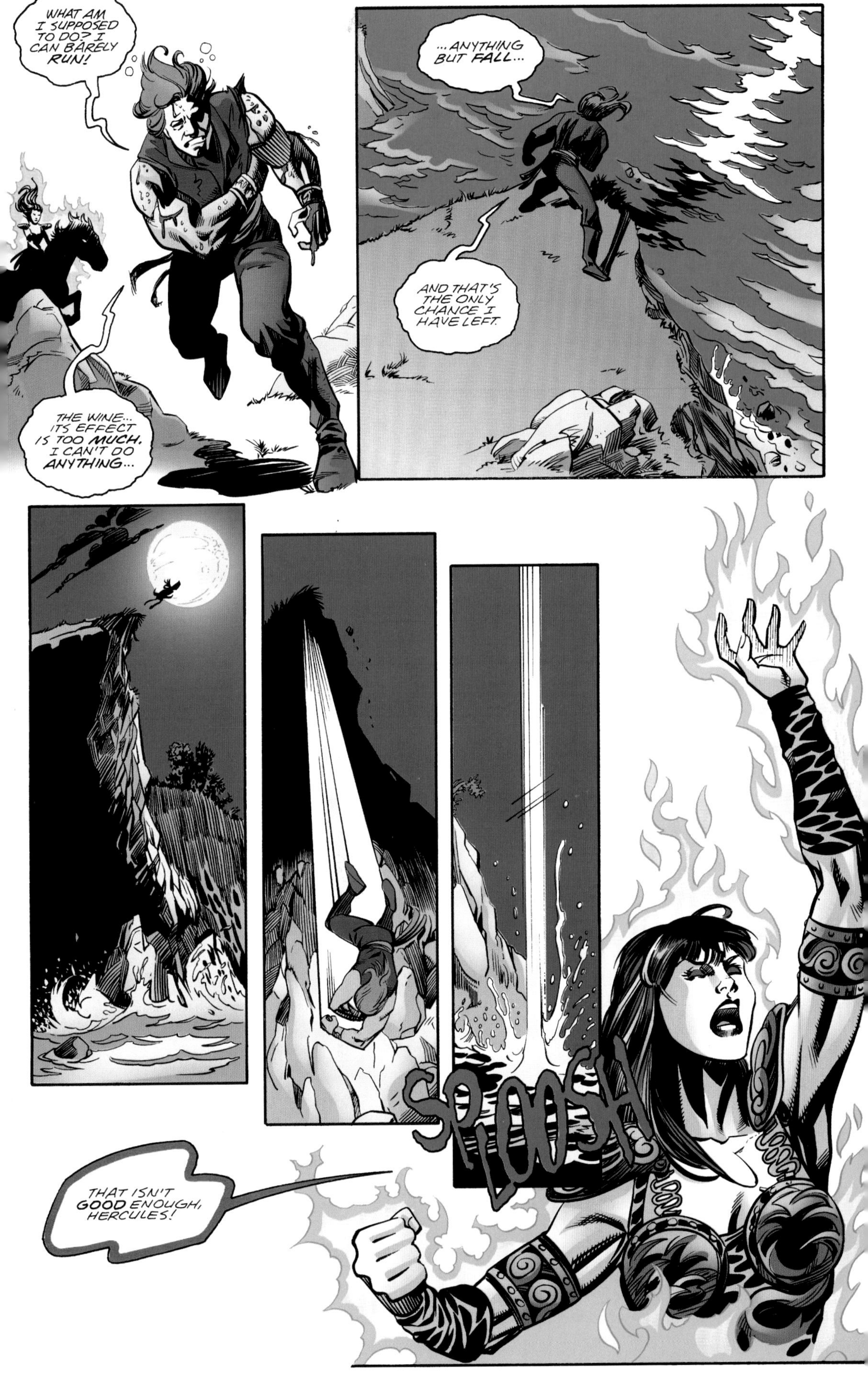
WHAT AM I SUPPOSED TO DO? I CAN BARELY RUN!
THE WINE... ITS EFFECT IS TOO MUCH. I CAN'T DO ANYTHING...
...ANYTHING BUT FALL...
AND THAT'S THE ONLY CHANCE I HAVE LEFT.
SPLOOSH
THAT ISN'T GOOD ENOUGH, HERCULES!

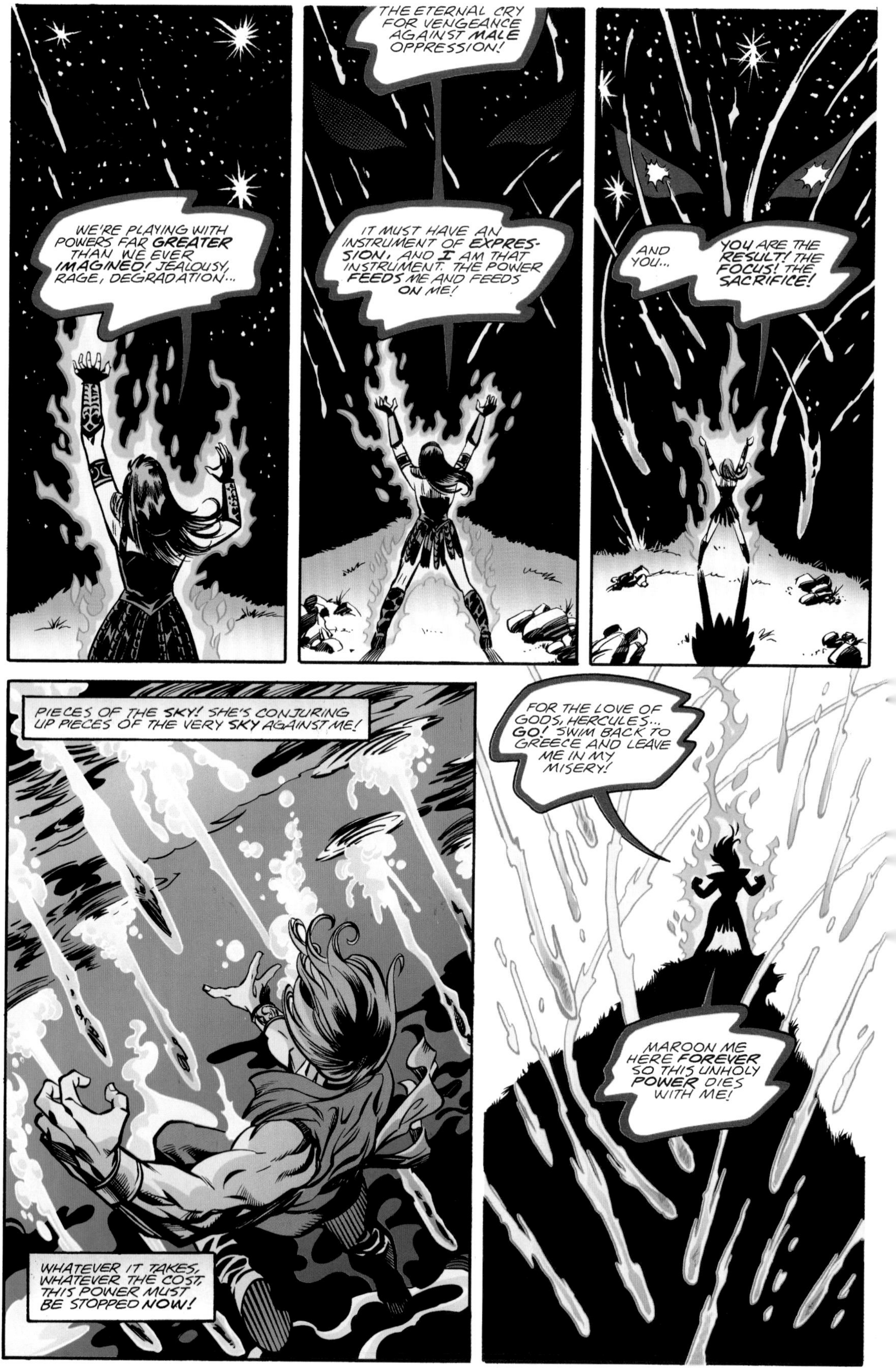
WE'RE PLAYING WITH POWERS FAR GREATER THAN WE EVER IMAGINED! JEALOUSY, RAGE, DEGRADATION...
THE ETERNAL CRY FOR VENGEANCE AGAINST MALE OPPRESSION!
IT MUST HAVE AN INSTRUMENT OF EXPRESSION, AND I AM THAT INSTRUMENT. THE POWER FEEDS ME AND FEEDS ON ME!
AND YOU...
YOU ARE THE RESULT! THE FOCUS! THE SACRIFICE!
PIECES OF THE SKY! SHE'S CONJURING UP PIECES OF THE VERY SKY AGAINST ME!
WHATEVER IT TAKES, WHATEVER THE COST, THIS POWER MUST BE STOPPED NOW!
FOR THE LOVE OF GODS, HERCULES... GO! SWIM BACK TO GREECE AND LEAVE ME IN MY MISERY!
MAROON ME HERE FOREVER SO THIS UNHOLY POWER DIES WITH ME!

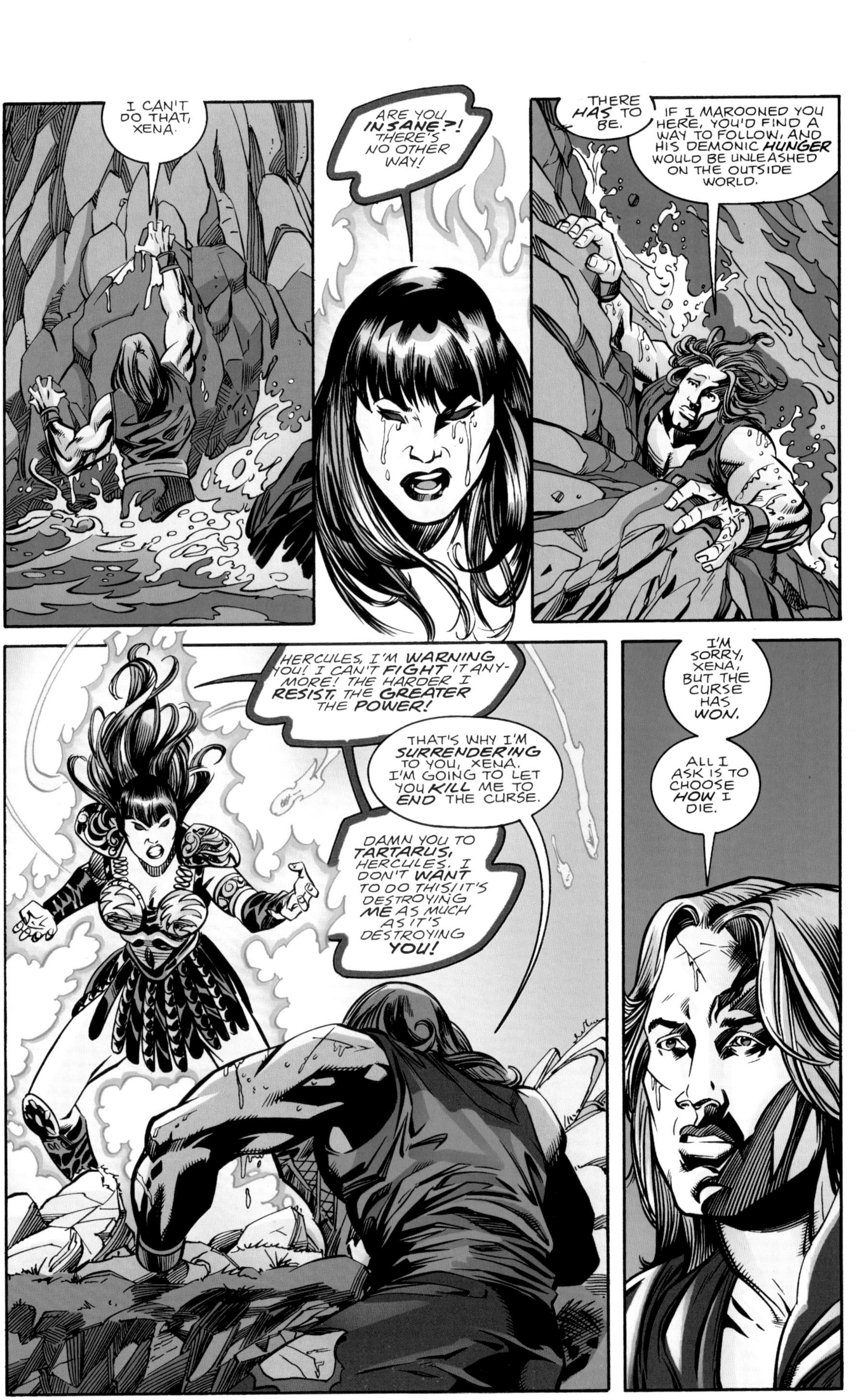
I CAN'T DO THAT, XENA.
ARE YOU INSANE?! THERE'S NO OTHER WAY!
THERE HAS TO BE.
IF I MAROONED YOU HERE, YOU'D FIND A WAY TO FOLLOW, AND HIS DEMONIC HUNGER WOULD BE UNLEASHED ON THE OUTSIDE WORLD.
HERCULES, I'M WARNING YOU! I CAN'T FIGHT IT ANY-MORE! THE HARDER I RESIST, THE GREATER THE POWER!
THAT'S WHY I'M SURRENDERING TO YOU, XENA. I'M GOING TO LET YOU KILL ME TO END THE CURSE.
DAMN YOU TO TARTARUS, HERCULES. I DON'T WANT TO DO THIS! IT'S DESTROYING ME AS MUCH AS IT'S DESTROYING YOU!
I'M SORRY, XENA, BUT THE CURSE HAS WON.
ALL I ASK IS TO CHOOSE HOW I DIE.

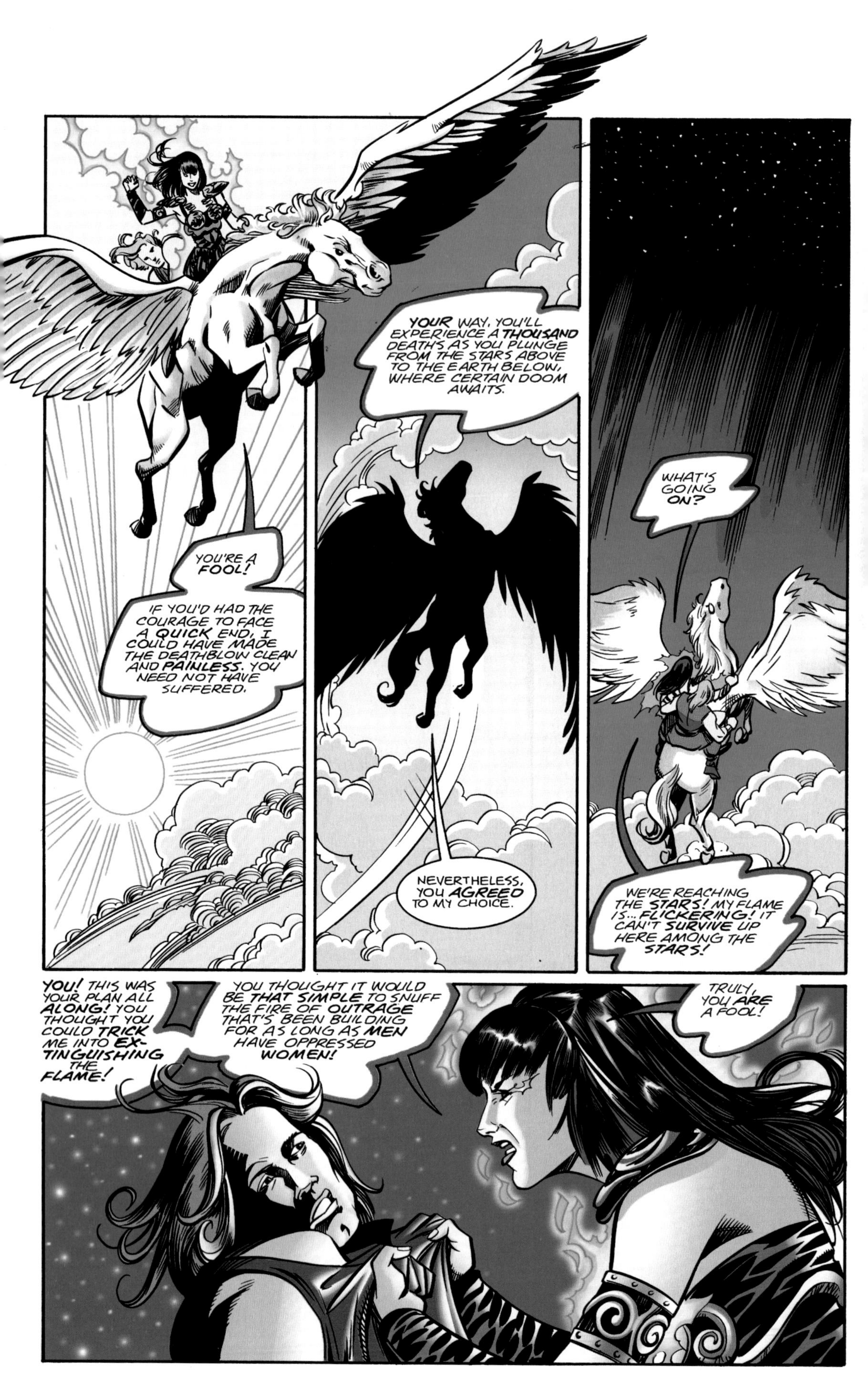
YOU'RE A FOOL!
IF YOU'D HAD THE COURAGE TO FACE A QUICK END, I COULD HAVE MADE THE DEATHBLOW CLEAN AND PAINLESS. YOU NEED NOT HAVE SUFFERED.
YOUR WAY, YOU'LL EXPERIENCE A THOUSAND DEATHS AS YOU PLUNGE FROM THE STARS ABOVE TO THE EARTH BELOW, WHERE CERTAIN DOOM AWAITS.
NEVERTHELESS, YOU AGREED TO MY CHOICE.
WHAT'S GOING ON?
WE'RE REACHING THE STARS! MY FLAME IS... FLICKERING! IT CAN'T SURVIVE UP HERE AMONG THE STARS!
YOU! THIS WAS YOUR PLAN ALL ALONG! YOU THOUGHT YOU COULD TRICK ME INTO EX-TINGUISHING THE FLAME!
YOU THOUGHT IT WOULD BE THAT SIMPLE TO SNUFF THE FIRE OF OUTRAGE THAT'S BEEN BUILDING FOR AS LONG AS MEN HAVE OPPRESSED WOMEN!
TRULY, YOU ARE A FOOL!

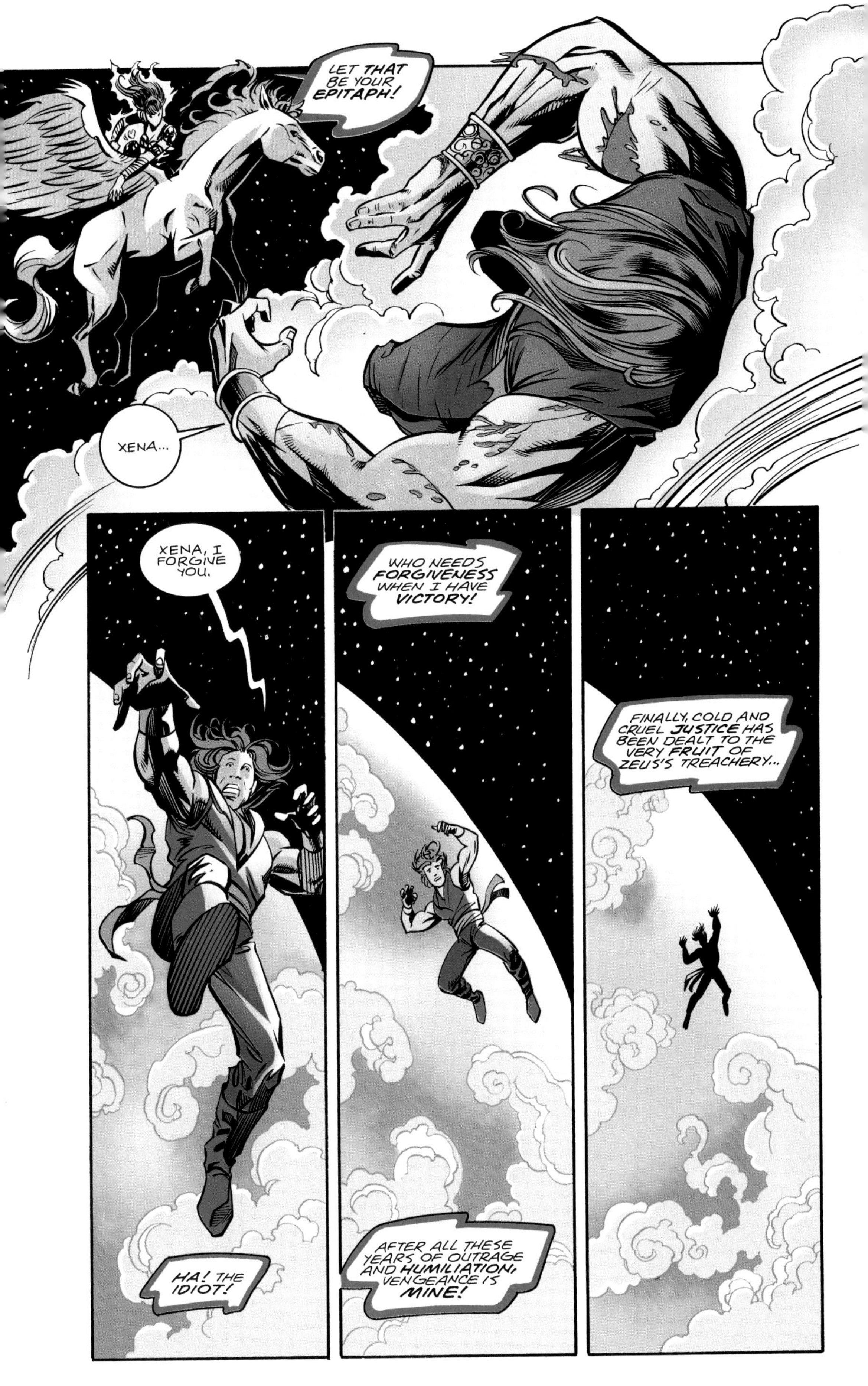
LET THAT BE YOUR EPITAPH!
XENA...
XENA, I FORGIVE YOU.
HA! THE IDIOT!
WHO NEEDS FORGIVENESS WHEN I HAVE VICTORY!
AFTER ALL THESE YEARS OF OUTRAGE AND HUMILIATION, VENGEANCE IS MINE!
FINALLY, COLD AND CRUEL JUSTICE HAS BEEN DEALT TO THE VERY FRUIT OF ZEUS'S TREACHERY...

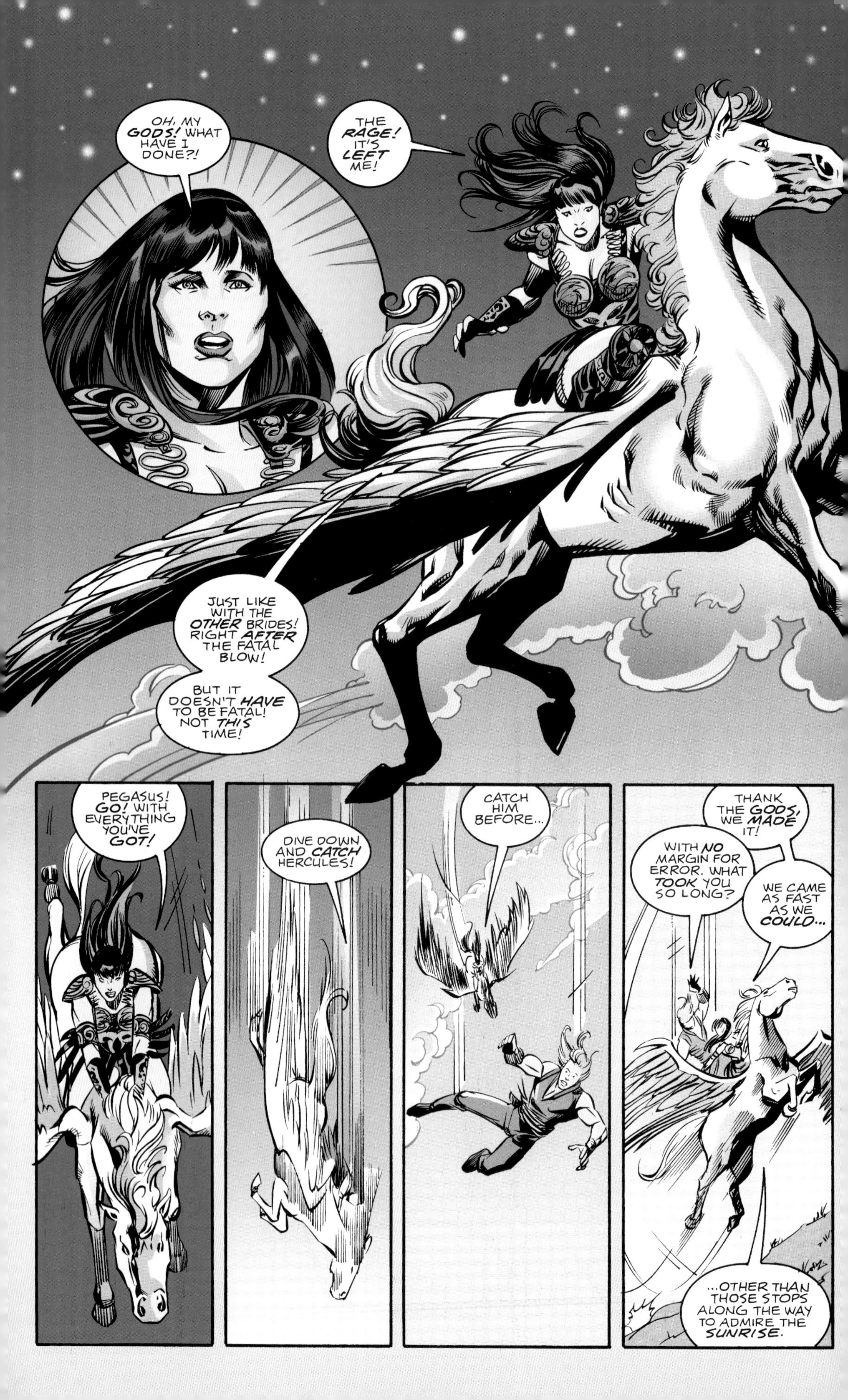
OH, MY GODS! WHAT HAVE I DONE?!
THE RAGE! IT'S LEFT ME!
JUST LIKE WITH THE OTHER BRIDES! RIGHT AFTER THE FATAL BLOW!
BUT IT DOESN'T HAVE TO BE FATAL! NOT THIS TIME!
PEGASUS! GO! WITH EVERYTHING YOU'VE GOT!
DIVE DOWN AND CATCH HERCULES!
CATCH HIM BEFORE...
THANK THE GODS, WE MADE IT!
WITH NO MARGIN FOR ERROR. WHAT TOOK YOU SO LONG?
WE CAME AS FAST AS WE COULD...
...OTHER THAN THOSE STOPS ALONG THE WAY TO ADMIRE THE SUNRISE.

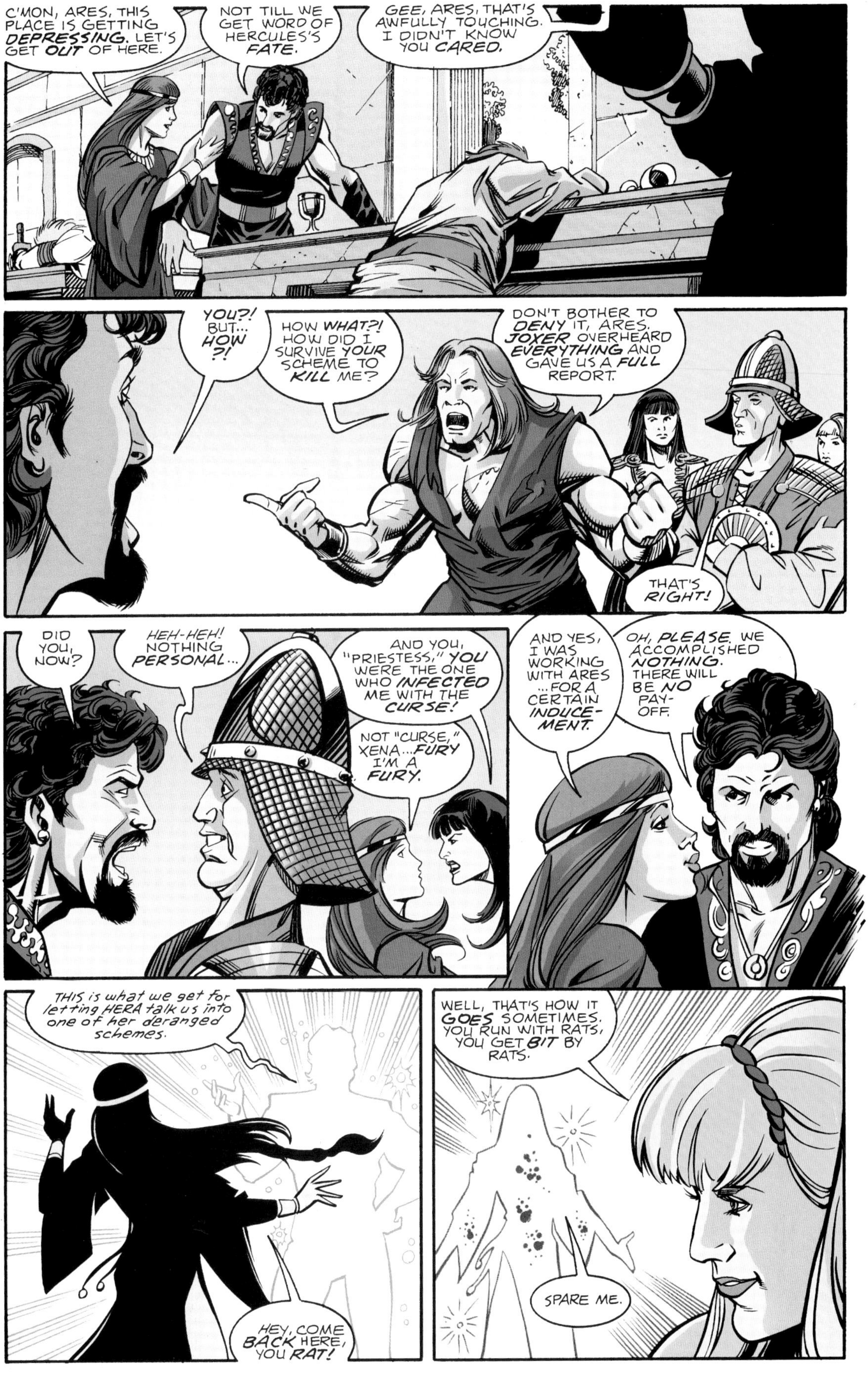
C'MON, ARES, THIS PLACE IS GETTING DEPRESSING. LET'S GET OUT OF HERE.
NOT TILL WE GET WORD OF HERCULES'S FATE.
GEE, ARES, THAT'S AWFULLY TOUCHING. I DIDN'T KNOW YOU CARED.
YOU?! BUT... HOW ?!
HOW WHAT?! HOW DID I SURVIVE YOUR SCHEME TO KILL ME?
DON'T BOTHER TO DENY IT, ARES. JOXER OVERHEARD EVERYTHING AND GAVE US A FULL REPORT.
THAT'S RIGHT!
DID YOU, NOW?
HEH-HEH! NOTHING PERSONAL...
AND YOU, "PRIESTESS," YOU WERE THE ONE WHO INFECTED ME WITH THE CURSE!
NOT "CURSE," XENA...FURY I'M A FURY.
AND YES, I WAS WORKING WITH ARES ...FOR A CERTAIN INDUCE-MENT.
OH, PLEASE. WE ACCOMPLISHED NOTHING. THERE WILL BE NO PAY-OFF.
THIS is what we get for letting HERA talk us into one of her deranged schemes.
HEY, COME BACK HERE, YOU RAT!
WELL, THAT'S HOW IT GOES SOMETIMES. YOU RUN WITH RATS, YOU GET BIT BY RATS.
SPARE ME.

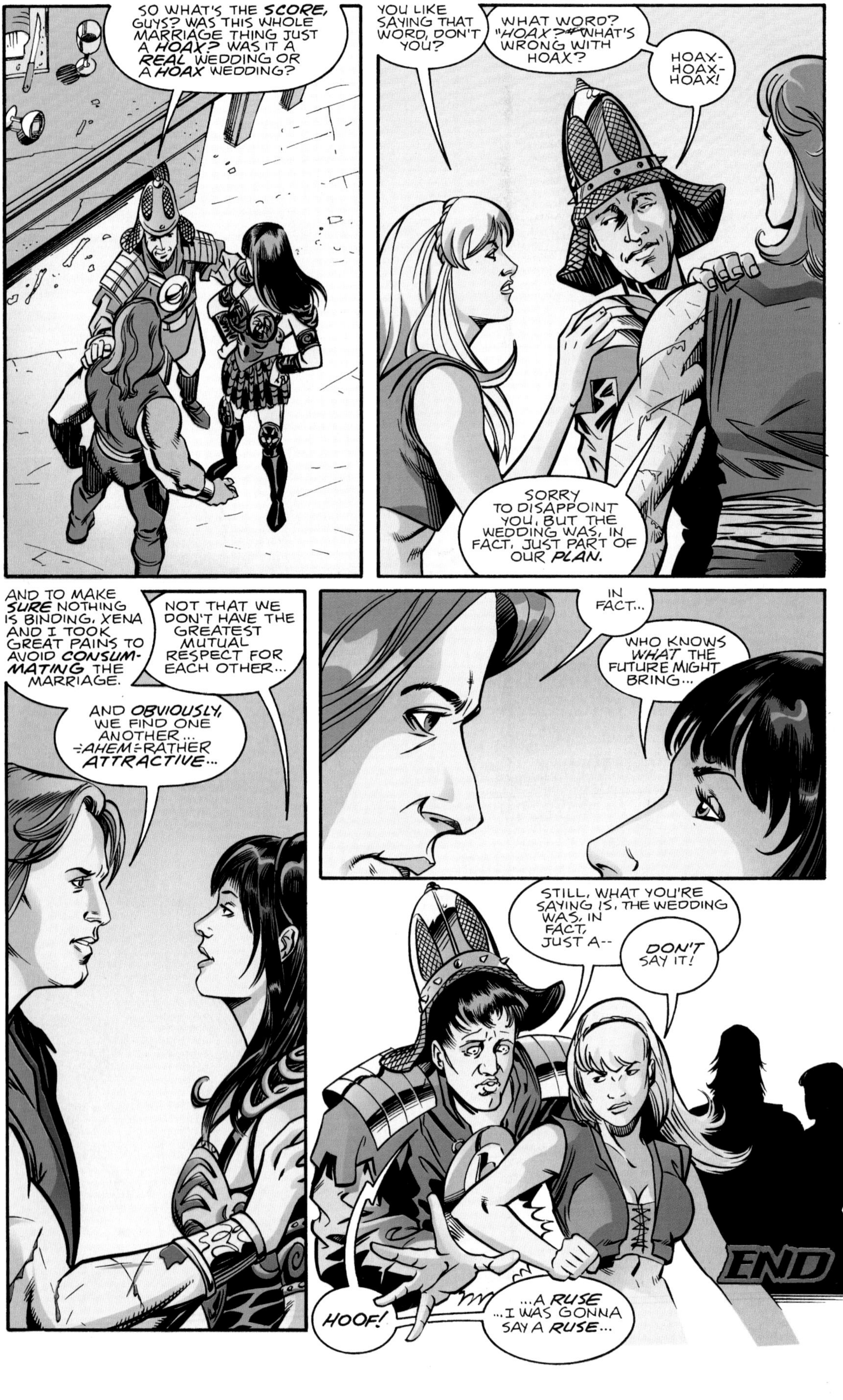
SO WHAT'S THE SCORE, GUYS? WAS THIS WHOLE MARRIAGE THING JUST A HOAX? WAS IT A REAL WEDDING OR A HOAX WEDDING?
YOU LIKE SAYING THAT WORD, DON'T YOU?
WHAT WORD? "HOAX?" WHAT'S WRONG WITH HOAX?
HOAX-HOAX-HOAX!
SORRY TO DISAPPOINT YOU, BUT THE WEDDING WAS, IN FACT, JUST PART OF OUR PLAN.
AND TO MAKE SURE NOTHING IS BINDING, XENA AND I TOOK GREAT PAINS TO AVOID CONSUM-MATING THE MARRIAGE.
NOT THAT WE DON'T HAVE THE GREATEST MUTUAL RESPECT FOR EACH OTHER...
AND OBVIOUSLY, WE FIND ONE ANOTHER... =AHEM= RATHER ATTRACTIVE...
IN FACT...
WHO KNOWS WHAT THE FUTURE MIGHT BRING...
STILL, WHAT YOU'RE SAYING IS, THE WEDDING WAS, IN FACT, JUST A--
DON'T SAY IT!
HOOF!
...A RUSE ...I WAS GONNA SAY A RUSE...
END

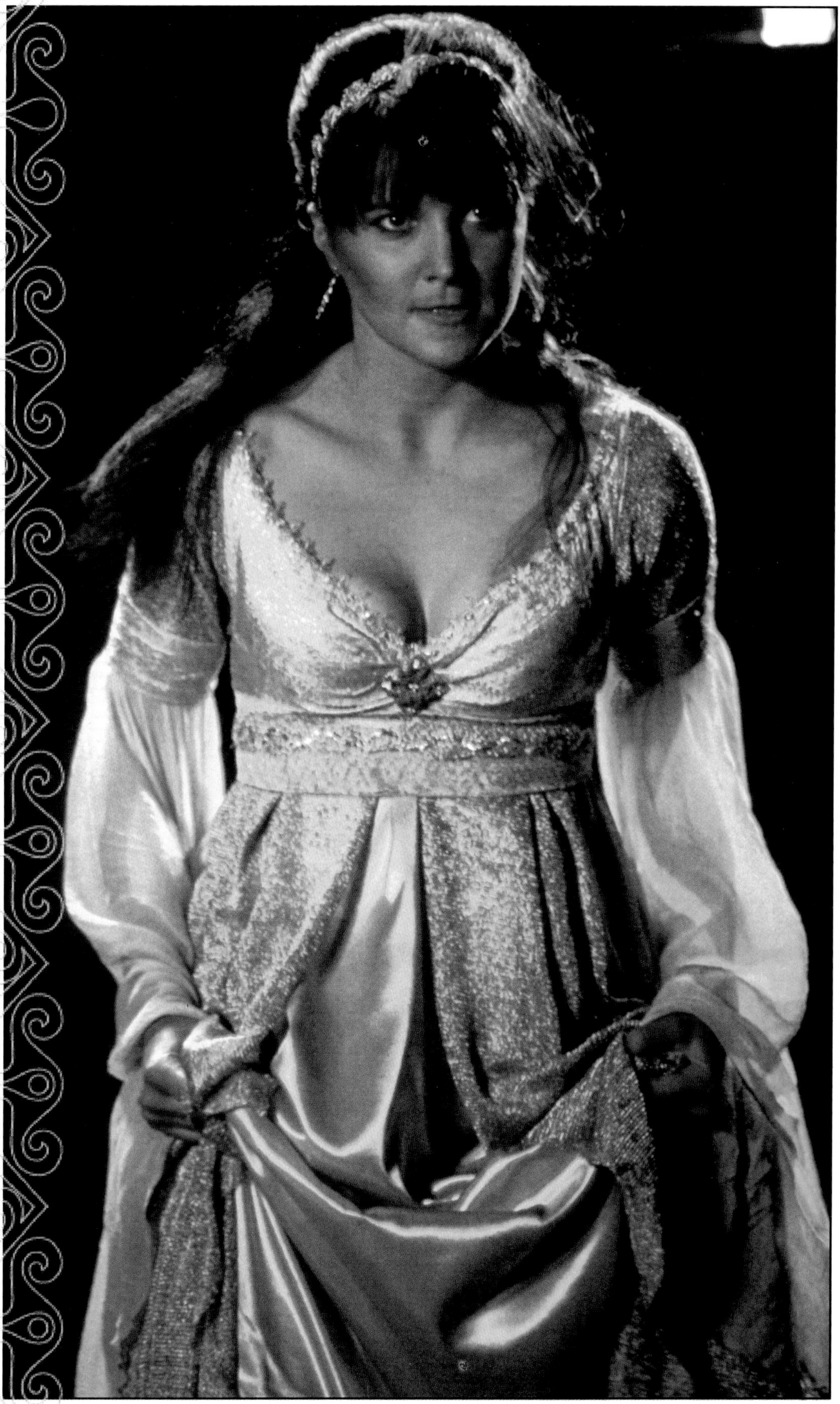

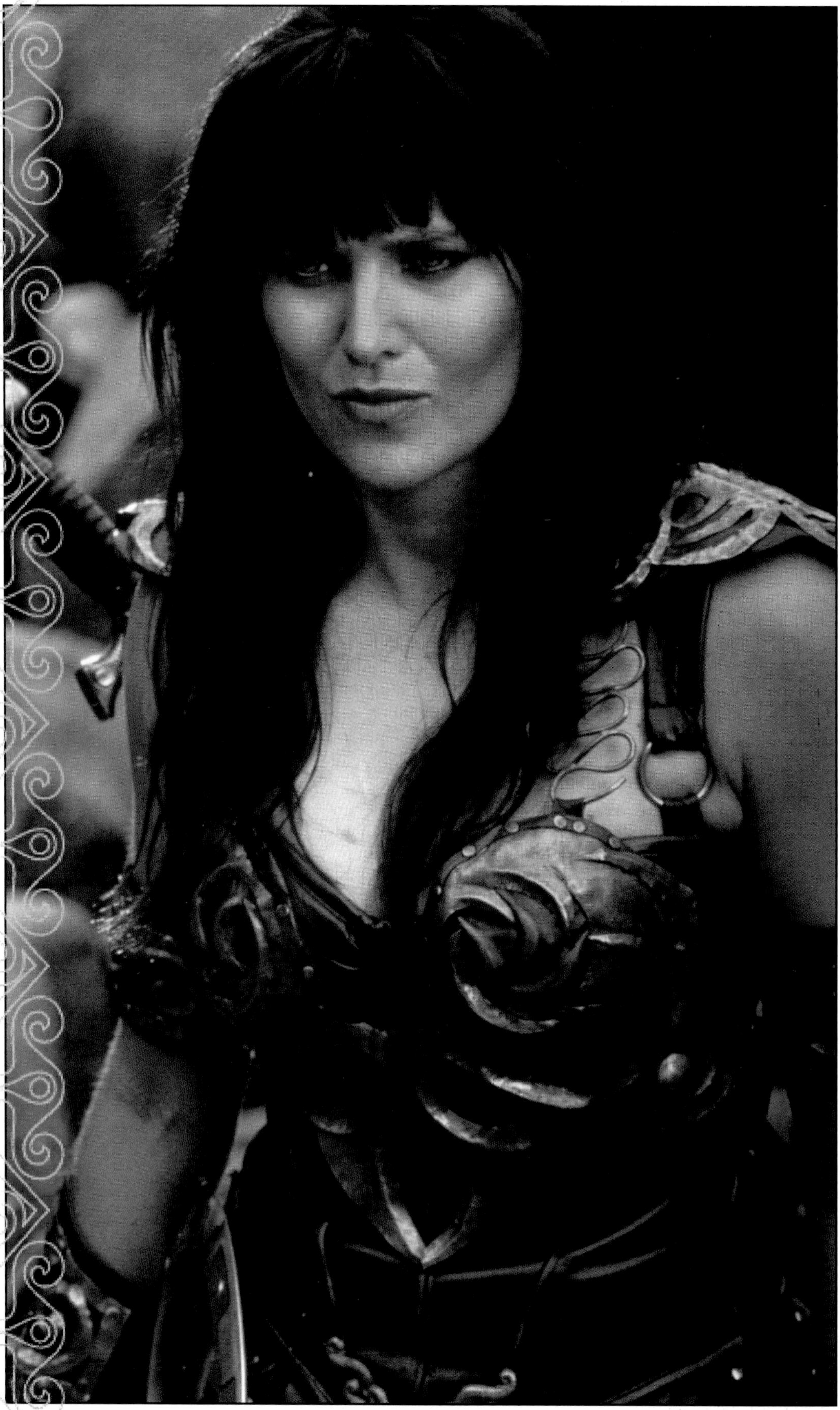

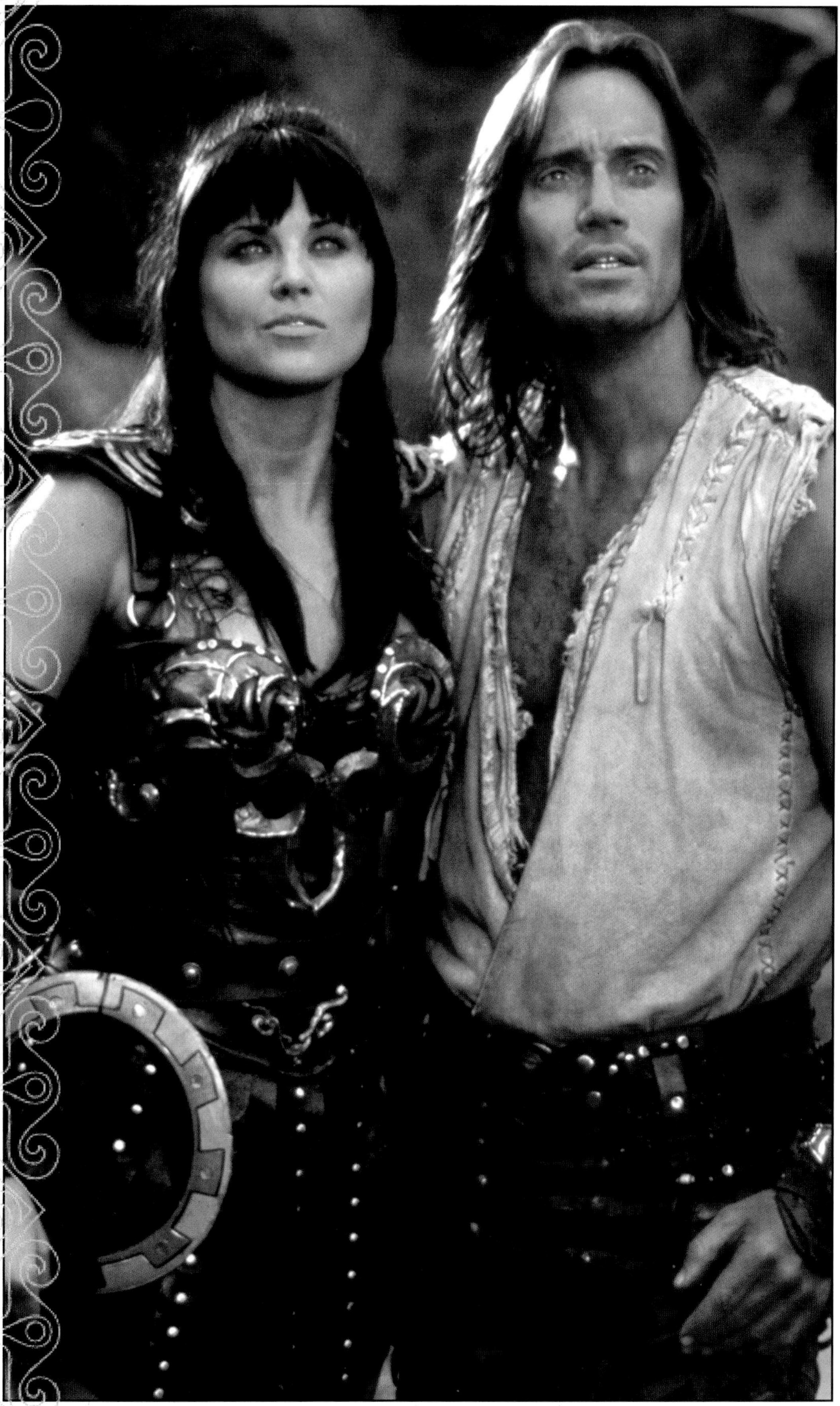